SHE COULDN'T SLEEP...
NOR COULD HER MOTHER

As soon as the lights were out, her fears returned. Her mind raced and slowly she became convinced she could smell the odor of corruption here in the bedroom.

She recognized it from the earlier occurrences. A putrid odor laced with the smell of sulfur. The smell started as a faint wisp. At first she thought it was her imagination. But it grew and grew until it filled her nose and mouth and lungs with its filthy, greasy presence.

She was too frightened to move.

Slowly, quietly, the door handle started to turn. The light from the hallway illuminated the angle of the door as it opened.

Mother. It was Mother.

She stood in the doorway in her long burial dress.

"Katherine..."

The voice was a moan for help...

RESURRECTION

William M. Valtos

ST. MARTIN'S PRESS/NEW YORK

Published by arrangement with Richardson, Steirman & Black, Inc.

RESURRECTION

Library of Congress Catalog Card Number: 88-061422

ISBN: 0-312-91720-1   Can. ISBN: 0-312-91722-8

Printed in the United States of America

Richardson, Steirman & Black edition published 1988
First St. Martin's Press mass market edition/October 1989

10 9 8 7 6 5 4 3 2 1

To Mother, who is out there watching . . .

One

THEY WERE THE wrong shoes for a cemetery.

The mud under the dead grass pulled at her heels and soaked through the expensive Italian leather, chilling her feet. She should have worn something sensible, like flat heels. Or better yet, boots.

Maybe even her Reebok running shoes, she thought, uncertain about what she'd find as she threaded her way among the tombstones. She was careful not to step on any of the old graves, partly out of almost-forgotten superstitions, partly out of fear that the ground might collapse underneath her. The air smelled of rotting leaves and the wet mushrooms that fed on them. Despite the raincoat, her slender body shivered in the damp October wind. She looked back to be certain the BMW was still there where she had parked it, at the end of the asphalt strip, below the flagpole and the life-size marble replica of Michelangelo's *Pietà*. The 735i engine purred beside the silent marble, its exhaust pipe emitting ghostly wisps of vapor. The door was still open, as she had left it, ready to welcome her back to the protection and comfort of German engineering.

It had taken Associate Professor Katherine Roshak eight years to make the two-hour trip from New York City to this cemetery. Eight years since the morning she had followed the cortege up the hill, behind the hearse in which Mother rested. It was during the funeral that Katherine started pretending Mother was still alive. She never allowed the undertaker to use the word "corpse" or "deceased," or, an apparent favorite of his, "the remains." It enabled her to preserve the illusion that Mother wasn't really dead, but somehow merely asleep. It was a harmless fiction. A comfortable delusion that had lasted for eight years, enabling her to ignore her guilt and push her grief to the back recesses of her mind.

Until four days ago.

Her twenty-eighth birthday.

That was the day Mother first appeared to her in New York.

And suddenly that harmless fiction turned into a reality that confused and frightened her. After all those years of pretending Mother wasn't dead, Professor Roshak was here to see if it could possibly be true.

She remembered only the general area of the grave.

The location she sought was at the far side of the cemetery, down a slope and along the back fence, out of sight of the BMW. Eight years ago it had been an empty part of the cemetery. Now that section was fully populated with crowded rows of tombstones, crosses, sunken markers, American Legion flags, and other emblems of death. This was a run-down part of the cemetery. The grass that covered the graves was thicker, overgrown in places and going to weed. The wild roses along the fence were dormant for the winter, but the few chrysanthemums on the graves were in full bloom, their yellow and purple cushions of color overpowering the nearby fading plastic flowers.

Nearing the last row of graves, next to the rusting iron fence that kept the hungry underbrush from consuming the helpless perimeter, she searched the markers for her family name.

What she saw in the last row confirmed her worst fears.

Without looking at the name on the tombstone, she knew it was Mother's grave.

The grave she sought, the section of ground under which Mother had spent the last eight years, the supposedly final resting place Katherine had seen only once before, on the day of the funeral, was an ugly open wound defiling the level ground of its neighbors.

She swallowed hard, forcing her fear back down her throat, back down to where the trembling was making it hard to breathe. She refused to allow herself to scream, afraid it might alert some unknown, unseen being.

It was impossible, she thought. Her mind must be playing tricks, as it had the past four days, when she kept seeing Mother. Hoping to dislodge the image, she closed her eyes and shook her head.

It was still there when she opened her eyes.

The grave was split in the middle, as if something had erupted from underneath and, once freed, allowed the soil to sink back until it was lower than the surrounding area. Chunks of mud and grass were tangled in the cavity. Black scorch marks ran down the slit in the middle.

Katherine backed away.

Slowly at first. Carefully. Afraid to take her eyes from the corrupted grave. Half expecting to see movement, some shifting of the broken ground to signal that there was life underneath. Her senses began to scream, urging her to run to the safety of the car. The soil pulled at her shoes, trying to delay her. The tombstones became a marbled gauntlet, forcing her to run over the awful soil with its subterranean chambers waiting to erupt beneath her. She slipped and slid until she reached the safety of the still-running BMW. Thank God. First check the back seat. No one there. Thank God. Slam the door. Press the lock. Hit the gas.

The sudden roar of the fuel-injected engine had a comforting sound. In the rush to get away, the front tires skidded off the asphalt into the mud. With a sickening whine, the tires spun deeper into the wet soil. In her panic, she slammed the accelerator pedal to the floor and held it there.

The engine screamed. The dashboard lit up with red lights as every indicator warned of the limits to which the car could be pushed. She prayed that the tires wouldn't explode from the heat and the speed and the stress. There was no way she would leave the protection of the car. The BMW lurched forward, slipped back, continued to scream, and jumped free of the rut, chipping the edge of the *Pietà* as she spun the steering wheel to regain control of the vehicle. With the squeal of burning tires, the BMW raced out of the cemetery onto the top of the hill that led down to the small town of Dickson.

As an authority on abnormal behavior, she knew exactly what was happening to her. It was a classic fight-or-flight response. Confronting the unexplainable caused a rush of electrical activity in her brain, as neurons fired in search of an answer buried in the synapses of the temporal lobe. Finding none, the neurotransmitters sent their message of alarm through the nervous system. The locus ceruleus in the brain stem released its norepinephrine, stimulating her heartbeat and signaling the adrenal glands to pump an oversupply of adrenaline into the bloodstream. These neurochemical secretions kept her flushed and trembling even after she reached apparent safety.

Slow down, she told herself.

To avoid being overcome by hysteria, she would have to get back in control of her emotions. A woman of her training should be able to handle a situation like this. Calm down. That was the most important thing. Breathe slowly. Tense the stomach muscles to force the blood supply back to its visceral functions. That's better. She could feel her heartbeat returning to normal.

The logical thing to do was to document, with witnesses, that the grave was empty. That was the first step. It was the easy

6

part. What would be harder would be to convince anyone that, eight years after having committed suicide, Mother was out of the grave and following her in New York. It sounded totally impossible. But the more she thought about it, the faster her heart beat.

Two

A LOUD ARGUMENT stopped when she entered the police station. Two men turned to stare at her. Neither of them wore police uniforms. One of them, the man against the wall, looked relieved by the interruption. He had a day-old beard, and haunted eyes that watched her from deep sockets.

Anger still colored the cheeks of the other man. He was an overweight, middle-aged man with a florid complexion. He wore an open leather jacket that revealed a holstered pistol tucked into the waistband of his trousers, pushing itself against a broad roll of stomach fat. He identified himself as the chief of police.

She told him her story.

When she was finished, he turned his leftover anger at her.

"What is there, a full moon out tonight?" he said. "You don't expect me to believe that, do you?"

"The grave is empty," Katherine insisted. "I know it is. I want it opened."

"But if you already know it's empty, why do you want it opened?"

He was going to try to make her look foolish, she thought.

"I want documentation," she said. "Independent witnesses. You understand the need for independent verification in a case like this."

The chief turned his back on her. He loosened his belt to tuck his shirt into his pants.

"Who said anything about a case? There hasn't been any crime committed. Do you know of any crime?"

"Technically, no," she admitted. "But I'd expect that you'd want to investigate, to find out what's going on."

The chief ran his black comb under the water from the drinking fountain. He bent his knees so he could fit his head into the top of a wall mirror's reflection. He didn't answer until he had finished shaping his hair with the wet comb.

"We're only interested in crimes, lady. We don't go out looking for weird stories like the *National Enquirer*. We just go after bad guys that break the law."

He turned back and gave her a well-practiced smile.

"Besides, I'm off duty for the night. You got here about three minutes too late."

Katherine took a step backward to block the doorway.

"Now, lady," he protested. "There's no crime been committed. Nobody's injured. No complaint's been filed."

"Then I'll make an official complaint. If you have a standard form, I'll fill it out."

The chief looked at his watch.

"I don't have time to play games, lady. I've got places to go tonight."

"You said you need a complaint. That's what I'm doing. I'm making a formal complaint."

"What's the crime? There's got to be a crime. Even if I believed your story, which I don't, coming back from the dead isn't a crime. A miracle, maybe, but not a crime."

"What about desecration of the grave?"

The chief chuckled.

"Now that's not really a crime, and you know it."

"I'm making a formal complaint. You have to investigate."

Katherine refused to move from in front of the door. She waited for him to make up his mind. He tried staring her down, but she didn't even blink. Finally, with a deep sigh that expressed his distaste, he nodded toward the man against the wall.

"He's not much, but he's the best I can do for you, lady. He'll take down your complaint and go to the cemetery with you."

The man against the wall hadn't moved during the conversation. He stared at Katherine with dark, tired eyes. The eyes were too old for his face, she thought.

"Dominic, stand up and say hello to the lady."

Dominic didn't stand up. He barely acknowledged hearing the chief. He was studying her with those ancient eyes of his. The pupils had long ago withdrawn into the protection of the deep hollows below his eyebrows. From the safety of those caverns, his black pupils seemed to be memorizing her, looking right through the expensive clothes she wore to enhance her figure: the small breasts and slim body and legs that gave her an almost boyish look. It was a body still waiting for a man to make it bloom. Not enough meat, Mother always said. Never find a man until you put on some weight.

But she had inherited Mother's high cheekbones and pale beauty, and that was enough to give her confidence in her appearance. She thrust out her chin and stared back in defiance.

"Dominic doesn't mind going to the cemetery at night," the chief said. "He spends so much time up there, he knows the gravediggers by name. Isn't that right, Dom?"

She judged his age at about thirty. About the same age as the other professors in her department. Unlike their lean, jogging-

11

style physiques, he was about five feet ten, with a powerful body and broad weight-lifter shoulders. Barely concealed by the stubble of beard was a mouth that looked as if he could be cruel. He watched her with silent interest.

"Is he a policeman?" she asked.

"Unfortunately, yes," the chief answered. "I've got his case in front of the civil service board, but until they take action, he's on the payroll."

The chief edged around to the door while Katherine studied the dark-haired man, who still hadn't moved.

"He's the perfect guy for your complaint. Dominic Delaserra. That's Italian, Delaserra. It means "of the night." That fits real good with your story. Dominic from the night goes to the cemetery with the lady from New York to look for ghosts. Well, I'm sorry I can't go with you," the chief said with another chuckle.

When he was gone, Dominic finally spoke.

"I don't believe in ghosts," he said. His voice was flat and emotionless. "I used to believe in all that stuff, ghosts and saints and holy water, but not anymore."

"How do I make out a complaint?" she asked.

"You don't need a complaint. That was just the chief trying to brush you off. I'll take you up to cemetery, if that's what you want."

He started for the door. When she stepped back, he smiled.

"You're afraid of me, aren't you?" he said.

She didn't answer.

It was getting dark outside. He led her to a police car parked behind her BMW.

"Don't pay attention to what the chief said. Like that stuff about my name. There's nothing special about Delaserra. It's just another Italian name, like da Vinci or spaghetti."

When he opened the car door for her, she hesitated again.

"Maybe we could wait until morning," she said. "It's getting too dark now."

"I've got a searchlight," he answered. "Might as well get this out of your system so you can sleep tonight."

12

A light drizzle was in the air, just enough for him to turn on the windshield wipers.

"Aren't you going to call anyone?"

"Like who?"

"Someone to open the grave."

"All we're doing is going up there for a look. There's probably a simple explanation."

"I doubt it," she said, sliding to the far side of the seat. She noticed that there were no handles on the inside of the passenger door.

"You really a professor?" he asked.

"You people don't believe anything, do you?"

"Well, you're driving a BMW. You're wearing expensive clothes. I didn't know professors got paid that much."

"I inherited money. It was held in trust until my twenty-eighth birthday. Why doesn't this door have any handles on it?"

"We take them off so we don't have to worry about prisoners getting out. You know, I wouldn't take you for a professor the first time I saw you."

"What did you expect? Tweeds and a pipe?"

"Now you're making fun of me. I get enough of that from the chief."

"I'm sorry."

The last daylight was fading as they turned up the hill to the cemetery.

"What kind of professor are you?"

"Abnormal psychology."

"Now I never would have guessed that. I would have figured art or music or something like that."

"Because I'm a woman?"

"Don't start in on that liberation stuff. You just don't look like you work around crazy people. It would show up in your face. I see that all the time in my line of work. Your job shows up in your face. But you don't have a hard face."

"I don't work with psychologically troubled people. All I do is lecture. I'm not a psychiatrist. I'm an associate professor."

"I don't need psychiatrists. Between the bartenders and priests, I've got all the help I need. I don't want to sound like I'm putting you down, but I don't need any psychiatrist."

"Consider yourself lucky," Katherine said. "Right now, I'm not so sure about myself."

"There's probably a simple explanation."

"I doubt it."

"Maybe you're just imagining things."

"You think I'm hallucinating?"

"I didn't mean that. I meant you're just letting your mind work too hard. You're looking for complicated answers to problems that don't exist. Life is a lot easier if you just look for simple answers. Common things occur commonly. That's the whole key to police work. It's just like fixing a car. You look for the simple answer before you start ripping apart the engine."

"The simple answer is that Mother isn't in her grave. She's out there somewhere walking around."

The light drizzle had grown heavier by the time they reached the cemetery. He left the headlights on.

"You can stay in the car," he said. "It gets real muddy around the graves."

"No. I want to come with you."

The truth was, she was afraid to stay in the car, but didn't want to admit it. He produced an umbrella from the trunk, and allowed her to lead the way.

When her heels stuck in the dense mud and she stumbled, he slipped a hand under her arm. He almost lifted her out of her shoes with that one powerful hand. He kept her in his grip as they moved along. It gave her a feeling of comfort.

They were beyond the range of the police car's headlights. Dominic produced a small flashlight and held it where she could watch her step. He seemed to know his own way without a need for lights.

At the end of the last row, she stopped.

"It's up there," she whispered.

The flashlight danced up the row of wet tombstones until it picked out the place where the grass broke open.

He moved cautiously to the edge of the grave.

"Well?" she whispered. "Now do you believe me?"

He ran his hand along the edge, feeling the break where the sod had separated when it dropped into the center of the grave. Holding the umbrella over him, she waited while he studied the site.

"It's recent, all right," he said in a soft voice. "The ground around the edges is still crumbling."

Rising to his feet, Dominic took the umbrella back.

"The coffin probably collapsed," he said. "It happens after a while, especially if there's been a lot of rain, like we had the last few years. The coffin deteriorates and the earth caves it in."

"There was a burial vault protecting the coffin," she said. "I paid extra for that, to protect the coffin."

"It probably had a defective lid. That must be why the ground settled so deep. I never saw a grave go this deep before."

"I want the grave opened," she said.

"You don't want to see what's down there. I'll just get the caretaker to put some fresh dirt on top and maybe a little sod. That's what your mother would want. Why disturb the dead?"

"I want the grave opened," she repeated.

"It's not that easy. You'd need the okay from the parish priest. This is a church cemetery. And then you'd need a certificate from the county health department."

"I want it done," she insisted.

Dominic continued staring at the grave.

"It's bothering you, too," she said. "I can tell."

"Me? No." He shook his head. "I was thinking of something else."

"Can we get it opened tonight?"

"It's just a settled grave. Why don't you forget about it? Go to church and say a few prayers. That's probably what your mother wants. It'll calm you down."

A cold wind blew the drizzle against their faces. Katherine struggled to keep the umbrella from being blown away.

"I can't rest until I know."

"I'm telling you, there's nothing to know. Let the dead rest in peace."

"The coffin is empty," she insisted. "I've seen Mother. She's not in the coffin."

"You're trying to wish her alive," Dominic said. "Why don't you just admit that she's dead and forget it. It happens to everyone. You'd think after eight years you could accept it."

"You could arrange to open the grave tonight, if you really wanted to."

"Lady, do you know what you're asking? Why can't you at least wait until morning?"

"I'll pay for it. I'll pay for everything. But I want it done tonight. We shouldn't be wasting time."

Later, when the floodlights were set up over the grave, Katherine began to have second thoughts. The lights sucked the color from the faces of the men Dominic assembled. He knew all of them on a first-name basis. They didn't like the idea of being called here in the dark and the rain, but Dominic had promised them triple the union rate. They waited for further instructions before starting their macabre assignment. Just beyond the circle of light, the tombstones waited, watching, Katherine thought, over their neighbor's grave.

"It's going to take a long time with these shovels," said one of the gravediggers. "We could do it in twenty minutes with the backhoe."

"I don't want to disturb anything you find down there," Dominic said. "As long as we're here, let's do it right."

He took a series of Polaroid photographs of the grave from various angles before the digging began.

"Just for the record," he explained to Katherine. "We always shoot Polaroids at the scene. Never know when they'll come in handy."

The rain stopped, only to be replaced by a rapidly dropping temperature. Katherine ached to sit in the car. It was already past midnight. The tension and fatigue burned at her eyes. Her feet were cold and wet. She couldn't stop her knees from trembling every time the wind blew her wet Burberry raincoat against her legs.

The slow, careful excavation process continued. Once the

16

gravediggers got past the muddiest layer of ground, the digging went faster. About three feet down, one of the shovels dug into a white silk pillow. Katherine refused to touch it when it was handed up to Dominic for examination. The gravediggers stopped talking after that. They dug silently until they struck a thin concrete slab lying on edge.

Dominic warned them to avoid moving around too much, but the gravediggers already knew that the vault was uncovered. The rest of the excavation was done more slowly. To avoid damaging anything, they used their shovels like trowels, pulling back the dirt before sliding the metal under it. They outlined the edge of the exposed vault. The cover rested against the side of the grave. Proceeding with the careful movements of archaeologists, they exposed the edge of the coffin. It was lying at an angle inside the vault. The coffin lid was open.

Carefully, carefully, they probed with their shovels, searching for the body. After an excruciating process of gentle excavation, they stopped.

"Nothing here, Dom. There's not even a piece of a body down here. Nothing in the coffin. Nothing in the vault."

The coffin was neatly outlined by the gravediggers, who stood in the mud around it. The white silk interior of the coffin, where her mother had rested for eight years, was stained with the color of the mud. Katherine felt a strange sense of relief as she stared at the empty coffin. At least she hadn't been hallucinating.

"Just what I was afraid of," Dominic muttered.

He reached inside his jacket for a crumpled pack of Camels.

"What is it?" she asked.

"Grave robbers."

"What?"

"Grave robbers. They must have been after her jewelry."

Katherine shook her head in disbelief.

"I know what you're thinking," Dominic said. "You're thinking I was wrong about the grave settling, and now I'm making up a story. But the only other thing that makes sense is grave robbers. You'd be amazed what people will do for money."

"There was no jewelry on Mother when she was buried. The undertaker even gave me her wedding ring."

"Maybe they thought otherwise. A diamond ring. A pearl necklace. Around here, that would be enough. You said your mother left you a lot of money. Word gets around. People get funny ideas."

A vague smell of sulfur and decay hung around the open grave. One of the gravediggers held a handkerchief to his nose. Dominic smoothed out a wrinkled cigarette, lit it, and took a slow, thoughtful puff.

"There's a funny smell down here, Dominic."

"After eight years, I'd expect that."

"No. It's something else. Like there was a fire down here. Smells like something was burning."

"It's your imagination," Dominic said.

"No. I've opened enough graves to know what it smells like. This is different."

"It'll go away," Dominic said. "All it needs is airing out."

Katherine put her handkerchief against her nose, breathing in the perfume to wash away the acrid odor coming from the grave.

"Come on out," Dominic said. He stepped back from the grave himself. "We'll examine it closer in the morning when the smell is gone. I'd like one of you guys to stay here, though. Just to keep an eye on things."

"She's been here eight years already," Katherine said softly. "If someone wanted to rob her grave, they would have done it long ago. Besides, where is her body?"

"Well hell, I don't know that. All I know for sure is that she couldn't get out of that grave herself. You've got a hundred-pound concrete cover on that vault, and a ton of dirt on top of that. You saw how long it took those men to dig it out. Nobody, especially a woman, could get out of that grave by herself."

He stopped suddenly.

"What am I talking about? That's impossible. People don't come back from the dead. It had to be grave robbers."

"Then how do you explain my seeing her in New York?"

Dominic threw his cigarette butt over the fence.

"I don't know. You're the one that teaches psychology, not me."

The bright floodlights were turned off, allowing the open grave to reenter the darkness that shrouded the rest of the cemetery. Flashlights flickered on around her, sending their beams in confusing directions. She was getting too tired to argue. She felt Dominic's hand under her arm again, leading her to the police car. He didn't need the flashlight to find his way back.

The car was warm and dry, a welcome refuge. She leaned her head back against the seat and closed her eyes. All she wanted to do was sleep. Sleep and forget the dreadful events of the last several days. If only she could sleep and wake up to a reality in which none of this had happened. But the image of the open grave and her mother's face prevented it.

"That didn't solve anything for you, did it?" Dominic asked. His voice was gentler now, more understanding of her.

"No. I think it only made things worse. I assumed if I could see the grave, the recognition of that reality would make it easier to cope with the situation. But now I'm even more frightened. I expect to see her everywhere. In a doorway. On the next corner. I don't know what to do now. All I know is she's out there somewhere."

The streets of the small town were empty. The old wooden frame houses were dark. It was still an hour before dawn. An emaciated yellow cat was frozen in the car's headlights, its eyes glowing green while it waited until the very last moment, daring the car to run it over, before leaping effortlessly out of the way.

"Would it help you to talk?" he asked.

"I thought you didn't believe in psychotherapy."

"Just pretend I'm a bartender. I'll take you for a drink. You could probably use one."

"It's four in the morning. This whole town is closed."

Still, the idea appealed to her. Maybe it would help her forget.

"We'll go to Eddie Elbows's place. He'll open up for me."

Eddie Elbows was in his mid-thirties, with flowing golden

hair and a soft peach-fuzz face. A handsome man with a big smile. There was only one thing wrong with him.

His forearms were missing.

His hands and fingers were perfectly shaped and normal in every respect, except that the wrists were attached directly to his elbows. They flopped at his ribs as he walked.

"He was one of those thalidomide babies," Dominic whispered while they followed Eddie to the bar.

The handicap didn't seem to interfere with Eddie's bartending skills as he set up two glasses for Dominic and poured a shot of Canadian Club into one. With a short hand, he expertly flipped the wooden handle that filled the other glass with draft beer. When he caught her staring at his hands, Eddie smiled and winked. He seemed to welcome the attention his hands attracted.

"And what'll you have, miss?"

"A glass of white wine."

"Give her a shot of whiskey," Dominic said. "She could use it."

Katherine didn't argue.

"Now tell me when you think you first saw your mother."

"That was on Monday."

"This week?"

She nodded and took a sip of the whiskey. It burned its way down her throat. It felt good after all those hours in the cold. She coughed before continuing.

"It was my twenty-eighth birthday. I was in Bloomingdale's coming down the escalator to the main floor. She was standing at the foot of the escalator, looking up at me."

Katherine shuddered at the memory, and took another sip of whiskey. This time she didn't cough.

"It was almost like one of those dreams I used to have. I was being taken down toward her, and she was standing there, waiting. But she wasn't smiling. That bothered me. It was as if she was angry at me. When I was halfway down the escalator, she disappeared into the crowd. I hurried after her, but she was gone. I thought maybe it was just mistaken identity—you know, someone who looked like her. I tried to forget it."

"You think you saw her again?"

20

"I did. It was Wednesday night. I was teaching my regular evening class. It was a session on schizophrenia in identical twins and parallelism as a factor in mental illness."

"Sounds complicated."

"It's not as complicated as it sounds. Being a policeman, you'd probably be interested, because it deals with the types of disorders that lead to crime. Starting with the German studies in 1929 and continuing through studies in Sweden, England, and Norway, it's been demonstrated that monozygotic twins have extremely high concordance rates for manic-depressive disorders and severe schizophrenia."

"What are monozygotic twins?"

"They're true identical twins. It means they came from the same egg, have identical genes, the same sex and appearance. Unlike ordinary twins, they're genetically the same person."

"So why should they have mental problems?"

"Some think it's because true identical twins tend to be on average weaker, smaller, and slightly less intelligent than single births. My own theory is that it has something to do with the unique mental bond between identical twins. Studies show some pairs of monozygotics know what each other is thinking through some unknown form of communication."

"You mean like telepathy?"

"Perhaps. Remember, their brains are identical, too. They often even share physical illnesses. The death of one can cause the death of the other through some unexplained form of sympathetic trauma. So it stands to reason they'd share mental illnesses, too. In some cases, the twin bonding is so extreme it becomes pathological. They'll take the same name and act like they're a single person."

"That's weird," Dominic said.

"The proper term is 'abnormal,' " she corrected him. "But it's extremely rare. I've been involved in a continuing life study of two hundred sets of monozygotic twins, and I haven't found a deviation that serious yet."

"You sound like you're disappointed."

She had to smile at his innocence. He just didn't understand the world of academia.

"You don't get famous studying normal people," she said.

21

"Not in my field. It's the aberrations that get the publicity. The more spectacular the aberration, the more publicity you get."

"Just like police work," he said.

He was doing a good job of keeping her talking, she realized. She studied their images in the mirror behind the bar. It was an old mirror, the silver backing tarnished in places. Its bottom was hemmed with an irregular row of whiskey bottles. In the dim light of the bar, the mirror softened his image and made him look friendly. She watched him looking back at her reflected image. Was he really interested in what she did? Or was he just doing police work? She took another sip. It really didn't matter, she thought. She just needed someone to talk to.

"I got involved in the study ten years ago, when I was an undergraduate. We've been following the subjects through their schooling, their jobs, their marriages, their illnesses, even their eating habits. I did my master's thesis on the study, and now I'm sort of in charge of it."

"Good for you," he said.

"It was boring at first. They just wanted somebody to do the detailing work. Interviewing all those twins four times a year gets repetitious. But I've built friendships with some of them, even the very secretive ones, like the 'D.' twins. I don't know their real names, but they call me, right on schedule, and we've gotten to be very friendly."

"But you don't know their names?" he asked with mild surprise.

"That was a condition of their continuing participation in the study. They wanted to protect their privacy. They didn't want to be treated like laboratory animals. They're real people. We talk about a lot of things. They know as much about me as I know about them."

"Isn't that dangerous? Letting strangers know too much about you?"

"Now you sound like a policeman."

"That's what I am."

"Well, I'm a psychologist. This is my life's work. I've got to give a little to gain their trust. It's the only way to learn more of the personal details that make a study like this more than just some musty old research report. I'd do anything to avoid losing track of the twins in this study. And besides, they're very nice. They even sent me a sympathy card when Mother died."

"No return address?" Dominic asked.

She made a face instead of answering.

"You said you saw your mother in a classroom," Dominic said, bringing her back to the original subject.

"She was there," Katherine insisted. "She stood in the doorway for a while. At first I thought it was a student trying to browse my class. They'll slip in sometimes to see if a particular teacher runs an easy class, so they can be sure of getting a better grade before they sign up."

"I didn't know they did that. I thought college was supposed to be tough."

Katherine smiled.

"College is just like everything else. Some people look for easy answers."

"That's supposed to be a jab, I guess."

She smiled. She could feel herself relaxing with him. The drink was catching up with her, she thought. Or maybe the tension, or the fatigue, or maybe just sitting here in the privacy of a bar that was closed to the public with a man she hadn't known before yesterday.

"So what happened?" Dominic asked. "Did she disappear again?"

Katherine asked for another drink. Eddie jumped up from his seat, manipulated the stubby arms, refused Dominic's money, and returned to his seat in the corner, his arms out of sight again.

"She came into the lecture hall and sat down in the very last row, right next to the door. She looked angry again, like she did that first night. I don't understand why."

Katherine took a long swallow from the glass. She waited until she felt the warmth of the liquid reach her stomach before she spoke again.

"I could almost feel the anger. Her eyes were so intense. I had a hard time coping with it. I mean the idea of Mother actually being there. All those years I wished she was still alive, and all

23

of a sudden there she was. I knew it was impossible, but there she was. Staring at me."

"What did she look like? Was she any different from the way you remembered her?"

Katherine tried to focus on the memory. Fatigue was making it harder to concentrate.

"She looked exactly like she did at the funeral. Of course, that would stand to reason, wouldn't it? She wouldn't look like she did when she was younger."

"How do you mean that?" Dominic asked.

Katherine closed her eyes, trying to remember details that she would have preferred to forget.

"I complained to the funeral director about the way she looked."

"Which funeral parlor was it?"

"It was a local one. She spent her last few days up here. I think it was called Kuranda's or something like that."

"Kuranda is right. Was it the old man or the son?"

"It was an older man."

"Too bad," Dominic said. "Old man Kuranda is gone now. He retired last year. His son runs the business now."

"Well, whoever it was, I didn't like what they did to her. They made her eyebrows too heavy and her lips too thin. It made her look mean."

"That happens. People never look the same when they're dead. Especially women." He stopped and took a long swallow of beer. His voice sounded distant. "You get someone else putting makeup on them, they look different than you remember."

"I gave them my favorite pictures of her to follow. They should have done better. And I never got the pictures back. I wrote to Mr. Kuranda, but he claimed he didn't know anything about them. The man who worked on my mother wasn't with him anymore."

"You mean it wasn't Kuranda himself?"

"No. He had an assistant. A young man just out of mortuary school. I remember he was very helpful. He said exactly the right things to put me at ease."

"Do you remember his name?"

Katherine couldn't recall it.

"Okay, let's get back to your mother. You say she looked just like she did at the funeral. Wasn't there anything unusual about her? Anything at all? After all, she was supposed to be dead for eight years."

"Her hair was kind of messed. My mother was the type of woman who never had a strand of hair out of place. It was always sprayed and set and neat. But that night at the university, her hair was wet and messy and her skin was gray, almost black."

The glass in front of Katherine was empty again. This time, Eddie Elbows let it sit without refilling. That was fine with her. She was having trouble remembering things now. Thank goodness. She was on the verge of falling asleep right there, at the bar.

"What was she wearing?" Dominic asked. "Anything unusual about her clothing?"

"No. It was a light blue gown."

"Sounds unusual to me. A blue gown would really stand out in a college classroom."

"But it wasn't unusual, because it was the same one she was buried in. I remember it was blue chiffon. She bought it herself, and had it wrapped in plastic and hanging in the closet so it would be ready when she passed away. I didn't believe her. I never thought it would happen that way. But it did."

She closed her eyes, tired of all the talking and remembering. It was nice to close her eyes and not have the image of her mother in front of her.

When she opened her eyes, she was no longer in the bar.

Afraid to move, she took a deep breath and listened. Someone was in the darkness with her. She could hear low voices from downstairs. But the steady breathing in the same room was what frightened her. She was in a bed. Moving her legs, she realized that her clothing had been removed.

A voice spoke when she stirred.

"You slept a long time," it said.

Katherine tried to locate the voice in the darkness. Across the room, someone rose. She could her the steps come closer.

"You'd better get up now," the man said.

The room was suddenly bathed in light as the drapes parted. Katherine squinted in pain at the brightness. Her head ached from the whiskey. When her eyes adjusted to the light, she could see Eddie Elbows standing by the window. He smiled down at her.

"It's almost ten o'clock."

"Have you been here all night?" she asked.

"Dominic wanted me to stay here. Said he didn't want you to be alone. Said you been seeing things."

Eddie crossed the room and tilted his shoulder to reach the door handle with one of his stubs.

"Get some air in here," he said as he opened the door.

The sounds of the bar downstairs were clearer now. The electric clicking of pinball machines. A TV with a game show on. Patches of conversation. It all sounded normal enough.

"Where are my clothes?" she asked.

"They were all muddy and damp. I figured you'd want something fresh, so I sent them to the cleaners across the street. They'll be done pretty soon."

She pulled the blanket tighter around herself.

"Don't worry, I didn't see anything." He smiled. "The lights were out, and I didn't want to disturb you. Dominic was afraid you'd have nightmares, but you slept real well, didn't you?"

The residue of the whiskey hurt when she tried to nod her head in answer. Her throat was parched. Her lips were dry and cracked. She wanted to go to the bathroom, but was too embarrassed to say so.

"Probably the bed helped you to sleep better. That's a Beautyrest mattress, you know. Top of the line. Seven hundred dollars, including the box spring and Harvard frame. But my wife said it's worth it. She always wants the best mattress, the best sheets. Nothing more important in the world than a good night's sleep, you listen to her."

Eddie handed her a bathrobe. It was a fine pink brushed-cotton robe with hand embroidery on the collar. Too flowery for Katherine's taste, but she knew it was expensive.

"She's up at the Mayo Clinic," Eddie said. "She goes there every year for a checkup. Takes a couple of weeks. She'll be back any day now."

The room was feminine, French country style, with ornate furniture in soft beige tones. Simulated holes were painted on the wood. The dresser was cluttered with perfume bottles, most of them sealed with wax to protect the precious fluids from evaporating. The wallpaper was an allover pattern of small yellow flowers. The radiator was painted yellow. Beside it, a large bucket of water waited for some mysterious purpose. It was a room for one person. Eddie's wife obviously slept by herself on the Beautyrest mattress.

"I can get you some breakfast," Eddie said. "You like eggs Benedict? Got some skinless, shankless smoked ham, sausage, cereal, whatever you want. I always cook for Phyllis. She'd rather eat than cook, and I'm the other way around."

"Where is Dominic?"

"I could open some Spanish sardines in hot sauce."

"Just a glass of tomato juice. I'm not a breakfast person. Where is Dominic?"

"It's hard to tell with him. He might be up the cemetery. Says it's a quiet place to think. A lot of people say he's crazy, the way he goes up there all the time."

He stopped at the doorway and turned to her with a quizzical expression.

"You're a psychiatrist. You think he's crazy?"

"He seems like a nice guy. Fairly normal. Maybe a little withdrawn, but nothing pathological."

"That's what I say, too. A little withdrawn. Nothing wrong with that, is there?"

"The cemetery part sounds strange, though."

"How do you mean?"

"You're the second person who said he's always at the cemetery."

"I didn't say always," Eddie corrected her. "I just said he goes there. I better get your tomato juice."

By the time he returned, she was washed and combed and lipsticked and feeling better about herself. The headache was mellowing out.

"Why is he so attracted to the cemetery?" she asked, picking up the conversation as if Eddie hadn't left the room.

"You said he was normal," Eddie reminded her.

"I just want to understand him better. He's a good friend of yours, isn't he?"

Eddie nodded and handed her the juice.

"Dominic always watched out for me. These flippers I've got? Most people make fun of them. Harmless jokes, maybe. But you know what they're thinking. Dominic, now, he's different. He even taught me to bowl, you believe that? You'd never think a guy with arms like these could bowl. And not only that, but now I'm damn good at it. I even took his place on the team when he quit. I'm a two-thirty bowler now."

"That's why you were willing to open up the bar for him last night?"

"I'd do anything for Dominic."

"That's why you're letting me stay here."

"No questions asked."

"If you think he's so great, then why does his boss think he's crazy?"

Eddie shook his head in frustration.

"He just stopped talking to people. Drives them nuts when he doesn't talk to them."

"He talks to me."

"I was surprised when I saw that last night. Hasn't talked like that in a long time. He was really interested in you. Maybe you're good for him.

"Maybe he's only interested because I wanted to go to the cemetery."

She was sorry as soon as she said it. Eddie gave her a look of disapproval.

"You know he's in trouble. And you talking like that won't help. They want to kick him off the police force. And the way he is, he won't be good for anything else."

"But what's his problem, Eddie?"

"Are you a real psychiatrist?"

"I'm not a practicing psychiatrist, if that's what you mean. But I do have a Ph.D. in abnormal psychology."

28

She waited while he decided whether that was good enough.

"Maybe you can help him, then," Eddie said. "He doesn't straighten out, I'm worried where he's going to end up."

"I was hoping he'd help me," she said. "Not the other way around. Maybe I've got the wrong guy on my side."

"Now don't think that way," Eddie said. "Chief didn't help you, did he? It was Dominic took an interest in your problem. When he gets going on something, he doesn't stop for sleep. He doesn't stop for nothing. Not until he's done. You'll see. It's just a question if he can take his mind off what's bothering him."

"And what's that? You've been talking about him all this time and you keep walking around it."

"I don't know if it's my place to tell you. He might not appreciate that."

"Do you want me to ask him myself?"

"No, no. Please. That would be too hurtful for him."

She waited as he studied her. What was he looking for? Something in her face that would show she could be trusted? If that was it, he took a long time to decide.

When he finally spoke, the words came slowly, with long pauses between the sentences. He didn't seem to enjoy telling another man's secrets.

"It was his wife," Eddie said. "Her name was Cara. She wasn't like my wife. She was a real honey. Skin so fair, you wanted to touch her face to be sure she was real. And dark hair so delicate and fine, my God, just your breath would make it move like there was a breeze. The kind of woman you just wanted to reach out and protect from the world. College-educated, like you. She could have been something, but all she ever cared about was Dominic. When they got married, we never saw Dominic except when he was working. All his spare time, every minute he spent with Cara. And you couldn't blame him. It wasn't like Phyllis and me. It was deeper. He dropped off the bowling team. We used to kid him about it when he was on patrol, but he was happy, so what the hell. He didn't need friends anymore. Oh, he didn't turn against them, he just didn't need anybody, as long as he had Cara."

Eddie lowered his voice at the memory of her.

"She died about eight months ago. A tumor on her spine. Nothing the doctors could do. Dominic watched her die. For two months he sat in that hospital, holding her hand. Wouldn't even go home. He'd just sit there, not even talking, just holding her hand, watching her die."

Eddie stopped and swallowed. He turned to look out the window. Embarrassed for him, Katherine stared at the floor. When he turned back, he sounded angry.

"You know what it must feel like to have a tumor chewing away at your spine? She couldn't even die on her back. They had her on her stomach the whole time. Morphine and all that stuff to keep her from screaming. She was so drugged up, the last three weeks of it, she wasn't conscious. They were afraid if they let her wake up, the pain would drive her crazy. But he stayed with her. He suffered right along with her."

The tears were flowing down Eddie's cheeks, and he made no effort to hide them.

"Now he goes up to her grave all the time. He says it helps him think, says it's so peaceful and quiet. He won't say what he thinks about, but I guess it's Cara. I don't blame him for that. But he's got to snap out of it."

"Unresolved grief," she said.

"Huh?" He turned, almost startled she was still there.

"Unresolved grief," she said. "The second stage of Kübler-Ross's five stages of grief."

"What does that mean?"

"The fact that he hasn't progressed beyond the second stage is an indication of pathological grief syndrome." The words came out easily, remembered from dozens of lectures. "That would explain the withdrawal from emotional connections with others. He's unable to transfer his emotional needs to another person. Until he does, that withdrawal will intensify his separation anxiety."

"You really know all that stuff," Eddie said in awe.

She shrugged off his admiration.

"It's not hard to learn. Putting it into practice is something else. Like I said, I just teach a college course. I'm not a working psychiatrist."

"But you could help him."

"I doubt it. I'm still in the denial stage myself."

Seeing his puzzled expression, she explained herself.

"That's the first stage. Denying that the person is dead. For eight years, I've been refusing to admit Mother was . . . dead. I never even used the word until yesterday."

"But you're a professor," he said with disbelief.

She shrugged.

"That doesn't make me anything special. People have to work through these things. It was just more comfortable to pretend she was still alive. I'm a lot like Dominic. I just found a different way to cope. Until I saw Mother. I really saw her, Eddie. And now I don't know how to handle it."

She shivered at the thought.

"I'm afraid. Why is she doing this?"

A siren sounded in the distance.

"Fire," Eddie said, his eyes growing wide.

He held up one of his arm stubs for silence, while counting the siren's wails.

"It's the middle of town. First ward," he said. "You can tell from the number of sirens."

Someone called him to the telephone downstairs.

When he returned, his face was grim.

"They're sending a police car for you."

"Dominic?"

"No. They wouldn't let me talk to him. The fire's at the police station, and the chief wants you there right away. They wouldn't tell me why.

Three

Having done their best, the fire engines remained on station, ready to attck again if needed. But there was nothing left to burn. At the center of attention, sitting in a puddle of white chemical foam, was the blackened hulk of Katherine's BMW.

Forty-nine thousand dollars, she thought.

Now it sat on metal rims, its tires burned away. The roof had buckled from the intense heat. The interior and seats were reduced to a smoldering tangle of wire springs and metal supports. The aftersmell of the fire hung in the air.

Less than four thousand miles on the odometer, she thought.

The chief of police came running out of the station when he saw her. His face was red with anger.

"I knew I shouldn't of let you two go off together last night!" he shouted.

Puzzled, she tried to understand what he was upset about. After all, it wasn't his car.

"You had no business leaving that car here. Police station isn't a parking lot. It's a good thing they were able to keep the fire from spreading."

The aftersmell had a sulfuric odor to it. It seemed vaguely familiar.

"Now we're going to have to repave the driveway. Damned asphalt is melted underneath."

"Where is Dominic?" she asked.

"Dominic? Ha. For all I know, he started the damn fire himself. Car was sitting there all morning, until he walked in. Then it just exploded. Don't try suing us, because that's a clearly marked no-parking zone. You had no business leaving it there."

She looked past the frantic chief of police.

At a window on the second floor of the building, she saw Dominic looking down at the scene.

The chief turned to follow her gaze.

"Don't look to him for any help. He's finished. He's off the force as of now. I should of done it months ago. It would of saved me a lot of trouble. That's what happens when you try to be a nice guy. But he's through now. Finished."

He turned back to Katherine.

"And so are you. I don't like the idea of digging up the cemetery at night without my okay. I think you better get back to New York, where you came from with your crazy story. Your insurance will take care of the car, but they better pay for the driveway, too."

"I came here to find out about Mother," she said.

"Whatever you saw, you saw in New York. All you found here is an empty grave."

"That empty grave is proof there's something going on."

"Proof? Proof of what? It doesn't prove anything, except that

Dominic opened that grave without authorization. That's a violation of the county health laws, village ordinances, and church regulations. I'm suspending him now, without waiting for the civil service hearing. Got all the evidence I need. And you better get out of town before I charge you with something, too."

Dominic remained at the upstairs window, watching.

"Don't blame Dominic," she said. "It was my fault. I insisted on having the grave opened."

"Doesn't matter. He had no business doing it without checking. And I want your address so we can send you the bill for the gravediggers. You're not going to stick us with that expense."

"What about my car?"

"What about it? Your insurance will take care of that."

"Isn't it strange that a car parked right in front of the police station bursts into flame?"

The chief's face got redder.

"You had no business leaving it there. That's a no-parking zone."

"You're evading my question," she said, her own anger rising in her voice. She would not let him deter her.

"Look, lady, I'm the one that asks the questions in this town, not you."

"You don't know how the fire started, do you?"

Up at the window, Dominic slowly shook his head before withdrawing into the shadows. His signal, if that was what it was, came too late.

The chief spun around and ordered the policeman to take her to the bus station in Scranton.

The policeman wouldn't let her call the university, her lawyer, anyone. He sat with her in the car outside the Greyhound station until the evening bus was ready to leave. When he put her on the bus, he cautioned her not to come back.

Katherine spent the trip through the darkening Poconos trying to apply some rational thought to what was happening.

Was she hallucinating?

35

Maybe she was trying to wish her mother back to life. Maybe eight years of denying her mother's death had altered her sense of reality.

But the grave was empty. That was a fact. Even the police admitted that.

An empty grave? Her mother back from the dead?

She couldn't say anything about that at the university. It wasn't what they'd want to hear from an associate professor of abnormal psychology who still hadn't been granted tenure. Her friends would recommend psychotherapy. And the New York police wouldn't be any more help than the chief of police who had just chased her out of town.

By the time the bus reached New York, Katherine's anger had given way to a recognition of her own helplessness. There was no one who would believe her story. Nowhere to go for help.

She was alone.

She was afraid to take the subway from the bus station. Afraid she might see that dead face in the crowded cars. There were too many opportunities to catch sight of her mother on a sidewalk, at an intersection, staring from the window of another car. She kept her eyes closed as the taxi took her to the Upper East Side.

It was a relief to reenter the cocoon of her condo building's security system. The doorman looked up from his battery of black-and-white TV monitors. He nodded and pressed the button that gave her entry to the lobby. On the silent faces of the monitors were the images of the laundry room, basement entrance, elevators, parking garage, and hallways. The doorman smiled a welcome at her.

No one could enter the building without passing his electronic barriers. She was safe now.

Alone, yes. But safe.

The condo was hot and stuffy, filled with air that had grown stale waiting for her to return. A familiar odor, probably from the building's incinerator, mixed with the stagnant air. It was a smell of old fires and charred ashes. She would have to complain to the building management again. For the price she was paying, she expected cleaner air. They'd probably blame it on the building next door again, she thought with resignation.

She turned on the air conditioning to purge the odor. The welcome whoosh sent its artificial breeze through the apartment. She turned on the TV. Not because she wanted to watch, but just for the sound of human voices. She went through the ritual of kicking off her shoes, turning on the coffeepot, stripping to her bra and panties, and slipping into the rough comfort of a terry robe.

The familiar routine helped her forget the last two days. She selected a frozen dinner from the dozen she kept in the freezer and put it in the microwave oven for the invisible rays to work their peculiar magic, cooking the meal without the use of heat.

The meal was like hundreds before. Katherine was used to eating alone. This time it was lobster Newburg, two hundred seventy-five calories, cooking time fifteen minutes. It was the first food she had eaten since leaving Eddie's place this morning. Maybe that was why she had the headache.

A few aspirin and a good hot bath would solve that problem. The bathroom door was jammed.

She pounded with her open hand. She twisted the doorknob. Finally, she threw her shoulder against the door. Once. Twice. On the third try, it came loose, sending her flying into the very center of the stench that had been seeping into the rest of the apartment.

Katherine yelled out in horror.

The interior of her bathroom, every square inch of it, was blackened and scorched, as if the very fires of hell had left their mark. A heavy, sulfuric odor mixed with the sour smell of fires strangled by their own fumes. The stench that had been bottled up in the confined space filled her mouth with its bitterness. Barely able to breathe, she stared at the evil that surrounded her. The plastic shower curtain was melted into a black crust inside the tub. The towels lay in neat little heaps of gray ash. Their plastic racks were melted into puddles, with bubbles frozen where they had formed. Every painted surface was blistered and burned. Bottles and tubes in the medicine cabinet had exploded. Their contents leaked from behind the mirrored door. And scrawled on the cracked and blackened mirror itself was a message.

She recognized the scrawl as her mother's.

Gagging from the foul air, Katherine began to sob. She ran to her bedroom and locked the door behind herself.

It took twenty minutes before the police and fire departments responded to her nearly hysterical calls.

The police arrived first.

Detective Arnold Russo, pockmarked face, mustache, balding on top, examined the front door for signs of forced entry. Katherine refused to enter the bathroom. He let out a low whistle when he saw the charred interior.

"This is arson squad business, lady. Strictly fire department. We don't have anything to do with fires that are out."

"I called the police for protection."

Russo scribbled something in his notebook.

"What kind of protection? Somebody threaten you?"

"That fire is a warning," she said. "I could have been caught in it."

"That's for sure," Russo said. "If you're not more careful, you could hurt yourself."

"I had nothing to do with it. I wasn't even home at the time. It was like this when I came back tonight."

"You must have left something on. A hair dryer, maybe."

Katherine showed her anger. "The hair dryer's in my bedroom. Look around. There are no appliances in there. Nothing that could have started the fire. I don't smoke. There aren't even any matches in the apartment."

Russo looked around and shrugged. He didn't seem to be too concerned.

"Maybe it's the wiring."

"You don't understand," she said. "There's nothing in there that started the fire. No short circuit, nothing."

He tried to suppress a grin.

"You mean it started sort of . . . by itself?"

"No. It was supernatural in origin."

38

The grin spread over his face.

"You mean spirits started the fire?"

"You'll see. There won't be any explanation for the cause of that fire. I'm certain of that. The fire was meant as a warning for me."

Detective Russo suggested she go back to the bedroom and rest until the fire department arrived.

The arson squad was led by Captain Edward O'Grady, a short red-haired man with a band of shiny scar tissue that wrapped around his neck. His eyebrows had been burned away in some long-forgotten fire. The squad's equipment filled three black suitcases. After photographing the scene, they began their examination. The policeman watched with curiosity as they worked. Katherine stayed in the bedroom, still too unnerved to go near them.

An hour later, Captain O'Grady came out of the bathroom. Behind him, the men were putting their equipment away.

"So what's the verdict?" Russo asked.

Captain O'Grady shook his head.

"Some sort of flash fire. All the burning is on the surface. High-intensity scorching. We took scrapings from the wood, and none of the scorching went deeper than a sixteenth of an inch. Normally in a flash fire of that sort there's an accelerant involved. Gasoline or naphtha or chemicals of a very specific nature. The kind that explode into tremendously hot flame. They're usually easy to detect. But we can't find any sign of chemicals."

"Where did it start?"

"Can't tell. Nothing really burned, except for the towels. Everything else is just charred. The surface damage indicates there had to be an intense source of heat. It takes a tremendous amount of heat to penetrate the medicine cabinet and make those bottles explode. The heat would have to be sustained, too. But we can't find any sign of the source. No part of the room suffered more damage than any other. There aren't any hot spots."

"You don't know what caused it?" Russo asked.

"Not at the moment. We've taken scrapings of the wood, samples of the ash, pieces of paint. We'll analyze those in the spectrometer. But I have a feeling we won't find anything."

He turned to Katherine.

"Those words on the mirror. Who wrote them?" he asked.

"Mother did."

"Your mother? Where is she?"

"She was buried eight years ago."

The policeman coughed.

"I don't think I heard you right," Captain O'Grady said. "Where is she?"

Katherine tried to keep her voice firm. It wouldn't help to sound out of control.

"She was buried eight years ago," she repeated. "But she's not in her grave now. I don't know where she is."

Captain O'Grady glanced at Russo, who held up his hands.

"She's a psychology professor," he said, as if it explained something.

"I hope you're not playing games here," O'Grady said in a suddenly suspicious tone. "A fire like that could spread to the entire building. You'd be endangering a lot of lives."

"It wasn't me," Katherine said. "I was out of town the last two days. I can prove it. I have plenty of witnesses. I came back tonight and found this . . . this manifestation of something I can't explain." She looked directly at him, challenging him to answer her. "You can't explain it either, can you?"

"Not yet," he said. "But if I find out what kind of fire that was, and I think you had anything to do with starting it, I'll charge you with arson, lady. I don't care where you were or how many witnesses you have, I'll charge you."

He signaled his companions to bring the suitcases.

"Whatever your game is . . . insurance or publicity or whatever . . . I'll see that it stops right here."

Russo lingered after the arson squad left.

Katherine didn't move. She was sitting in the center of her bed. Her knees were folded up under her chin, her arms wrapped around her calves in a protective, almost fetal posture.

His voice was gentler when he finally spoke.

"What kind of protection did you want?"

"You see what's happening here," Katherine said.

"It's not easy getting protection. You'd have to make a formal request. It would have to go through the precinct and, if they okay it, get bucked up to the commissioner's office. I could bring you the forms. But you'd have to be very specific about why you need the protection."

"It would be a waste of time, wouldn't it?"

"You'd have to write down who you think is trying to hurt you."

"They'd think I was crazy, wouldn't they?"

"It wouldn't be the first time someone claimed they saw a ghost in New York."

Katherine rubbed her chin against the top of her knees. Her voice was low, almost a whisper.

"It's Mother," she insisted. "She's doing all this."

"I deal with muggings and rapes and murders," Russo said. "This is out of my league. I can't deal with ghosts."

"You're going to leave me now? What if Mother comes back?"

"You want my opinion?"

When she didn't respond, he gave it anyway.

"I wouldn't hang around here, if I were you. Why don't you take a nice long vacation? The Caribbean or Mexico. Get a change of scenery. Get this off your mind."

He started for the doorway.

"You let it eat at you, you'll only be hurting yourself."

He stopped in the doorway and looked back.

"And no more fires," he said. "That O'Grady comes back, he'll take you in."

Huddled in her protective position, Katherine stayed on the bed. She stared at the open bathroom door. Beyond it, invisible from this angle but burned into her mind, was the message on the mirror.

Four words.

They were scrawled on the blackened glass with agonizing clarity.

"No one can help."

41

What did it mean?
Was it a threat?
A warning?
Or some strange cry for help?

Four

"**N**O ONE CAN help."

She remembered the words from eight years ago. She was a graduate student then, at NYU. It was a Friday night, April 11. They brought her from the library to a room where a priest waited for her. Father John Ritter. She didn't know where he was from. She never met him before, and hadn't seen him since. Apparently they thought it was better for her to hear it from a priest than from some disembodied voice over the telephone. Or from one of the university's administrative staff.

The black clothing of the Catholic priest made her nervous even before he spoke. Afraid to look him in the eye, she concentrated on the square inch of starched white Roman collar that was exposed at his neck.

He might have been a very good priest, but he hadn't known Mother, so there was no way he could really understand what had happened. All he knew was what the police had told him about finding her in the bathroom of a motel in Pennsylvania. They had told him about the fire. About the message scrawled on the mirror. Did she know what the message meant?

She remembered it was all so unreal, she didn't even cry. It was a peculiar feeling, one that made her feel guilty. The next morning in Pennsylvania, she refused to go with the police to see where Mother was found. She refused to see Mother at all until after the funeral director had completed his work. And when she finally saw Mother, it was impossible to believe she had been asphyxiated. As the funeral director said, she was in repose.

Asleep.

Asleep and now awake.

Perhaps she was never really dead.

But why come back, after all these years?

Was she angry?

The unanswerable questions went through Katherine's mind in an endless round.

It was the ringing of the telephone that finally snapped her out of it. Her legs were stiff and painful from hours of sitting in the same position. It was daylight already.

"Katherine? You sound strange. Are you all right?"

She felt better at the sound of Dominic's voice.

She tried to keep her voice calm as she told him about the fire, but it was trembling despite her effort.

"Dominic, I'm frightened. Why is she doing this?"

"I don't have any answers. All I know is you're in danger. I'm not even certain I can help you."

"But you've got to help. No one else will listen to me. They all think I started the fire myself."

"Now calm down, Katherine. If you want me to help, you'll have to follow my instructions. Will you do that?"

"All right. Just tell me what you want."

"I'm going to come to New York to pick you up. I'm going to bring you back to Dickson, where I can try to protect you."

"Try? You mean you're not sure you can?"

"Katherine, just listen to me. I don't want you to stay in that apartment alone. I want you to go down to the lobby of your building. There's a security guard in the lobby, isn't there?"

"Yes, there is."

"I want you to sit by that guard and wait for me. Don't go out into the street. Don't even go near the door. You sit in that lobby where the guard can see you. I'll be there as soon as I can."

"But it's a two-hour drive from Dickson. You expect me to sit in the lobby for two hours?"

"Now listen to me. You're in danger as long as you're alone. I'll tell you why when I get there. But I want you out of that apartment now. Don't change your clothes. Don't waste any time fixing your hair. Don't do anything except go down to the lobby, as fast as you can, and wait for me there. Do you understand?"

"Yes."

"Then do it."

She held on to the telephone with both hands, as if this link to his voice conferred some sort of protection upon her. She wanted him to keep talking, to explain what was happening, to promise her that he could help. But all he would do was repeat his warning to leave the apartment.

She didn't want to let go of the telephone, even after his voice was replaced by the angry buzz of the dial tone.

What did he know?

Why wouldn't he tell her?

And why wasn't he surprised when she told him about the fire?

Each unanswered question led to another. She was upset by his secrecy. But she did what she was told.

She went down to the lobby in her bathrobe, not even bothering to put on her makeup.

The security guard, too jaded to be surprised by anything the tenants did, tried to be polite.

"You're the apartment that had the fire, aren't you?" he asked.

"That's right."

"The police asked me about you, but I told them you were out of town when it must've happened."

"Thanks."

"I think they were trying to pin it on you."

"Probably."

"There's guys selling dope right on the corner here, but the police don't bother them. They got no business coming in my building trying to pin stuff on decent people."

"I agree."

"Well, they won't get anything from me. You can count on that."

By the time Dominic arrived, the security guard's friendliness was gone, replaced by irritation at her unwillingness to talk.

Instead of a police car, Dominic arrived in a once-elegant Buick Riviera. The battered car wore the rusted bruises, dents, and faded paint that come not from age, but from lack of care. Dominic didn't look much better himself. She guessed from his face that he hadn't slept last night. His eyes glowed with an intensity that reflected inner demons at work. They went up to her apartment.

But whose demons were they? she wondered, when the charred bathroom brought a smile to his lips. There were no Polaroids this time. He seemed to be memorizing the scene. His fingers moved quickly along the blistered surfaces.

"What did the police say?" he asked.

"They can't do anything about it."

"And the arson squad?"

"They think I did it. They threatened to arrest me."

"Typical New York police," he said. "They should be out arresting the scum instead of threatening you."

"That's what the security guard said downstairs."

"It's just a trick to get you off their backs. If they scare you a little, they figure you'll be too afraid to call back and bother them again."

He rubbed his fingers lightly over the message on the mirror.

"What does that mean?" he asked. "Who wrote that on the glass?"

"It had to be Mother. It's a message from her. Maybe she wants help."

"And maybe it's a warning."

"I considered that." She shivered at the thought.

"Does it look like her handwriting?"

"It's identical. As if a handwritten note was enlarged. Her letters always tipped over to the left. She used to make excuses about her handwriting."

"*No one can help.* You saw that same message before, didn't you?"

Katherine stiffened as he turned to face her, the intensity of those dark eyes boring into her, searching for her weakness.

"You saw it in another bathroom just like this. The one where your mother died eight years ago in Pennsylvania."

"No," she murmured weakly.

"Or maybe you didn't see it yourself. You only saw the photographs."

"Please don't . . ."

"Why didn't you tell me your mother committed suicide?"

"Stop it."

"I went to the county health department yesterday. Your mother died of asphyxiation. But she didn't feel a thing, thanks to a few dozen sleeping pills. I read the coroner's report. Why didn't you tell me?"

"Because I never believed it. Mother wouldn't take her own life. She never exhibited any self-destructive tendencies."

"It's all in the coroner's report. She's dead, Katherine, dead. Why don't you accept it?"

He spoke with gentleness, the tone men reserve for those helpless moments when they share another's pain. It reminded her of the private agonies Dominic himself must have endured.

"I know you're trying to help," she said. "But I'm too upset to talk about it now."

He nodded and went back to his examination, digging into the woodwork with the sharp edge of a nail clipper.

"Fire stayed right on the surface," he said. "It must have been tremendously intense, but fast. Otherwise it would have burned deeper."

"That's what the arson squad said."

He twisted around to look under the sink basin. She heard him grunt. Quickly he looked under the toilet tank.

"Did they say there was anything unusual about the fire?" he asked.

"Pretty much what you said. Intense heat. Short duration. They looked for chemicals or gasoline residue, but didn't find anything."

"So they don't know the cause?"

She shook her head.

"I told them Mother did it."

"You shouldn't have done that."

"I know. Now they think there's something wrong with me."

"There's nothing wrong with you. You just have an overactive imagination. You think too much. Too complicated."

"You're saying I imagined all this?" she asked, waving her hand at the seared walls. "It's all in my mind, is that what you're saying?"

Dominic came up from under the sink with a smile. He brushed some cobwebs off his hands. His interest in the bathroom was over.

"No, you didn't imagine it," he said. "Come on, dress up and let's get out of here."

"I've got to pack."

"We'll come back. After we visit a cemetery here. I've got to get the location from the police."

Katherine shuddered at the thought of another cemetery, but did as she was told. Going with Dominic, wherever he was headed, was better than sitting here alone.

As they drove to the precinct station, the car was slowed by double-parked vehicles that reduced the crosstown street to a single lane. Beyond the unbroken rows of parked cars, brown plastic garbage bags were stacked against the buildings.

"This is supposed to be the good part of town, isn't it?" he asked.

"It's the Upper East Side," she answered. "Not exactly Park Avenue, but it's what you'd call the high-rent district."

"I don't believe it." He curled his lip in disgust. "It's like living in the town dump, except for the fancy buildings. There's garbage everywhere. Look at it."

"You think Dickson is so terrific?"

"Well, it's a lot cleaner."

They stopped in the middle of the block to wait for the uptown traffic to clear the intersection. The traffic light ahead turned from green to red and back to green again, but the intersection was still blocked by a bus and taxis that refused to give way. The cars behind them set up a chorus of angry horns.

Dominic was watching a woman walking a dog.

"Is that one of your successful New Yorkers?" he asked. "The lady with the mink coat? What do you think she pays for her apartment?"

"If she lives around here, at least a thousand a month."

"And that's not for a fancy place, is it?" he asked. "I read they pay that much for a hole in the wall in this town."

"Everybody wants to live in Manhattan," she answered. "There's a housing shortage, people from all over the world come here. Successful people."

She emphasized the word "successful." Why was she suddenly getting defensive?

"So she's paying a thousand a month," Dominic said. "She looks terrific. Lives in a location so desirable, the whole world wants to live here. But she's got to keep a fifty-pound German shepherd in her apartment for protection, feed him five pounds of dog food every day, and go out and walk him twice a day when she'd rather be home watching TV."

"What's wrong with that? A lot of people have dogs."

"Yeah, but twice a day that woman has to go out with her plastic gloves and pick up dog shit off the sidewalk. All because she's too scared to live in her thousand-dollar-a-month apartment without a watchdog."

"You sound bitter."

"Bitter? No. I'm realistic."

The intersection finally cleared and the traffic started moving again. They made it to the corner before the light turned red again.

"This city's out of control," he said. "Too many people. Too much filth. It's amazing what people give up to live here."

"You sound like Mother. She was always trying to get me to move back to Dickson."

"She had the right idea."

"Maybe if I did . . ." Katherine stopped and shook her head. "No. It wouldn't have made any difference."

He parked the car in a no-parking zone, between two police cars.

"Look at that building across the street," he said. The building he pointed to covered the entire block. Forty stories of small windows punctuated the soot-covered brick walls. "You could probably fit half the people of Dickson in that building. But it's like a prison. Everybody passes a checkpoint in the lobby, rides the same elevators, and hopes to God nobody broke into their apartment while they were gone. They're too suspicious of each other to even make friends."

"They're happy," Katherine said. "A lot of people like the anonymity of a big building."

"And if something goes wrong? What happens then? You've got five thousand strangers trying to beat each other out of the building if there's a fire. A lot of people are going to get hurt. It's not right for so many people to live like that."

"Does it make you nervous? Too many big buildings for you?"

"You think I'm a hick, don't you? Well, it doesn't bother me as long as I know I can turn my car around and I'm out of here. Back to where people live the normal way. In houses, where they know each other."

Katherine was going to respond. But she stopped when she realized that at this moment, in the city where she had lived most of her life, the only person she could rely on was this ex-policeman from Pennsylvania, whose fiery eyes and bitter words hinted at psychological problems. She decided to let him ramble on.

"Take that security guard in your building," he said. "He couldn't protect his mother in this town. You say the most successful people in the world come here. Well, so do the most successful criminals. And the craziest. And you know what? Nobody cares. You can do anything in this town and get away with it."

He lowered his voice as they entered the police station.

"You listen to this cop we're going to see. He won't care about us. He'll just want to move us in and out as fast as he can. Probably never even checked back with Dickson to see if I was really a policeman myself. The whole town is overloaded with people and problems. That's why the cops hardly even bother chasing the bad guys anymore. The prisons are full, the courts are full, and the cops are too busy with paperwork. If they catch anybody in this town, it's the exception. You watch."

Dominic asked for Lieutenant Orestes Coleman. A policeman in the crowded entrance area pointed him toward a low cubicle just beyond the open clerical area.

Lieutenant Coleman was a tall black man with short steel-wool hair and a beard that curled into itself.

Dominic shook hands and introduced Katherine as a detective on the Dickson police force. When Coleman didn't ask for her identification, Dominic winked at her.

"You called about those graves," Coleman said. "Here's the file, and here's a map. I'd go out there with you, but I just haven't got the time to spare."

"Busy, huh?"

"There's not enough hours in the day."

"I know what you mean," Dominic agreed, as he looked through the file. "What about the next of kin? You said you'd check into that."

"Yeah, I guess I did say that. So far, we don't have anything more than I told you on the phone."

Coleman answered his telephone, made a few comments, and put his hand over the receiver.

"Everything we have is in the file. Three suicides and one

woman committed to an institution. As a result of the stolen bodies. A real trauma, I guess. If you need anything else, just call me. I've got to talk to this fellow on the phone."

He reached out to shake hands with Dominic, dismissing them.

After glancing at the file, Dominic led her out of the station.

"I'll bet he never even went out to the cemetery to check," Dominic said. "According to the file, the coroner made the gravesite inspections. Maybe somebody out there knows what's going on."

"Do I have to go to this cemetery with you?" Katherine asked.

"Does it bother you?"

"It frightens me, yes."

"A cemetery is the safest place you can be. Everybody's dead there. They can't hurt you. You'd be in more danger just crossing the street."

A vague grin came to his lips. It made her remember what the chief had said about him.

He took the Fifty-seventh Street entrance to the lower level of the Queensboro Bridge. The morning rush was over, but repair work on the aging structure forced the eastbound traffic into one overcrowded lane.

"How did you learn your way around town?" she asked.

"I used to come every Christmas with my wife," he answered while the traffic crept along. "She liked to see the Christmas lights on Park Avenue and the department store displays. We used to watch the skaters in Rockefeller Center and listen to the bells at St. Patrick's. She'd buy perfume at Lord and Taylor and gifts for her nephews at Macy's."

"I thought you didn't like New York."

"It was different in those days. Or maybe it was just being with Cara. I saw everything through her eyes, and it was all beautiful. Now all I see is the garbage."

They finally broke free of the construction traffic, only to have the bridge exit deposit them into an industrial area where the streets were clogged with trucks. It took a half hour to travel the five miles to St. Mark's Cemetery. Katherine had seen the cemetery hundreds of times from the Long Island Expressway. She hadn't even known the name of it until now. It was always just another one of those vast anonymous tracts of New York that meant nothing to people who had no reason to go there.

But seeing St. Mark's at fifty-five miles an hour from the far lane of the Long Island Expressway was different from entering its wrought-iron gates at a crawl. The narrow two-lane road wound among overcrowded rows of monuments that filled every available piece of ground, a silent farm of marble that followed the contours of the rolling land for acre after acre, all the way down to the distant expressway.

The monuments were far more elaborate than those in the small cemetery in Pennsylvania. Angels towered over the road in frozen flight. A scale model of the Temple of Diana sat on a knoll. Obelisks and statues, crucifixes and slabs were aligned according to the eternal discipline imposed by the subterranean rows of coffins. The only relief from the marble fields was the isolated, now leafless trees, eunuchs whose roots were regularly trimmed to avoid toppling nearby markers.

They found the caretaker's building, where Dominic waved the police file before a suspicious old man. It was identification enough.

"I've got a fresh one," the old man said. "Must have happened last night. The coroner's man didn't even show up yet. They don't give a damn anyway."

They rode with the caretaker in his pickup truck. It took almost five minutes down winding roads before they reached the gravesite.

"This is the fifth one," the caretaker said. He blessed himself quickly, not caring whether they noticed.

The grave had a frightening similarity to the one in Dickson. The center was collapsed into a long depression whose middle had been violently torn open. Clumps of grass and mud were strewn around the neighboring graves, as if they had exploded from the ground, thrown up by some strange force.

"It happens like this at night," the caretaker said. "Always at night, and in the morning another body's gone. The dead can't sleep in peace anymore."

"Did you ever see anybody?" Dominic asked. "Or hear anything?"

"There's forty thousand graves here. The cemetery is two square miles. And these tombstones block everything. There's no way you can watch every grave. And you can't pay people enough money to stay in a cemetery overnight. They added security guards after the first one, but the guards were staying in the equipment barn all night, drinking and watching portable TV. So they stopped that. Waste of money, that's all."

Dominic examined the debris on the adjoining graves. He took the usual Polaroids, while Katherine watched, puzzled by what she was hearing.

"All five coffins were empty, I suppose," Dominic said.

"This is the fifth," the caretaker reminded him. "The first four, I know for sure, because I saw them. Wasn't anything left in them. Just some stains on the coffin linings, where the bodies had started to rot, but no signs of anything else. This one, I'd expect the same once we open it."

Katherine shuddered at his description.

"Lieutenant Coleman said it must be grave robbers. Is that what you think?" Dominic asked.

The caretaker looked around before answering.

"They're just guessing. They don't know what's going on."

"Is it something else? Do you have a different idea?"

"The police don't follow this stuff up. They just want to close the case. If they followed it up, they might think different."

Katherine felt a cold shiver. She had a sensation that someone was watching.

"You don't think it was an ordinary grave robbing?" Dominic asked.

"I didn't say that. You been around cemeteries as long as I have, you see a lot of funny things. All the weirdos you've got on the streets. They used to put them in loony bins, but now they let them wander around town. Saves the city money, I guess. I've had one or two try to dig up graves. But it's not that easy."

"How do you mean the police don't follow up?"

"Well, if they came out here, they'd see the people that showed up right after the graves were opened."

"Like who?"

"Oh, different people. Sometimes the widow. The son. The father. The partner."

Dominic was fingering the edge of the grave, where the grass was torn away.

"Of course they'd come," he said. "I'm sure the police notified them the bodies were missing."

"Not the police. It's the cemetery that notifies them. The police have nothing to do with it. You see, the law says the plot really belongs to the cemetery. The heirs just have an easement. That's all they buy when they buy a plot. They don't own the land. And it's the heir that the cemetery contacts."

"So they come out to visit the grave, see the site themselves. What's unusual about that?"

"Well, they'd come here before the cemetery notified them. It was like they already knew the grave was empty."

Five

THE FEELING THAT they were being watched grew stronger. Katherine spun around to examine the cemetery behind her, but all she saw was a gray squirrel running between the rows of tombstones, hoping to find the shelter of a tree before being caught. By whom?

"I'll tell you something else," the caretaker said. "I've seen lots of people come to visit graves over the years. I couldn't begin to count how many. They cry. They talk to the tombstones. They bring flowers. Sometimes they just stare. But these folks were different. They were scared."

"Maybe they were just upset," Dominic said. "After all, the graves were open. That must have been upsetting."

"I can tell when a person is scared," the old man insisted. "These people were shaking, I tell you. They looked like they expected something to tap them on the shoulder. I went up to one lady and she about jumped out of her skin, she was that scared."

"Like she saw a ghost?"

"It's not funny," the caretaker said. "You've got to remember what these people went through. Somebody dies, and there's a lot of grief involved. Then, when it's all over, the corpse disappears. No wonder they were scared."

A wind that started somewhere out on Long Island Sound came gently in, carrying with it the muddy smell of the tidal flats, blowing shriveled oak leaves into the grave. The dead leaves sounded like something stirring nearby. Katherine didn't want to listen to what the old man was saying.

"Can we go now?" she asked.

Dominic raised his hand, unwilling to be interrupted.

"Those people you saw. Did you know that four of them committed suicide?"

The caretaker's eyes widened. He turned away, kicking a loose piece of sod into the grave.

"God rest their souls," he said, half under his breath. "That's why they stopped coming here, I guess. I wondered about that."

The old man stared out across the cemetery. Katherine shivered in the silence. The first drops of rain blew against the back of her raincoat, making a soft flicking sound.

"I'm not surprised," the caretaker finally said. "But it's a terrible thing for a person to do. Especially if they're afraid of the dead."

As the rain started up, Katherine raised the collar of her raincoat and moved closer to Dominic, using his body as protection against the wet wind.

"I'd like to get this grave taken care of," the old man said. "But now with the rain, I don't guess the coroner's people will be out here today."

Back at the equipment barn, Dominic scrawled his name and phone number on a piece of paper and passed it to the old man.

"Do me a favor," he said. "Anybody shows up at that grave, ask them to call me. Or at least get their name and call me yourself."

The caretaker studied the paper.

"This is a long-distance number," he said.

"You can call collect."

"Where are you folks from?"

"Pennsylvania."

"What do you care what goes on here?" He grew suspicious, now that he was being asked to involve himself. "You got relatives buried here?"

Dominic reached into his wallet for some money.

"We have a similar case up there," he said. "Body missing from the grave. We want to see if there's a connection."

There was a small window in the back of the equipment barn. While Katherine waited for Dominic to finish with the old man, she went to the window. The feeling of being watched wouldn't go away. The wind was beginning to blow the rain against the dirt-coated glass. She looked for some sign of movement among the tombstones. Was someone out there? Was it just fatigue, playing tricks on her senses?

Or was it the first creeping tentacles of paranoia?

That was how it started, she knew. Vague suspicions at first. Tendrils of doubt. Insidious feelings. They had a way of sneaking up on the mind and finally knitting together into a rational and coherent fabric of beliefs that were compellingly real. The beliefs were mere delusions, masquerading as reality.

Was all this part of some paranoid delusional pattern?

It was impossible to tell, because the delusions existed in the mind without impairing intellectual functions. Freud had demonstrated that paranoids were capable of fully coherent behavior, vigorously defending their illusions. Just as she did now, turning from the window.

"Somebody's out there," she said.

Delusion or not, she was convinced of it.

The two men halted their transaction and joined her. The

rain had melted the dirt into a gray sludge on the glass, making it difficult to see through.

Dominic went to the door. After a while, he shook his head. "I don't see anything," he said. "Maybe it's just the rain."

"Cemeteries will do that to people," the caretaker said. "They make your mind work in a different way, seeing things that don't exist. Everything so quiet, and you know that under the ground are all those people, some of them here for fifty years. You start to wonder if they can hear your footsteps on their graves."

Katherine was quiet until they were back in the car, heading for Manhattan.

"Now I know why you called this morning," she said.

"So you think you figured it out?"

"You didn't want me to be alone. You were afraid I might commit suicide, like those other people."

"That was one of the reasons," he admitted.

She knew a shorter way back to the Queensboro Bridge, but she let him retrace his earlier route.

"You think I can't handle this," she went on. "You don't have to worry about me. I'm a psychologist, remember?"

He gave her a low, derisive chuckle.

"Is that supposed to give you some kind of protection?" he asked. "You think it makes you immune? Well, everybody's a little crazy, and that includes professors and psychiatrists, too."

"You don't know anything about psychiatrists."

"I know enough to tell they're a waste of time. All they do is listen."

"Maybe if you went to one, you wouldn't have the problems you do."

As soon as she said it, she was sorry.

"You think I'm crazy?"

"I didn't say that."

"You don't really know me. You don't know what I've been through."

"I know about your wife," she said in a gentle voice. She didn't want to argue with him.

"You don't know anything about Cara. Nobody does. They

60

all talk, but none of them know what it was really like. Not at the end."

"Tell me about it. Maybe I can help."

"You help?" He laughed. "You've got more of a problem than I do. At least I can admit Cara is dead. She's dead and buried, and I know she's never coming back. But you still pretend your mother's alive."

"The grave was empty," she said in a flat voice. "You saw that yourself."

"All that means is the body is gone. It doesn't mean she's alive."

"I saw her twice."

"I went through that too. After Cara died, I used to smell her perfume, hear her voice. I'd see a woman in a car and swear it was her. I'd wake up at night and think she was in bed with me. It was just my mind playing tricks on me. I wanted her to be there, and my mind pretended she was. It was just echoes of her. And that's what you're going through."

"What about all those other open graves? Can you explain that?"

"Not yet," he said. "Not yet."

Paranoia, she thought. She had just vigorously defended what could be a delusion.

The buildings of Manhattan appeared across the East River, white marble columns pasted against the blackening clouds. They drove through the gloom of wet crosstown streets to her apartment. It took only a few minutes to pack. She didn't want to spend any more time in the apartment than necessary.

They reached the George Washington Bridge before the afternoon rush hour. The cold rain hitting the warm waters of the Hudson River created a foggy layer that covered the bottom of the New Jersey Palisades.

"Look, I'm sorry," she finally said. "I know I sounded ungrateful, but I'm under a lot of stress."

"That's okay," he grunted.

"I want to thank you for coming to help me. When I heard your voice on the phone, it was such a relief. I don't know what I would have done."

"It's part of my job," he said.

"But you don't have a job anymore. You were fired. That's why you didn't have a badge to show to Lieutenant Coleman or the caretaker. You're not a policeman anymore. And it's all because of me."

"Taking away the badge doesn't change anything. You saw me work. I got all the information I wanted without a badge. I can still do my job."

"But you don't have a job anymore," she repeated. "You were fired. You're not a policeman now."

"You keep calling me a policeman. I wasn't a policeman. I was a detective."

"Sorry."

"This is the only work I know. And I used to be good at it, too."

"You still are," she said. "You found out about those other empty graves."

"That was easy."

"But you did it so quickly. I left Dickson yesterday, and you knew all about the graves this morning."

"That was simple. Anything weird like this, it's bound to happen in New York if it happens anywhere else. They say New York has more of everything. Well, I figured it's got more dead people, too. So I called police headquarters, and bingo!"

They broke clear of the last of New York City's most distant commuter suburbs, and entered Pennsylvania through the massive gates of the Delaware Water Gap. Ahead of them, the tops of the Pocono Mountains were cut off by low-hanging rain clouds.

"Doesn't it frighten you, what you found?" she asked.

"All those empty graves? No. That doesn't bother me. What I'm worried about is four people dying after the graves were opened."

"You can't go on pretending you're still a detective. You can bluff your way in New York, but they know you in Dickson."

"I've still got friends."

"And the chief of police isn't one of them, from what I saw. You could get in trouble trying to help me."

62

"He can't stop me from asking questions," Dominic said in a defiant tone. "Everybody has the right to ask questions."

"He chased me out of town," she reminded him. "He won't be glad to see me again."

"Nothing he can do about it. I know the law as much as he does. I won't let him bother you. Besides, you can't stay in New York. The police there don't give a damn, you saw that. I want you where I can keep an eye on you."

The road took them higher into the mountains, up above the honeymoon resorts and ski chalets and the ski runs that were shaved into the sides of the mountains. Gradually the trees along the road were erased from sight by the thickening clouds. Dominic turned on the headlights and slowed down. Soon the road itself disappeared into the fog.

"You don't mind staying at Eddie's place, do you?"

"I don't have any choice, I guess."

"There's no hotels in Dickson."

"That's all right, I don't mind. He scared me at first, the way he looks."

"A lot of people are like that with Eddie. He has to put up with a lot of crap because of his hands. But he's used to it. You've got to admire him. He runs that bar and makes a good living. A lot of people with two good hands couldn't do that."

"And the bowling, too. He's a two-thirty bowler."

"He told you that?"

"It's really amazing the way he overcame that handicap. He must really love to bowl."

"He's not a good bowler," Dominic said. "He tells everybody he is, but he's basically a lousy bowler. They only keep him on the team because he gives them free drinks after they bowl."

"You're being cruel."

"No. I'm being honest. You think a guy with arms like his could ever be a good bowler? It takes a lot of control to put that ball where it has to be to make a strike, or a seven–ten split. And the control comes from the lower arm and wrist action. That's why he'll never be a good bowler. The highest he ever rolled was one thirty-five. I wouldn't call that good."

"So he exaggerated a little. What harm is there? I still admire him for doing it. It takes courage to expose himself to the possibility of ridicule."

"He sucked you in with one of his stories and you believed him. Now you're trying to defend him. You're really naïve."

She answered his bluntness with silence.

The windshield wipers became the loudest noise in the car. Their mindless back-and-forth movement had a hypnotic effect on her. She struggled to keep her eyes open. With the gray fog ahead, there was nothing to focus on, nothing to distract her attention. She didn't want to look at Dominic. As thankful as she was that he had come to her rescue in New York, there was still something about him that frightened her. She didn't know why he was taking this sudden interest in her problem. He wasn't a policeman anymore. And he was suffering from some sort of withdrawal. That was obvious. Yet he had become very free in talking to her. And in bringing her back to Dickson, he was risking further trouble.

It was dark when they reached the Lackawanna Valley. The lights of the towns below were thickest in the center of the valley, thinning out as they climbed the hills on both sides. The fog hung over the tops of the mountains in a canopy that reflected the glow of the lights.

"How long will I be here?" she asked.

"I don't know," he answered in a tired voice. "As long as it takes to clear this all up."

"You can't arrest someone who's come back from the grave."

"I don't believe in ghosts," he said. "I already told you that. Besides, I don't have the authority to make arrests anymore."

"You're dealing with the supernatural, Dominic. Whether you want to admit it or not. Mother can do whatever she wants, and you have no control over it."

They started down the long hill that skirted the edge of Scranton, passed a row of green and red neon motel signs, intersected with a short expressway, and deposited them on the two-lane road that served as Dickson's Main Street.

"You mean well, but you have no control over any of this," she repeated.

"I know there's something . . . or someone . . . out there. I don't think it's your mother. It can't be, because she's dead. She's been dead for eight years. I'm going to find out what's behind those empty graves and those four deaths. I don't know what it is, but I'll find out."

Dominic parked the car in front of the red-neon-lit windows of the Valley Inn. He took her baggage around the back way.

"No point in letting the chief know you're here," he said.

He pressed a button under the kitchen windowsill. A buzzer sounded inside, bringing Eddie Elbows to unlock the back door.

"It's the Sunday entrance," Dominic explained. "Also for after hours."

Eddie Elbows took her hand with his short arms and drew her inside.

"I'm glad you're back," he said with a big smile.

They went up the rear stairs. Katherine caught a glimpse of the crowded bar as they passed the doorway. A few customers turned to look at them.

"I moved some of Phyllis's clothes out of the closet, so you'd have more room," Eddie said.

The bed was turned back, to reveal new sheets that were still creased from the package in which they were sold.

"I brought up a small TV for you, in case you get bored," he said. "It's only a small one, but it's color."

He switched on the TV to demonstrate.

"I'll get you some food," he said. "You must be starving."

"I'm not hungry," she said, looking around the room.

"Don't be bashful," Eddie said. "There's plenty of food downstairs. I serve ham sandwiches and kielbasi at the bar on weekends, so I've got that, plus potato salad and coleslaw. You know where the bathroom is, so when you freshen up, come on down to the kitchen. I'll be waiting for you."

When he was gone, Katherine sat down on the bed, running her hand over the smooth new sheets. From the open doorway she could hear the electronic music of video games and the hollow click of balls on a pool table. An occasional shout rose above the barroom din.

"It's noisy here," she said. "Is it like this every night?"

"It's the weekend," Dominic said. "It'll be noisy until

around midnight, when the crowd heads for the bars in Scranton."

"I hope I can sleep."

"At least you'll have plenty of people around. It's better than staying alone in a hotel room."

"Am I permitted to go downstairs to the bar?" she asked.

"You don't want to go down there. It's just a bunch of drunks."

"What about going outside for a walk?"

"You'll be safer in here."

"How far away do you live?" she asked.

"A couple of miles, but you'll be okay. Eddie keeps a shotgun behind the bar, and I can be here in a few minutes."

"What do you expect to prove by keeping me here?" she asked. "These are supernatural manifestations. They're beyond human control. There's nothing you can do about it."

"You keep saying that. But I wouldn't be here with you if I didn't think there was something I could do."

He stood by the window, positioned in such a way that he could look out without being seen. A smile slowly spread across his face.

"There's nothing you can do," she repeated, trying to draw his attention.

"I've already done something," he said without turning.

"I don't understand."

"I brought you here," he said.

His smile made her uneasy.

"And it's working already," he said. "Faster than I thought it would."

"What are you talking about?"

"Your so-called supernatural manifestation. Whatever it is, it followed you here from New York."

She hurried to the window. He held her back, to prevent her from being seen. A cold draft came through the poorly fitted window sash. Outside, the wind was drying the last of the water from the street. The weather had changed.

"Look between the buildings across the street," he said.

"I don't see anything."

"It's in the shadow. Let your eyes get accustomed to the dark. You'll see it."

The spot that he indicated was a narrow passageway between a white frame house and an appliance store. Like all the other buildings on Main Street, they were separated by less than ten feet of empty space. She stared at the darkness between them, until the shadows began to take on indistinct shapes. What had been solid black turned into shades of gray. But the mass was still indiscernible.

"What is it?" she asked.

"There's a figure there. Standing between the buildings."

"Are you sure?" she asked. "It's too dark for me to see."

"Keep watching. There! Did you see it move?"

"I'm not sure."

"There. Do you see it now?"

The headlights from a passing car lit the shadows briefly. Anticipating that, the figure drew back into the shadows. Katherine jumped forward to see better.

"Mother!" she screamed.

Dominic tried to pull her back.

"Mother!"

The figure across the street withdrew into the shadows.

Katherine trembled in front of the window, trying desperately to look through the blackness to see the figure again.

"Don't leave this room," Dominic said. "I'm going to lock the door. I don't want you going down to the bar, or out to the bathroom or even out into the hallway. You just stay here and don't open the door for anyone except Eddie or me. Do you understand?"

She nodded, unable to speak.

"I'll send Eddie up to keep you company."

From the window, she could see Dominic race across the street. The glow of his flashlight stopped to search the ground where the figure had been. She watched the light disappear between the buildings, to reappear as a vague glow behind them. She waited until the light disappeared again.

She stayed at the window, watching for what seemed like an hour, leaving only to open the door for Eddie.

He came in with a bar tray: a platter of thick ham slices, a plate of rye bread, a small bowl of coleslaw, a jar of mustard, and a bottle of wine. She hurried back to the window. Dominic's flashlight was still not visible.

"You need to eat," Eddie said. "Dominic told me you didn't have anything all day."

He set the tray on a folding stand and pulled up a chair for himself. He motioned for her to sit on the bed.

"You don't have to stay," she said. "I'll be all right."

"Dominic wants me to stay," Eddie told her.

His short hands opened the bottle of wine as expertly as she had ever seen it done. He offered her the cork, and then poured a small amount into one of the glasses for her to taste.

"That's the way they do it in fancy places," he said. "I don't ever do that in the bar, because they'd think I was trying to act high-hat."

To humor him, she took a sip and nodded approval.

"It's a Sebastiani Pinot Noir," he said, filling the two glasses.

The cold sweet smell of the ham was hard to resist. It had a smoky flavor. Real smoke, not like the canned hams she was used to in New York.

"Tomorrow I'll bring you some nice food," he said. "This is just what I serve in the bar."

"I don't need anything fancy," she said.

"You being from New York, and a professor, you know all about good food. I don't get the chance to entertain people who appreciate the finer things. Do you want more wine?" He refilled her glass before she could answer. "With my wife away, I don't have anyone to cook for. I'm a gourmet cook, but if it's just for me, I don't usually bother. It takes too much time to prepare a meal for just one person."

Katherine had forgotten how hungry she was. After a few nibbles of the ham, she made herself a thick sandwich. The meat was tender, the rye bread pungent, the mustard sharp. It was better than any deli sandwich she could remember. The Pinot Noir was a sweet way to wash it down.

"Your wife is lucky to have a man who cooks like this," she said.

He looked pleased at the way she enjoyed his food.

"I'm the lucky one," he said. "Phyllis is a beautiful woman, the most beautiful woman in town. And she has style. Real style. You can see it as soon as she walks into a room. The way she carries herself, you know what I mean?"

He sat back and grinned.

"People are jealous of me. They don't know how I can attract a woman like Phyllis. They make fun of me, because of my arms. But that doesn't bother Phyllis. No sir."

The figure across the street was temporarily forgotten as they talked.

"She must really love you," Katherine said.

She thought she could see tears forming in Eddie's eyes. He emptied his wineglass.

"I like to think so," he said. "God knows, we have a wonderful marriage."

He jumped up when Dominic's footsteps came running up the steps. She was surprised at his reaction.

"I've got to get back to the bar," he said. "If you want anything, just tap on the radiator with that wooden hammer. That's Phyllis's signal. I can hear it real clear downstairs, because the pipe comes right down through the corner of the bar."

Dominic's pants were soaked from the wet grass. His shoes were muddy. He was breathing heavily from the exertion of running through the yards.

"Did you find her?" Katherine asked.

Dominic shook his head.

"But it was her, wasn't it?"

"Hard to tell," he said as he crossed the room.

He carried a small see-through plastic bag.

"There were footprints," he said. "Woman's shoes. But I lost them."

He handed her the evidence bag.

"This look familiar?" he asked.

Katherine suddenly lost her appetite.

"It's Mother's rosary," she said.

Six

INSIDE THE BAG was an old rosary with black wooden beads on a silver chain. The figure on the crucifix was partly worn away from years of use. It brought back memories of life with Mother. Mass on Sunday mornings. Fish on Friday. Ashes on Ash Wednesday. All those rituals Mother followed. Heaven, Hell, and the Devil. The Devil was real to her, Katherine remembered. He was waiting right around the corner, ready to work his evil. Only her guardian angel and prayer could help. The best prayer was the Rosary. Saying the Rosary every night was a guarantee of the last rites before dying. But it hadn't worked for Mother, had it? The Five Glorious Mysteries of the Rosary, those were her favorites. The first was the Resurrection from the tomb.

Was that what was happening now?

"I found it between the buildings."

"She had that rosary since she was a child," Katherine said. "It was buried with her. I remember it in her hands in the coffin."

She refused to touch the bag.

"What does she want from me?" Katherine asked in a weak voice. "Why is she doing this?"

Her shoulders began to tremble. Dominic sat on the bed beside her. She didn't resist when he put his arm around her and drew her close.

"Why?" she repeated. "What does she want from me?"

"Now take it easy," Dominic said. "It couldn't be your mother. Your mother is dead."

"She's out there, Dominic. You saw her."

"I saw a figure in the shadows. It could have been anyone."

"You said it was a woman. Why would a woman be watching me, if it wasn't her?"

"I don't know."

"You found Mother's rosary. Can you explain that?"

"No. I can't."

"Then why do you refuse to admit it's her?"

"Because it's impossible."

Katherine pulled away from him, unwilling to accept his attempt to soothe her.

"I've studied parapsychology," she said. "There are hundreds of fully documented cases in which the dead have communicated with the living."

"You don't really believe that, do you?" he asked.

"I don't know what to believe anymore," she said. "I don't know what's happening to me. I don't trust what I see."

He reached for her again. She tried to resist, but he pulled her close. He started to rock her back and forth, the way a parent comforts a child.

"What does she want, Dominic? If I only knew what she

wanted, I'd do it. Anything so that she could rest in peace."

"Don't let yourself think like that," he said. "Don't give in to it. There's got to be a logical explanation."

She sighed. "I wish there was."

"You've got to accept that she's dead. That's the first step," Dominic said in a gentle voice. "Once you accept that, you'll know she can't come back."

"You sound like a psychologist."

"It's something I had to come to grips with after Cara died."

"That's what it says in the textbooks. But did it really make things any easier for you?"

"No," he said. "It was easier to pretend that she was still alive. I did that a lot at first. I'd lie in bed at night and listen for her and pray that she'd come to bed with me. Or I'd come home from work and call her name to see if she'd answer. There were a lot of things I used to do. Some of them seem silly now. But I couldn't help it."

"How did you get over it?"

He stopped rocking her.

"I'm not sure I'm totally over it. Not yet. There are times that I want to see her come walking through the door so badly that I start crying."

His voice cracked on the last word. She was afraid to look at him, afraid to expose herself to his grief.

"I love her so much," he said, "even though I know she's dead and never coming back. I still love her. Oh my God, I love her."

His body started to shake with his violent, masculine sobs. She put her arms around him and squeezed as tight as she could, trying to comfort him.

"I can't help it," he sobbed. "I'm sorry, but I can't help it."

She held on while he shook with grief for his dead wife. She couldn't think of anything to say that would calm him. Holding this man in her arms, she could feel the sorrow that shook his body in a way that made it her own.

His tears eroded what little control she still had over her emotions. A wall melted within her. She felt hot tears surge into her eyes. And suddenly she was crying with him. For the

73

first time in eight years, she was crying for her mother. Tears of sorrow and fear, tears of anguish and guilt, they mixed together to cleanse her mind. Long-suppressed emotions poured out with a sense of relief.

"It was my fault," she sobbed. "If I'd come with her, she wouldn't have done it."

She heard him disagreeing, telling her not to blame herself, but she repeated the accusation over and over again.

"I let her down," Katherine moaned. "I didn't help her when she needed me. I'd do anything to make it up to her."

Dominic offered her a handkerchief already wet with his own tears.

She blew her nose and wiped her eyes. Taking a deep breath, she cleared her lungs.

Dominic rose and went back to the window.

"It's getting late," he said. "I hate to leave you here alone."

"I'll be all right. I feel better now."

She wiped the last traces of moisture from her eyes with the back of her wrist.

"A good cry helps," he said in a gentle tone. "But that's not what I meant. I'm worried about your safety. Maybe I shouldn't have brought you here."

"I'm glad you did."

She tried to look cheerful, to make it sincere.

"I don't know if it was right." He shook his head. "You're in great danger here. More than I thought. It's all happening faster than I expected."

"What do you mean?"

He kept staring out the window. From his expression, she couldn't tell whether he saw anything outside.

"I brought you back from New York because those manifestations, as you call them, seem to follow you. But I didn't expect it this fast."

Apparently seeing nothing outside, he turned away from the window. The serious look had returned to his face. He was back in control. It was impossible to imagine that he had been crying in her arms just moments ago.

"That figure across the street," he said. "It was there within minutes after we arrived. Yet no one knew we were coming."

"There's an answer," she said. "You just don't want to believe it. You're looking for an explanation that doesn't exist."

"Maybe it doesn't. But I'll feel better if you have some protection."

She was shocked when he pulled the small pistol out from under his armpit. It must have been there all day, hidden under his jacket. She had never noticed it, even when she was holding him.

"It's my own gun," he quickly explained. "They took away the three-fifty-seven Magnum I used when I was on the police force."

He flipped open a black cylinder, removed the copper-headed bullets, snapped the cylinder back in place, and offered it to her, handle first.

"Get the feel of it. It's unloaded. See how it fits your hand. It has a small grip, so it should fit you pretty good."

She pulled away from it.

"You said Eddie has a shotgun."

"He'll use it, too, if he has to. Don't worry about him. This is for extra protection. Just in case."

He offered it to her again.

"I don't believe in handguns," she said.

"It's for your own protection, Katherine. Take it."

"I'd really rather not," she said, putting her hands behind her back.

"Okay, don't take it. Just watch. All you have to do is pull the trigger, like this."

The gun made a sharp click as he demonstrated.

"I think you'd better use two hands. The trigger will be hard for you to pull, because it has to turn the cylinder as well as move the hammer back."

"I have no intention of using a gun."

"You don't even have to aim," he said. "You just wait until they get as close as I am to you and bam . . . you're in business. The two-handed grip helps with the recoil. That gives you more control for the next shot."

He held out the six bullets, their brass cases shining in the light. They made dull clicking sounds when he inserted them in the open cylinder.

"You'll have six shots. No point in giving you any extra bullets, because you won't know how to reload."

"You're not listening to me," she said.

"I heard you. You don't believe in guns."

He snapped the cylinder shut and placed the gun on the night table.

"I'll leave it right here, where you can reach it fast. You don't have to touch until you need it, if that makes you feel better."

"You think I'm going to point a gun at Mother? For God's sake, don't be ridiculous."

"If it really is your mother, if that's who you really think it is when someone comes after you, then don't shoot," he replied. "But if it's not, these bullets are flat-nosed and have an X filed across the tip. They're designed to flatten on impact and split apart. They'll stop anything." He paused. "Anything, dead or alive."

She stared at the gun, at the small hole in the short barrel that was designed to spit the deadly chunks of metal.

"There's no way I'd ever use it."

"If you get scared enough you will. I promise you that. You'll forget all your rational, logical thoughts, and you'll jump for the gun."

"I doubt it."

"See, that's where you're wrong. I know how people react in these situations. I know that better than you, no matter how much you know about psychology and all that abnormal-behavior stuff. I know it, because I study people, not books. I don't waste my time on what people say to me. I watch what they do. I've been watching you. You're a smart woman. But you're on the edge right now. You're letting your imagination work overtime. You better get hold of reality."

"And you think that gun is reality?"

"I wouldn't be able to sleep if I left you unprotected. The gun stays. If you don't have to use it, well and good. But if you do need it, you'll have it. You've got nothing to lose."

Maybe he was right, she thought. Why was she making a big deal out of it?

"You're right about me being on the edge, Dominic. It's funny, I know the symptoms, and I know the psychological reasons for it and the clinical description. I'm heading for a breakdown and I know it and there's nothing I can do about it. Maybe I should go check into a hospital like Eddie's wife did."

"Like who?"

"Eddie's wife."

"Who told you he had a wife?"

"Eddie did. He told me all about her. She must be a wonderful person. He loves her so much."

"You've got to be kidding me."

"What do you mean?"

"Eddie's not married. Never has been."

"He told me her name was Phyllis. He said she was a beautiful woman."

"For an educated person you're really gullible. The only Phyllis around here was a woman used to work in the bar. And she wasn't good-looking by any stretch of the imagination. She was your basic ugly. She had no jaw and her upper teeth stuck out. But she was never married to Eddie. She used to make fun of him."

"He said she was up at the Mayo Clinic for a checkup."

"That's another one of Eddie's stories. The Phyllis I know ran away with some guy who came into the bar. A complete stranger. She was tending bar one afternoon while Eddie was sleeping off too many beers. Some guy driving a load of furniture for Allied Van Lines came in for a beer and directions to I-80. He was headed for California. Phyllis said she'd show him the way. Personally. She took off her apron, and that was the last anyone saw of her. Didn't even send Eddie a card. Far as I know, she's still there."

Katherine looked around the room with a puzzled expression.

"But what about the clothing and things? There's perfume on the dresser and women's clothes in the closet."

Dominic looked as if he was sorry he had said what he did.

"The guy's lonely. He builds dream worlds for himself. You should understand that, you being a psychology professor. He doesn't mean any harm. He invents stories to make himself feel better. It's not that he's really lying, not in his own mind. He's just making things come out the way he'd have liked them to be. You can't blame him for that."

"I guess not," she murmured.

But the revelation bothered her. That was twice now that Eddie had deceived her. Why did he do it? She was a stranger to him. There was no reason to lie to her. Unless he wanted to make himself seem more important. But he must have known Dominic would tell her the truth.

"I know what you're thinking," Dominic said. "Now you don't trust him and you're worried about staying here. That gun is probably looking better now, isn't it?"

She didn't respond, not wanting to admit that he was right.

"You don't have to worry about Eddie. He'll protect you with his life. Just don't believe what he says when he tells you about himself."

And you, Dominic, what about you? Can I trust you? Two days ago, he had showed classic psychotic symptomatology: withdrawal, emotional flatness, the haunted look that comes with insomnia. Yet he had left the shelter of Dickson to come seeking her out in New York City. He had dealt with casual assurance to get what he wanted from Lieutenant Coleman and the cemetery caretaker. He had shown confidence in himself and displayed none of the apathy of their first meeting. A little earlier, he had shown the only sign of emotional conflict in his tearful breakdown, but she shared that grief herself. It was impossible to fault him for crying at the memory of his wife.

But was this all a serendipitous reversal, a sudden emergence from a depressive grief disorder?

Or was it a sign of dementia praecox, the sudden and sometimes dangerous personality change of the schizophrenic?

She stared at the gun he had left behind. It was a menacing piece of metal, shaped into a strangely appealing design. Something about the gun attracted her. The metal was cold. The grip had a checkered design, with hundreds of tiny teeth that bit into the palm of her hand. The bluish-gray coating was worn down to a shiny metal on the trigger housing. The gun had been used a lot.

It bothered her that she hadn't known about the gun until he showed it to her. What other secrets did he have?

Frightened by her thoughts, she propped a chair under the doorknob. It might not stop anyone from entering, but it would make enough noise to wake her.

After all her protests about the gun, she placed it under her pillow, where she could sleep with her fingers touching it.

She awoke in the morning to the smell of breakfast.

The bitter aroma of strong coffee mingled with the sweetness of fried eggs and bacon. Eddie Elbows was setting up a breakfast tray in her room.

Through barely open eyelashes, she watched his movement in the room. He opened a folding table. With a flourish he obviously enjoyed, he swung out a fresh tablecloth, allowing it to float down into position. Smoothing it out with practiced gestures, he could have been a waiter in an elegant restaurant, except for the peculiarity of his arms. He set the table with silverware, put out the plates, and added a small vase with a rose. When he was done, he turned and smiled.

"Breakfast is served, Professor."

"How did you get in here?" she asked. "I had a chair in front of the door."

"I didn't notice any chair," Eddie said. "I didn't want to wake you up before breakfast was ready. I made eggs Benedict for you and bacon and eggs for me."

The food looked inviting, but Katherine kept herself wrapped in the bedsheets.

"The door was locked," she said.

"I have extra keys for all the rooms."

"You should have knocked."

"Like I said, I didn't want to disturb you. Come on now, let's eat."

The chair she had put against the door last night was standing beside the bed. It was only a few feet from where she sat. Almost within arm's length. She wondered if he had been sitting there, as he had the other night. How long had he been in the room, watching her? He could have reached out to touch her from the chair. The room didn't seem safe anymore. Instead of a refuge, it was beginning to feel like a trap.

Eddie sat down at the breakfast table.

"Your food is going to get cold," he said. "Come on, let's eat."

Katherine kept her legs tightly closed under the sheets.

"Did you come in here last night?"

"I just came in a few minutes ago," he insisted. "All I did was bring you breakfast. I didn't want you to get mad at me. Are you mad?"

She slipped her hand under the pillow, reaching for the gun.

"You don't want to eat with me, do you?" Eddie said.

The gun was missing.

Eddie smiled at her.

"You probably want to eat by yourself. Is that what you want?"

She nodded, and watched while he took his plate and backed toward the door.

"Just call me when you're done," he said.

As soon as he was gone, Katherine spun around and searched the bed. All that was under the pillow was a small grease smudge where the gun had been. She threw back the sheets.

Nothing.

The gun wasn't under the bed. It wasn't on the night table. It was gone. Only the smudge of grease proved it had been there at all.

"You'd better eat," Eddie called out. "Your food will get cold."

She was convinced he was watching her through some secret peephole. She decided to test him. Although the fear had taken away her appetite, she drank a cup of coffee. The eggs Benedict were perfectly prepared. Yolks soft and runny, skin firm, muffins crisp. But she had no taste for it. She broke the yolks and watched the yellow contents run across the plate. She pushed the tray aside and returned to her bed.

"Are you done?" Eddie called out, right on cue.

Katherine looked around the room, wondering where he was watching from.

"Can I come in now?" he called again. "I'll take away the dishes."

When she didn't answer, he opened the door partway and peered in.

"Is everything okay?" he asked. "You're not still mad at me, are you?"

Without a word, she took her makeup kit and went to the hallway bathroom. Her hands trembled as she applied her mascara. She felt exposed, watched, violated. She rushed through her cleansing process as quickly as she could.

When she returned to the room, the food and the folding table were gone. The bed was neatly made. On closer inspection, she saw that the sheets had been changed.

"I thought you'd want some clean sheets," he said from behind her.

He was close. So close, she could feel the warmth of his breath on the back of her neck.

"Phyllis likes clean sheets every day," he went on. "I'm used to changing sheets."

She moved across the room, trying to put a safe distance between them.

"You're still mad at me," he said with surprise. "Why are you mad? I'm only trying to be nice to you. Dominic wants me to take care of you."

"I can take care of myself," she answered.

"I didn't mean it that way," he said. "I mean he wants me to treat you nice."

She spun around to face him.

"What did you do with the gun, Eddie?"

"What gun?"

"You know what I'm talking about. Where did you put the gun?"

She looked for some sign in his face, some flicker of an eye or twitch of a lip that would reveal his deceit. But his face was blank. He raised his short arms in a helpless gesture.

"I don't know what you're talking about. I keep a shotgun under the bar. Is that what you mean?"

"There was a gun under the pillow when I went to sleep last night. This morning it was gone. You were the only other person in this room. What did you do with it?"

"Maybe you misplaced it. Did you look around?"

"Don't play games with me, Eddie. You came into the room last night. You must have taken it while I was asleep."

"I only came in to bring your breakfast. Maybe there wasn't any gun. Maybe you just imagined it. You were pretty tired yesterday."

"The gun belonged to Dominic. He gave it to me for my protection. He'll look for it when he gets here."

A troubled expression danced across Eddie's face. It came and went so fast, she wasn't sure if it was guilt or fear.

"Dominic's gun, is it? We'd better find it then. He'll get mad. Did you check under the bed?"

He was down on his knees, lifting the bedspread to see better. She watched his sudden burst of interest without moving.

"You know it's not there," she said.

"Did you look in the closet?"

He jumped up and darted across the room.

"Maybe you left it there when you were unpacking."

"There's no point in looking in the closet. The gun isn't there, and you know it."

He turned with a painful expression. His eyes searched the room, looking for other hiding places.

"That's not fair, accusing me of taking Dominic's gun. I'm just trying to be nice to you, Professor. That's the reason I didn't wake you up when I came in. I wanted to be nice to you."

This was going nowhere, Katherine thought. She decided to give him a chance to return the gun without acknowledging he took it.

"I'm going to go out for a walk, and when I get back, I expect the gun to be here. Do you understand?"

Eddie backed toward the door, shaking his head.

"Oh no, you can't leave here, Professor. I'm sorry, but you can't."

Katherine reached for her coat.

"You can't keep me here," she said.

Eddie blocked the doorway.

"No, Professor. You have to stay in the room. Dominic said you can't be seen outside. It's too dangerous."

"I'll decide what's dangerous," she said. "And I'm starting to think it's dangerous staying here."

Thrusting her arms through the sleeves, she turned to check herself in the mirror. Too late. Before she could turn back, she heard the door close and the lock slide shut from outside.

"Eddie!" she shouted.

"You have to stay in there," he called through the locked door. "I can't let you go out."

She ran to the door and pounded on it with her fists.

"Let me out of here, Eddie! You have no right to do this."

"I'm sorry," he called out. "But I have my orders. You have to stay in there, where I can watch you."

She pounded the door until her fists hurt. She slammed the chair against the door. She smashed again and again, until the chair legs broke off. The door shuddered, but withstood it all.

"Breaking things won't help," he said when she stopped. "You can't get out. Why don't you just calm down?"

"Let me out of here," she screamed.

"You'll have to wait for Dominic. He's the only one who can let you out."

"This is illegal."

It sounded silly, but she couldn't think of anything else to say.

"You're only making things worse on yourself, Professor. Just relax. You're not going anywhere."

Exhausted by her efforts, Katherine slumped to the floor. She picked up one of the chair legs and hurled it against the wall.

Trapped.

She looked around the room. There was no telephone. Outside the window was a ledge leading to an adjoining roof. She struggled to raise the window. It wouldn't budge. She tried using the broken chair leg as a lever. The warped window frame refused to yield. It was jammed at an angle against the sash. Jammed by someone carelessly closing it the wrong way.

Frustrated, she threw herself on the bed.

There was nothing to do but wait.

Stare at the ceiling.

And think.

Think about how foolish she was to allow herself to be lured here. She closed her eyes, trying to shut out the images of her captors. A deformed bartender with a tenuous grip on reality. Was he watching her through some peephole? She pulled the bedsheet over herself to hide. All she could do now was wait for a probable schizophrenic to release her.

The room was warm with the afternoon sun when Dominic's voice woke her.

"Katherine, are you all right?"

She didn't answer.

He banged on the door and shouted for her to open it. A whispered voice outside conferred with him.

A key slipped into the lock with metallic precision. The door opened to reveal Dominic and Eddie. Dominic was clean-shaven, hair combed, wearing a tweed sport coat instead of his old zippered jacket. He was a handsome man, except for the haunted hollows of his eyes. But it would take more than a shave and a change of clothes to disguise what she saw there. Insomnia. Anxiety. Depression. Dementia.

She pulled away as he came toward the bed.

"What's wrong?" he asked.

She pulled the sheet around her.

"Why are you doing this to me?" she asked.

"What are you talking about?"

Katherine looked around the room. The remnants of the broken chair were gone. Another chair was in its place. Her coat was back in the closet. There was no sign of the earlier mess. Her shoes were placed neatly by the side of the bed.

"I didn't take off my shoes," she said.

"What?"

"I didn't take off my shoes."

"Are you okay?"

She jumped up to keep the bed between herself and the two of them.

When he started to come around the bed, she backed away.

"Why are you frightened?"

"Don't come any closer."

She pressed herself into a corner. Eddie remained by the door, watching her.

Dominic stopped and held his hands out, as if to show he meant no harm.

"You must have had a bad dream, Katherine. I'm not going to hurt you." His voice was soothing. "Tell me what happened."

"You gave me a gun last night. You told me I needed it for protection. You said I was in danger."

"That's right."

"Well, the gun is missing. It was under my pillow when I went to sleep, and when I woke up it was gone."

A flicker of something appeared in his eyes. Fear, she thought. But it was gone before she could be certain.

"Eddie must have taken it," she said. "He was in here while I was asleep last night, and he was in here when I woke up. I don't know why he took it, but Eddie has your gun."

She looked up at the doorway. Eddie had disappeared.

Dominic frowned.

"Eddie wouldn't do that. He's got some funny ways about him, but he wouldn't steal anything."

"He's a pathological liar, living in a fantasy world. He's a psychopathic personality. Stealing would be perfectly natural for him. He scares me."

"Eddie's harmless," he assured her. "He talks funny, but he wouldn't hurt you. Did you look around the room? Maybe you misplaced the gun."

"That's what Eddie said. But I know he took it."

Dominic circled the room, examining the closet, opening the dresser drawers, throwing back the bedsheet.

"I already looked there," Katherine said.

He paused at the window.

"Not only did he steal the gun," she said. "But he locked me up in here. He wouldn't let me leave the room."

"I'm sorry, that was my fault. I told him not to let you go out. It could be dangerous."

Dominic ran his fingers along the window sash. He tried to raise the window, but it was still jammed.

"I don't like him coming in here when I'm asleep. If he tries to project his fantasies on me, he could be dangerous."

Dominic hit the top of the window frame with his fist, popping the warped wood. With a mild grunt, he was able to open the window. Cold air flooded into the room.

"Sometimes Eddie gets carried away, but he doesn't mean any harm. You have to get used to him."

He thrust his head outside the window and took a deep breath of the afternoon air.

"I don't want to get used to him," she said. "I want to go back to New York."

He looked back into the room.

"I can't let you do that," he said.

She wanted to scream at him, but that would only make it seem as if she was losing control. She tried to keep her voice calm and steady.

"You have no right to keep me here. I want to go back to New York."

"I'm trying to protect you," he said.

"I'll be as safe in New York as I am here," she answered.

"You know what happened last time you went there."

"I won't go back to my apartment. I'll go to a hotel. In the morning, I can get a flight to Puerto Rico. No one will know where I am."

"The risk is too great. I can't let you do it."

"I'm not asking for your permission."

"I can't let you go, Katherine. I'll keep you here by force if I have to."

He stood between her and the doorway. His arms hung loose at his sides, ready for any move she made. She tried to reason with him.

"You're not a policeman anymore. You have no authority to keep me here."

"That's right, I don't. I'm asking you to stay, so that I can protect you. But if you try to leave, I'll stop you."

He seemed to be switching between two moods, his words alternately pleading and threatening.

"If the chief of police knew what you were doing, he would arrest you," she said.

He nodded.

"He's just looking for an excuse."

"But you'd risk that to protect me?"

He nodded.

"There's something you're not telling me," she said.

When he didn't answer, she started to circle him. He was no longer protecting the door.

"That's why you didn't come here this morning," she said. "You found out something you don't want to tell me."

He didn't respond.

"What is it? What are you hiding from me?"

His eyes studied hers.

"I don't think you want to hear about it."

"Try me. I'm a big girl."

He reached into his jacket pocket for his cigarettes. He carefully straightened one out, stroking it gently. He watched her while he lit the cigarette. He didn't answer until he had taken a long puff and exhaled the smoke.

"That old caretaker at the cemetery in New York," he said. "He called me this morning."

Dominic took another puff on the cigarette. Again the slow inhalation of smoke followed by the gentle exhalation.

"They found the widow of the man whose body disappeared from that grave. The caretaker discovered her this morning when he came to work. She was wearing a black dress and veil, like she was dressed for a funeral."

He stared at her. She could sense him watching for her reaction as he spoke.

"She was hanging from a tree behind the open grave. They figured she was dead about six hours."

Seven

THE SHOCK took the breath from her throat. She suddenly felt giddy and lightheaded. Dominic reached out to stop her from collapsing. He led her to the bed.

"Another suicide?" she asked.

"That's what they're calling it."

Sitting on the bed, she took deep breaths to calm herself. She gripped Dominic's hand for support.

"Isn't it unusual, all those suicides?"

"Not according to the New York police. Lieutenant Coleman

said they average about fifteen suicides every twenty-four hours. Most of them at night. They're found in the morning, but they do it at night. This one was the tenth suicide called in this morning. Didn't seem to bother the police. The only guy who was upset was the caretaker. He doesn't like people killing themselves in his cemetery."

"The police aren't going to investigate?"

"They said it's a waste of time. But they're going to alert their squad cars to put the cemetery on their patrols. They think they can scare off the grave robbers with a police presence."

She shook her head.

"They're not going to accomplish a thing that way," she said. "A police car won't stop what's going on. The entire police force can't stop it."

"You're still on that supernatural stuff, aren't you?" he said. "Rising from the dead and all that."

Dominic smoked his cigarette down to the point where she thought it would burn his fingers. He turned the cigarette at an angle to get another puff from it.

"Personally, I'd be a little suspicious of the suicide angle," he said. "We only get one or two suicides a year in Dickson. But it's always a person you'd expect. I could probably make a list of four or five names and be sure one of them would stick their head in a gas oven in the next twelve months."

"You're very certain of yourself," she said, irritated by the casual way he spoke of death.

"I've seen enough of them. I've seen them hanging, which isn't very pretty, the way the pressure bulges the eyes out. Carbon monoxide, which is a little better, gives the skin a healthy pink glow. Of course, the newer cars have more sulfur dioxide in their exhaust, so the skin color is a little paler. Then you've got the real impulsive ones. They'll swerve their car right off the road into a concrete abutment. Too much of a rush to get home and close the garage door. Or maybe they're out for the double indemnity on their insurance, I don't know. There's a lot of different ways they do it. But their reasons are different, too. That's why I'm suspicious about those five suicides. I never saw two people kill themselves for the same reason, never mind

90

five. That's not even a coincidence, that's almost an impossibility."

"They all had something in common," Katherine said. "They've all been through traumatic experiences. Situations like that can trigger acute depressive reactions."

She was going to say something about his own admitted depression, but changed her mind.

"They were caught up in grief over the death of loved ones," she went on. "It can take a long time to get over that. When they found the bodies missing, the stress became too much to handle. A shock like that, a disruption of the normal grief pattern, the sudden confusion could be enough to send a lonely widow or widower over the edge."

"You're saying they were scared into it?"

"That's a simple explanation of what could have happened. The human mind is too complicated to know for certain. Although it looks like the same reason, it was probably a little different in each case. For some, it could have been a desire to join their loved ones. Some people just can't let go when their spouse dies."

She stopped, realizing she was getting dangerously close to describing Dominic's symptoms.

He finally ran out of space on his cigarette and dropped the small remnant into a water glass on the dresser. She made a face as the butt sizzled and then turned brown in the water.

"It's an ashtray," Dominic explained. "Eddie doesn't like people smoking up here. He's scared to death of fires. He keeps glasses of water in each room instead of ashtrays. Says it's safer."

"I noticed the bucket of water by the radiator."

"He was also the first guy in town to buy smoke detectors. Got them all over the place, even the closets."

"He must have had a bad experience," she said.

"His mother was burned on the arms in a house fire when she was pregnant with him. He thinks that's why he was born without elbows."

"That sort of trauma doesn't affect the fetus. Besides, you said it was thalidomide."

91

Dominic shrugged.

"Eddie believes what he wants to believe."

"That's a psychological disorder," she said. "He's trying to create his own reality."

"And what are you doing? You're trying to tell me those graves are empty because people are coming back from the dead."

"You have no other explanation," she said.

"I have explanations, but you won't accept them."

"I know what I saw," she insisted.

"The dead don't come back, no matter how much you want them to, no matter how much you pray for it and beg God for it."

He stopped, as if he was afraid of revealing too much of himself. As suddenly as it had come, the storm that raged through his mind dissipated. His face and voice softened.

"You want the reality of death?" he said. "I'll show you reality. I'll show you why your mother will never come back."

He took her to the Kuranda Funeral Home.

It was on Main Street, halfway between the Valley Inn and the old brick road that led to the Visitation of Mary Church. Katherine recognized it as the funeral home where Mother had rested for the traditional three days before being taken to the cemetery.

The main part of the building, the original house, was covered with sandstone facing. Joined to it without any thought of design was a wide one-story structure clad in white aluminum siding. That was where the main activity of the funeral home was conducted: the visiting of the body, which was supposed to be a psychological catharsis for the bereaved. The building sat isolated from its neighbors by an asphalt parking lot large enough to park sixty cars. A florist's van was parked by the double doors through which the coffins were removed.

"I already know Mother was buried," she said. "Nothing the undertaker has to say will change the fact that I saw her."

Dominic nodded to the florist. The inside of the funeral parlor opened into a large reception area with velvet chairs and a guest book near the second set of double doors. Beyond them were rows of chairs facing a display of floral bouquets behind a gold-and-white casket. Part of a woman's forehead was visible above the edge of the casket. The smell of fresh roses and gladiolas hung in the air.

"I'm glad you came early," Walter Kuranda said. He spoke in a hushed tone, as if afraid of disturbing the woman in the casket.

"As you can see, we have a funeral under way. It's the first evening of visitation, and the family will be here soon."

He steered them quickly into another room, a smaller one with a couch and two chairs. A packet of smelling salts was on the table.

"This is the Grief Room," he said. "We can talk here."

Walter Kuranda was a shiny little man.

Light glistened from the polished skin of his bald head and the clear enamel on his manicured fingernails. Clear blue eyes sparkled behind gold-rimmed glasses. He wore a glossy black three-piece mohair suit cut to make him look slimmer. He could have been an affluent banker, except for the perpetual smile on his face.

"Dominic tells me you've been having visions of your poor dead mother," he said.

"They weren't visions," Katherine said. "I saw her three times in the last week."

"Grief can do strange things to us, Miss Roshak. As a psychology professor, surely you understand that."

"It's been eight years since she was buried," Katherine said. "I never saw her during that entire time. Not until last week."

"Sometimes the longing for a loved one stays with us, remains dormant, as it were, to come forth when we visit familiar surroundings again. Is this your first visit to Dickson since the funeral?"

He leaned forward in his chair, close enough so that she could feel the warmth of his breath. It was probably a technique they taught in classes on the Psychology of Bereavement, she thought. Sure enough, he reached out to take her arm. Closeness. In times of stress, physical closeness can be the most effective therapy. That was from Kübler-Ross, she remembered.

And it was true. She found she didn't pull away. His touch was soothing.

"I came here because I saw her in New York," she said. "I know about delusions and hallucinations. I know how the mind works, just as I know what you're attempting to do right now. And I'm telling you, it was Mother. We have evidence to support it."

The undertaker raised his eyebrows in disbelief.

"But that's impossible, Miss Roshak. There's just no way on earth such a thing could happen."

"She's not in the coffin," Katherine said.

The undertaker turned to Dominic, who nodded in agreement.

"She's not in the coffin," Katherine repeated. "She's out there somewhere. We found her rosary across the street from where I'm staying."

Walter Kuranda removed his hand from her arm. His eternal smile dimmed a little.

"You're not accusing me of burying the wrong body? If this is some sort of malpractice accusation, I have all the proper documentation. I checked it after Dominic called."

"Take it easy, Walter," Dominic said. "She's not accusing you of anything. She just thinks her mother's out there walking around."

"She looks exactly like she did in the coffin," Katherine said.

"See what I mean?" Dominic said. "She's convinced she's seeing her mother. I brought her here so you could tell her why that's impossible. She doesn't understand what happens to a body before it's buried."

The undertaker ran his hand across his mouth in an unconscious bit of body language.

"I don't discuss such matters with the bereaved. It's not ethical."

"I know you don't like to take people behind the scenes," Dominic said. "But it might help in this case. She's got to understand that all this is impossible."

"But we have evidence," Katherine protested. "It's not just

my word. There's the rosary, and the fire in my apartment . . ."

"Why don't you just let your mother rest in peace," the undertaker asked. "Why don't you just go back to New York and forget about all this? Perhaps all that's needed is a few prayers. Sometimes when we think about the departed, it's because they're asking us to pray for them. Go to church and say a prayer for your mother."

"Did you tell him about the other missing bodies?" Katherine asked Dominic.

The undertaker sighed.

"I think you've been seeing too many horror movies, Professor. First your mother and now other missing bodies. That happens only in Hollywood. People like me, who deal with death on a daily basis, don't like to see cemeteries used as devices to frighten people in cheap thrillers."

"The part about the missing bodies is true," Dominic said. "There are five empty graves in New York City. The bodies are missing, just like her mother's."

The frozen smile finally melted. Without the smile, Walter Kuranda looked older and unsure of himself. He was no longer the confident counselor, dispensing support and tired clichés to next of kin who barely listened to the words. He was just another businessman in his middle thirties, who suddenly had discovered that there might be unsettling questions about his business.

"You didn't tell me about that," he said.

"I didn't want to discuss it on the phone," Dominic said.

"Did all this happen recently?"

"About the same time her mother's body disappeared. At least the last one did."

"There must be a logical explanation," the undertaker said.

"I'm sure there is," Dominic answered. "That's why I want you to explain to Katherine what you do to a body before the burial. Why it's impossible for her to be seeing her mother now."

"I'm not certain Miss Roshak will want to hear such things."

"I think she needs to hear it. It's the only thing that will convince her. I've been trying for three days and I haven't succeeded in changing her mind."

"It's against my better judgment."

"Consider it a favor to me, Walter."

"And it's also against every principle of mortuary science."

"I can tell her about it myself, but I probably wouldn't get all the facts right."

"Very well, but I won't be responsible for any trauma. Do you understand that, Miss Roshak?"

They followed him past the Slumber Room. The first of the mourners had arrived: an old man, probably the husband of the woman whose head was visible in frozen profile. He sat straight-shouldered and stiff-legged, staring at the corpse. Outside, car doors were opening and closing.

"We'll have to hurry," the undertaker said. "This is the first night of the wake, and it's usually the most difficult. I'll have to be there if any of them break down."

Below the Slumber Room, they passed a display area of caskets, each with its own color chart and swatches of silk linings that showed the options available.

A hospital gurney rested against the far wall, its black padded top partially covered with a fresh strip of white paper.

Walter led them through another set of double doors into a large room with gleaming stainless-steel fixtures and powerful overhead lights. It was cool inside. The room smelled of antiseptic.

"Looks like a hospital operating room, doesn't it?" Walter said. His voice echoed off the hard surfaces of the room. The overhead light gave his mohair suit an iridescent glow that shifted when he moved.

"Remodeled it five years ago," he said. "Put in all new fixtures, new floor, new cooling units. They had to bring in another two-twenty line for the extra power we needed. I had to take out a second mortgage, but I figure this is where I work, so it's worth the money."

The floor was easily scrubbed ceramic tile. It reminded Katherine of a restaurant kitchen floor. Glass cases contained assortments of forceps, scalpels, and other medical instruments. Built into one wall was a stainless-steel door whose thickness identified it as the entrance to a refrigerated room.

"This is our prep room," he said. "Only qualified personnel are ever allowed here—doctors, other medical personnel, and, of course, our assistants. As you can see, the room is spotless. Every piece of equipment is sterilized after use. We operate in a germ-free environment, to protect us as well as those who come in contact with the remains."

He circled the room, pointing out the sterilization equipment and the huge metal sinks.

"I really never get the chance to show this to outsiders. No one seems to be curious about it."

A machine that resembled a heavy-duty vacuum cleaner with a flexible metal hose rested in a corner. The end of the hose narrowed to an opening no larger than a straw.

"I like to consider myself a doctor to the dead. Where a regular medical doctor finishes his work with a patient, that's where mine begins. I take up where he leaves off. And I approach it with the same professional standards and concern for the patient and the family as any doctor does. The only difference, of course, is that my patient is deceased."

In the center of the room, directly under the lights, were two inclined stainless-steel tables, each over six feet long. Around the perimeter of each table was a channel that drained into a funnel positioned over a large plastic container.

Walter snapped on a pair of transparent rubber gloves.

"Handling of the body is always done with gloves, of course."

He stepped between the inclined tables.

"I kept the old tables when we remodeled. You can't get stainless-steel tables like this anymore. These days they try to sell you lightweight stainless and pretend it's just as good."

He ran his hands along the polished metal, looking for a moment at his reflection in the table.

"This is where it all starts, right on these tables. The deceased is brought here, stretched out, and the clothing removed. We examine the body for any unusual cuts, bruises, or puncture marks. At that point, the body is usually stiff with rigor mortis. We have to massage it to overcome the stiffness. By loosening up the body, we can work with it better and position it later on. The Catholic Church requests that the hands be clasped over the chest, or folded as if in prayer."

Katherine had a sudden image of her mother's hands, pale and blue-veined, with the black-beaded rosary wrapped around them.

"There are a few housekeeping chores we do before the embalming process starts."

From a small drawer, he removed two plastic devices. They were small half circles with tiny teeth on the outside. He held them up to his eyes.

"These are eye caps. They're inserted under the eyelids and cemented in place to keep the lids closed. They also maintain the natural shape of the eyelids."

From another drawer, he removed a spool of wire.

"Surgical wire," he explained. "The same kind a doctor uses to wire a broken jaw. I could use plain old copper wire and nobody would know the difference. Except me. I like to work with quality materials."

He snipped off an eight-inch length of the silvery filament. It was the same thickness as the gold rims of his eyeglasses. He held it up to the light.

"This little piece of wire helps us give the deceased that peaceful look. We pierce the jawbone, insert the wire, and twist it until the jaws are drawn together and the lips meet. It depends on the aesthetics we want. Men look better with their jaws clamped really tight. Gives them that firm, determined look. For women, we leave about a quarter-inch between the teeth. It gives the lips a better shape. The excess wire is cut off and the ends are folded up between the teeth."

Dominic sat down in a chair. His face was pale.

"Are you all right?" Walter asked.

"I'm fine. Don't worry about me."

"Perhaps I shouldn't continue," Walter said, although his voice indicated that he didn't want to stop.

"Go on." Dominic waved his hand. "I want Katherine to hear all of this."

Walter pulled an instrument cart to the table. A scalpel appeared in his hand. He turned it slowly in the light, catching the reflection on the sharp point.

"It takes a great deal of study of human anatomy to become a mortician. Actually, we're called demisurgeons in some circles. Myself, I studied at the Jefferson College of Mortuary Science in Columbia, Missouri. That's a long way from Dickson, but it was my father's idea. He wanted me to learn the most sophisticated techniques. Jefferson is the Harvard of mortuary science."

As he spoke, Katherine thought of her mother lying on the cold metal table, naked and helpless, the wire being slowly tightened in her jaw. Mother had had upper dentures. She wondered if they were removed before the wire was inserted.

Walter Kuranda had his jacket off. His shirt sleeves were rolled up. He was obviously enjoying himself.

"Pretend there's a body on the embalming table," he said.

Dominic turned paler. He was staring at the ceramic floor.

"There are two parts to the embalming process," Walter said. "The first part, the one most people know something about, is arterial embalming. This involves the removal of the blood and its replacement with preservative fluids."

He raised the scalpel and plunged it down in a quick stroke at about the midpoint of the imaginary body.

"I start with an incision at the groin. Every demisurgeon has his own favorite drainage and injection points. There are three major ones to choose, where a major vein and artery come together. That allows the body to drain faster. I generally use the conjunction of the femoral artery and femoral vein near the groin. Other demisurgeons use the axillary artery and subclavian vein near the armpit, or the jugular vein and carotid artery at the neck."

He pointed out the other two locations on himself.

"It's extremely important to drain the body as soon as possible after death, because it's the blood that causes most of the disfiguration and discoloration of the remains. With the proper training, a skilled demisurgeon can accomplish the necessary incision without mutilating the body in any but the most minor way. The artery and vein are raised from the adjoining tissue, and each vessel is circled with string. I use only surgical string for this process. The vessels are then tied from both directions to avoid any leakage after the embalming process is completed."

He attached a hollow steel needle to the flexible metal tubing of the pumping machine.

"This is an injection needle. It goes into the artery and pushes the embalming fluid to the heart."

He placed another instrument on the table, close to the injection needle. It was about ten inches long, with a small hole at one end and a larger flared opening at the other. It was long enough to reach to the deep channel at the end of the table.

"This is a drainage instrument. It's inserted into the vein. Everything, as I said earlier, is completely sterilized, the same as in a hospital."

Pressing a pedal, he turned on the pumping machine. It made a rhythmic, pulsing noise.

"The injection machine simulates the pumping of the heart. I usually set it at a pressure of about seven pounds per square inch. It forces the blood out of the body into the channels on the side of the table. The average person takes about four or five gallons of embalming fluid. It's basically formaldehyde, but it's perfumed to help overcome the smell of death."

He paused, and for the first time showed some distaste for what he was doing.

"The smell of death, that's something I never got used to. I can smell it as soon as I walk into a room where someone died, even if they've only been dead a short time. But once the fluid goes into the body, the smell disappears."

Katherine stared at the edges of the table, at the gutters that collected the blood and channeled it down to the funnel. She thought of her mother on this table, her body slowly draining, as so many hundreds of bodies had drained before her on this same cold metal.

"The embalming fluid goes through the arteries, fills the heart, enters the veins, into the capillary system, and into the very cells themselves, tracing the path of the blood it's replacing. The fluid can be tinted any shade we need. It's just like mixing paint. We just add in some Suntone, Special Cosmetic Tint, Lyf-Lyk Tint, or other shades. We try to adjust the coloration to the individual's particular needs. When they come out of the hospital, they're usually really pale to start with. The family likes them to look more natural. It's really fascinating, watching the color come back into the deceased, the glow coming back into the cheeks as the fluid pumps in."

Dominic took a handkerchief from his pocket. He blew his nose, but she suspected he was trying to hide his tears. Walter Kuranda didn't seem to notice.

"The second part of the procedure is cavity embalming."

He brought out the machine that looked like a vacuum cleaner. He slipped a stainless-steel tube into the end of the metal hose.

"This is the trocar. We make a small incision below the solar plexus to insert it. The trocar is connected to the aspirator pump to draw blood and fluids from the entrails and chest cavity. If the deceased had internal bleeding, this is where much of the blood would have collected. When the cavity is cleaned out, we inject a very powerful formalin concentrate, more powerful than the one we put in the veins. It's an antiseptic procedure, because the intestinal cavity is always filled with microorganisms. Embarrassing things can happen to the corpse if we don't treat the cavity properly."

By now the stainless-steel table looked like an operating table, with various instruments on its surface and the metal tubes leading to it. Walter Kuranda looked up and smiled.

"Any questions?"

Dominic shook his head.

"Then that's it. We wash the remains, put little plastic plugs in the incision areas, dress the remains, and restore the deceased cosmetically. The entire process takes less than three hours."

He pulled off the operating gloves with a rubbery snap and tossed them into a clean metal basket.

"I think it's disgusting," Katherine said. "Why does all that have to be done? If I'd known you were going to do that to Mother, I never would have permitted it."

She felt Dominic's hand on her arm, squeezing tightly.

"I'm sorry, Walter," he said. "Maybe I shouldn't have brought her here."

"That's quite all right," the undertaker said. "You don't have to apologize for her. I'm used to that sort of reaction from people. The funeral industry gets a lot of it from consumer advocates, and even the FTC. But they don't understand the tremendous contribution we make to public health. A number of studies prove how vital embalming is to eliminate pathogenic bacteria that can survive in the earth for years. I'm accustomed to such criticism, and I can ignore it, because I know it's misguided."

"You drained Mother's blood and filled her with your bleaches and chemicals. I had no idea how primitive all this embalming business is."

Dominic pulled her through the door and out past the caskets to the stairway.

"I'm sorry I put you through this," he told her. "But I wanted you to understand that your mother is dead. Her body may be missing from its grave, but it's filled with formaldehyde. There's no way it could be moving on its own."

"Then how do you explain me seeing her?" she asked.

"I don't have an explanation," Dominic said.

"You saw her too. You even found her rosary."

"All this is impossible," Walter Kuranda said impatiently.

He guided them to the kitchen. The Slumber Room was already filling up with mourners.

"I've done all I can to help you," the undertaker said to Dominic. "I've really got to attend to the bereaved family. They'll be looking for me."

"Who worked on her mother?" Dominic asked. "Did you do the embalming?"

Kuranda shot a quick look at Katherine before answering.

"It wasn't me. If there was anything wrong with her mother's burial, it wasn't my fault. I was still in mortuary school eight years ago. I wasn't even here."

He took some notes from his pocket.

"I assumed you'd be asking about that, so I checked the records. That was before my father retired. He's down in Fort Lauderdale now. You can call him if you want to, but I've got all his records here."

He adjusted the wire glasses on his nose, and squinted at the penciled notes.

"The actual embalming was done by an apprentice. Name of Effenbeck. David Effenbeck. Good-looking young man. Blond hair. German background, from what my father told me. I never knew him very well, but my father said he had a real gift for working with the dead. Most young people are turned off by it. I know I was. But Effenbeck really enjoyed it."

"Do you know where he is now?"

"He was only here for a short time. Dad wanted to keep him on. Said he was the hardest-working assistant he ever had. He was a terrific cosmetologist, too. That's real important, because it's the only way the family can judge whether you did a good job. If the corpse doesn't look right, they think the funeral director isn't competent. They don't know about everything else we do."

"He didn't do a good job on Mother. She didn't look good at all."

Katherine's voice was still resentful, even now, eight years later.

Walter shrugged, not visibly concerned with her complaint.

"It was probably the photographs you supplied. When restorative work is done without personal knowledge of the deceased's appearance, we have to rely on supporting photos. If they're out of focus or show the deceased with an odd expression, it causes a problem. It certainly had nothing to do with Effenbeck's skills. His restoration work was magnificent. I spent most of that summer watching him work."

"I never got the pictures back, either."

"Well, that happens. When you want the photographs back, you have to tell us."

She was going to argue with him, but Dominic interrupted.

"Do you have his Social Security number? Maybe I can trace him through that."

"That's illegal, isn't it?"

"Giving me the number isn't illegal. Let me worry about the rest of it. I know somebody at the Social Security Administration in Wilkes-Barre."

"It'll take a while to get the number. I'd have to go into the financial records. That far back, eight years ago, all those financial records are in storage. The only records we keep on hand have to do with funerals. But I do know where he went to mortuary school, if that will help." He brightened at the idea that he might have remembered something important. "It was Knoxville, Tennessee. I remember that because he was so secretive about it. You know, when people try to hide things, it makes you remember more than if they didn't."

Through the kitchen door, Katherine could hear the sounds of the family and friends of the woman in the coffin as they greeted each other.

"I'm really going to have to go," the undertaker said. "I have a responsibility to the family. They'll be looking for me."

"Why was he secretive about it?" Dominic asked. "Why would he try to hide where he went to school?"

"I don't know," Walter said. "He was just a very secretive type. He was always making long-distance telephone calls, always collect, even though Dad told him he could bill them to us. It was like he didn't want us to know who he called."

Impatient now, he straightened out his jacket, adjusted his tie, and patted the hair on the sides of his bald crown.

"Why did he leave?" Dominic persisted. "Did your dad fire him?"

"Of course not. I told you what Dad thought of him. We never knew why he left. One morning he was just gone. Clothes and all. Of course, that was only one suitcase. He always wore a black suit and a white shirt, must have had a spare in his suitcase. When he was gone, he didn't leave a trace behind. It was as if he was never here. Frankly, if I knew where to find him, I'd hire him tomorrow. Make my life a lot easier."

"How soon after the Roshak funeral did he leave?" Dominic asked.

The last light of afternoon was fading quickly. The kitchen was growing dark. No one moved to turn on the lights. She could see the undertaker's eyes narrow with suspicion.

"What are you trying to establish?" he asked. "You trying to say he did something wrong? Broke a law? Health law? Is that it?"

"I'm just asking a question."

"My dad never would have allowed that. The only difference between funeral directors is your reputation, and Dad took real pride in the reputation we have. I'm the third generation in this business."

"When did he leave?" Dominic persisted.

"You know, I don't have to answer any of your questions," Walter said. He started for the door to the reception hall. "You're not with the police anymore. It's all over town how you got fired."

He glared at Katherine, as if trying to signal her that he knew it was her fault. She stared back at him with barely disguised contempt.

"Did he leave after the Roshak funeral?" Dominic repeated.

"I consider you a friend, Dominic. I know you're having a rough time since your wife died. That's the reason I took the time for you. I'm really busy."

His hand was on the doorknob.

"Just answer the question and I'll leave."

"All right. That was the last funeral he worked on before he left. But so what? The woman was dead. And that was eight years ago. Even if he did do something wrong, it's too late to bring it up now. The statute of limitations says anything over seven years, you can't bring any charges or sue. Is there anything else you want? I've got to go light the candles in the Slumber Room."

"You sound like a lawyer, Walter."

He shrugged before leaving the room.

"Everybody has to be a lawyer these days. Too many people looking to take your money if you let your guard down. You've got to protect yourself, Dominic."

They went out the kitchen entrance, not wanting to make their way through the mourners. Katherine took a deep breath of the cool air, trying to wash the smell of formaldehyde and flowers from her throat. The short November day was already gone. The hills above the valley were turning from gray to black.

"That was your version of shock therapy, wasn't it?" she asked.

"I'm sorry," he said. "Maybe I shouldn't have put you through all that."

"If you thought you were going to shock me into accepting Mother's death, it didn't work."

"I noticed. You don't show much emotion when it comes to your mother. Except for fear."

"I never did," Katherine said. "I tried to feel some emotion at the funeral, but I couldn't. We never had that kind of relationship. And it's bothered me ever since. I feel guilty, even now."

"It wasn't your fault," Dominic said as he started the car.

Katherine leaned her head against the back of the seat. She wanted to sleep and forget all this. But she was afraid of what awaited her when she closed her eyes.

"I remember that apprentice he was talking about," she said. "Effenbeck. I thought he was the funeral director. I don't remember Walter's father being there at all."

"Walter's father was an alcoholic," Dominic said. "That's why they always needed an apprentice. He'd take over when the old man was on a bender. They have him in a rest home down in Florida now. The mother lives a block away and visits him every day."

They went to the Mid-Valley Diner for coffee. Dominic said he wasn't hungry after the lesson in embalming. She ordered a chef's salad and toast.

"If I knew what they did in there, I never would have had Cara embalmed," he said.

"At least they comfort you. I appreciated having someone to talk to, not knowing anyone in Dickson. And that apprentice sat there and listened to me for hours, working out my grief. He said exactly the right things to make me feel better, almost as if he knew me."

"Your mother had no relatives up here?"

"None."

She stared down at her coffee cup, swirling the brown liquid around the bottom.

"Mother was an only child. So were both of her parents. She thought that made her unique. When she got married, she refused to have more than one child herself. She said it would break the line. That it would be unlucky."

"What did your father think about that?"

"He divorced her. I don't know if that was the reason. I was only three years old at the time. You should really have something to eat, Dominic."

The waitress brought her salad, a big plate of lettuce covered with strips of ham and cheese.

"I don't have any appetite," he said. "I don't eat much anymore."

He pulled out his crumpled pack of cigarettes.

"I don't smoke much anymore, either," he said. "Used to be a pack and a half a day. Now I'm down to one or two cigarettes a day. By the time I finish a pack, the last few cigarettes are stale. You know, you should eat real food, not just salads. You'd look better if you gained weight."

He ordered fresh coffee for both of them.

"After the divorce, my father made a fortune in the real estate market when prices in New York City took off. He owned half of the Flatiron Building at one point, according to Mother. And he was one of the first developers in on the warehouse conversions in Soho. But he never gave Mother a cent, so she wouldn't let him visit me. I barely remember the man."

"Where is he now?"

"He died in that DC-10 crash in Chicago in 1978."

She waited in silence for the waitress to finish pouring their coffee. Dominic lit his cigarette. He blew the smoke out of the side of his mouth to keep it from drifting in her direction.

"Mother wouldn't let me go to the funeral. It was a total denial on her part. Complete repression of emotion. She wouldn't even let me see his picture on the obituary page of the *New York Times*. I looked it up years later on the microfiche."

He was studying her as she spoke, she realized. He was smoking his cigarette and studying her across the Formica table.

"This sounds like *True Confessions*," she said with an embarrassed laugh.

"Talking about it helps," he said. "It does for me."

"Well, it's obvious you loved your wife. But Mother and I never learned how to be close to each other. The maternal bonding never took place. Under the best of circumstances, she was hard to get along with. But after my father went down in that plane crash, it got worse. He didn't leave her anything. Not a cent."

"What happened to all the money he made in real estate?" Katherine nibbled on a strip of ham.

"You want some salad?" she asked. "I won't eat the whole thing."

He waved it off.

"It was my father's one chance to get even with Mother. He left everything to me. He must have assumed she'd try to get at the money, so he found a way to put it out of her reach. He set up a trust fund that wouldn't pay off until after Mother's death or my twenty-eighth birthday, whichever came later. I won't tell you how big the fund was, but the yearly interest payments to me were over seventy thousand dollars."

He let out a low whistle.

"That's why you can afford a BMW and a fancy condo on a professor's pay," he said.

She nodded, and began nibbling at the corner of a slice of toast. She was hungrier than she had thought.

"That really pissed off your mother, I bet."

"She resented the hell out of it. I think that's what drove her over the edge, always thinking about the money."

She pushed the plate toward him.

"You really should get something into your stomach. You haven't eaten all day."

He finally gave in, and she felt good watching him eat. He finished each of the half slices in two bites. She ordered more toast, watched him devour most of it, and salvaged one slice for herself.

"I told you you'd feel better if you ate."

He wiped his mouth and smiled, and for a brief instant she thought she saw something more in his eyes, a warmth she hadn't seen before.

"It wasn't your fault, what happened to your mother," he said. "Most people in your situation think they're somehow responsible."

"Subconsciously, I think that's why I studied psychology. I wanted to understand Mother."

"Did it help?"

He paid the bill and left a dollar for the waitress.

"I know all the scientific terms. I can teach a class in Psychopathic Susceptibility in Abnormal Symbiotic Relationships. I know all about psychoses and neuroses and the latest psychodynamic trends."

"But you spent the last eight years pretending your mother was still alive. What do psychologists call that?"

He held the door open for her. The evening had the cold wet smell of impending winter. The few cars that passed the diner had their windows rolled up tight, hurrying home to escape the night.

Katherine looked up at the blackened hills that rose above the town. Dim strands of light marched halfway up the hill, marking the progress of the streets. Beyond the last string of house lights was the cemetery.

"She's up there right now," Katherine said. "I can feel it."

"You know that's impossible," he said. "Don't keep torturing yourself."

He opened the car door, but she didn't get inside.

"She's after me," Katherine said. "I don't know what she wants, but Mother is after me."

She started to shiver.

"Isn't there something you can do?" she asked.

"I'm doing everything I can. I've been to doctors, pathologists, the coroner's office, the health department. We just left the funeral home where she was laid out. I've even taken samples from the coffin liner to a microbiologist for spectrographic analysis. Everybody confirms that your mother died eight years ago. The corpse was already decomposing in that coffin."

Katherine stared up at the cemetery. "She's come back for some reason. She won't rest until she does what she set out to do. Mother was always like that."

"You're giving me the chills now."

"Then do something to help me. All you've been doing is trying to prove she's dead. I don't believe you. The only way to disprove me is to find her body."

She squinted her eyes, trying to focus them better on the blackness far up on the hill, where the cemetery was.

"Don't you think I've been looking?" His voice was angry. "But I can't go to the TV stations and tell them there's a dead woman walking around the valley. They'd laugh at me, just like the chief did."

In the blackness beyond the last row of street lights, she saw a smaller light moving.

"There's a light in the cemetery, Dominic. I can see it."

He came around the car to look at the cemetery from where she was standing. It was just a faint glow that she saw. At first she thought it was a house light. But while they were talking, she had been watching it move slowly, dimming as it passed behind trees, brightening when it came into the clear.

They stood in silence, close enough together for her to feel the warmth radiating from his body. The faint light finally stopped. The glow remained steady.

"It's probably just some kids fooling around," Dominic said.

"I want to go there, Dominic. If it's Mother, I want to see her, talk to her."

"It could be some nut. We had a guy up there once who sprayed his body blue and walked around the cemetery naked, starting fires on children's graves."

"Are you afraid to investigate?" she asked.

The question caught him off guard. He turned to look at her. It took him a while to decide on an answer.

"I'm afraid for you," he said. "I'll go there alone, but you'll have to wait where I tell you. I don't want you exposed to any danger."

"And where do you think I'd be safe?"

"In church."

The Visitation of Mary Roman Catholic church was the tallest building in Dickson, a monument to the Polish miners who had settled the community at the turn of the century. At night, floodlights illuminated the huge red brick structure, with its twin gold-leafed spires that rose nearly two hundred feet above the street. The church was familiar to Katherine. It was the same church where Mass had been said for her mother eight years ago.

"There'll be a few old ladies in there saying vespers. I want you to stay in there and don't leave until I come back for you. I'll be five, ten minutes. Fifteen at the most."

"I'd rather go with you."

"You'll be safer in church. Nobody will bother you there. And while you're inside, you can say a few prayers for your mother."

It was the first time Katherine had entered a church since the funeral.

The smell of candles in the stale air made this church seem as familiar as the ones she used to attend as a little girl. Automatically, she reached out to the life-size plaster angel holding the shell of holy water. She touched her finger to the wet sponge and blessed herself as she passed through the vestibule.

The interior of the church was softly illuminated by candles. There were banks of small votive candles before both of the auxiliary altars. Along the side walls, between the statues of the saints and the confessionals, were the larger seven-day candles

111

with their more powerful glows. And in the center of church, hanging high overhead below the darkened frescoes of the vaulted ceiling, was a single candle encased in red glass: the Eternal Light. The familiar surroundings triggered old memories of other churches at other times. She felt at home.

She knelt beside a pew before taking a seat in one of the back rows.

As Dominic had said, there were a few people in the church. Four old women in veils huddled in the front row, saying the Rosary. A man and woman knelt together across the aisle from her. Making her way through the rows, a nun was arranging hymnbooks and missals in their holders.

Katherine watched the black-robed nun shuffle from one pew to another. She was surprised to see the starched white linen that surrounded the nun's face. From what she had read, she had thought that today's nuns all wore normal street clothing and makeup, just like other women. Perhaps that was only in New York, she thought. In small towns like this, the Catholic religion was probably still practiced in the old ways.

When the nun was finished, Katherine realized that she was alone in the church. The couple beside her was gone. The old women had finished their Rosary and left.

She checked her watch.

The ten minutes were up.

Dominic would be coming soon. She wasn't in any rush. It was warm and comfortable in the church. It was odd how comfortable she felt. That was one of the strengths of religion, she knew from her classes. It provided a comfort for the troubled.

Someone entered a pew behind her. At least she wasn't alone anymore.

She stared at the crucifix above the altar, remembering those hundreds of Sundays at Mass with the rest of her parochial school class. They were always finding ways to talk to each other without being caught by the nuns. It was so long ago, she thought. So much had changed in her life.

From behind her, she could hear the heavy breathing of the other visitor. A bad case of asthma, she thought. It was the wheezing sound of lungs that had to struggle for every breath.

She checked her watch again.

It was fifteen minutes since Dominic left.

She leafed through a hymnbook to take her mind off the wait. In the dim light, she could make out the song titles. Many of them were in Polish, a symbol of the fourth and fifth generations trying to hold on to their immigrant roots.

Gradually, the smell of candles and incense gave way to a new odor. It was an odor that seemed out of place in a church. There was something vile about it: sulfuric and filthy. It grew stronger in the still air of the church, enveloping her with its stench until she covered her mouth to avoid breathing it in.

She was afraid to turn.

Afraid of what she would see in the pew behind her.

Her handkerchief was able to blot out part of the smell. But the sound of tortured breathing grew louder.

She started to pray for Dominic to return, to save her from having to face whoever was behind her. It was all in her mind, she thought. Creeping hysteria. But she was afraid to turn her head and confront the reality.

The voice, when it came, made her stop breathing.

It was unlike any human voice she had ever heard.

Eight

THE SOUND WAS guttural and raspy, torn from a throat that seemed to be in agony at the effort of forming a single word.

"Kathy . . ."

She knew.

She knew without turning.

Her flesh tingled at the realization of who it was.

The words were drawn out in a slow-motion sound that filled the spaces between them with painful sighs.

"No . . . one . . . can . . . help . . ."

Feeling a wave of dizziness, Katherine clutched the pew for support.

It was the message from the mirror.

The stench grew stronger.

The sighing continued. It had a hollow, dry sound, as if the air were being propelled through a passage no longer used for breathing.

Katherine gagged on a sudden surge of nausea that left a bitter taste of bile in her mouth.

"Look . . . at . . . me . . ."

Although every fiber of her mind screamed at her not to turn, Katherine found herself unable to resist. A power greater than logical thought took over. She found her body moving in response to the voice, slowly turning to face the reality of what she had seen only from a distance. Until now, she had been unsure. The only way to learn the truth was to turn and face it.

What she saw made her vomit into her handkerchief.

"Kathy . . ."

It was Mother.

Putrefied. The hair streaked with mud. The face flat on one side, puffy on the other. The flesh dark gray, rubbed open in places.

She vomited again.

It was Mother.

Not the living Mother. Not the Mother who had argued with her, who had complained about her father, who had brought her to church as a little girl, who used to sit and watch television reruns until four in the morning.

This was the Mother from the coffin.

This Mother, Katherine admitted, looked dead.

Dead, but back from the dead.

Her mouth hung open, with her tongue apparently unable to move. A stainless-steel wire protruded from the side of her mouth. The end, once twisted, gleamed in the candlelight.

The words that came had to fight to form themselves in a mouth that had long ago breathed its last. And now, here it was, desiccated muscles, blackened lips, foul-smelling, trying to breathe again.

Katherine wanted to scream. But, unlike the figure she faced,

116

she couldn't force a sound out of her throat. She could barely breathe. Her heart pounded. The veins in her head throbbed with panic.

She watched the jaw drop, the head stiffen as the words formed from painfully exhaled air.

"No . . . one . . . can . . . help . . ."

The eyes were clouded and milky. The ears were shriveled. She was wearing the same pale blue gown in which she had been buried. The shoulders of the gown were muddy. The sleeves were torn, shreds of the fabric sticking to the skin of her forearms. Eight years after Katherine had stared at her through the long hours of the wake, after sitting beside the coffin in this very church while the priest intoned the final prayers, she was staring at Mother again. Mother with the stench of death in full bloom and her flesh barely hanging to her bones.

"You . . . must . . . must. . . . do . . ."

Was it really happening, or was she going crazy?

". . . what . . . I . . . say . . ."

"Yes, Mother," Katherine whimpered.

The sound of her own voice was weak and frightened compared to the voice that emanated from the figure before her.

"Yes, yes, yesyesyes," she repeated again and again, until she burst into breathless sobbing. The tears that had never come at the funeral poured out now, eight years after the fact, eight years of repressed emotion washed away by her breakdown.

She cried herself out, until all that was left was the violent sobbing that continued after the tears were gone.

A hand touched her shoulder.

She started to shake.

She kept her eyes closed, afraid to look.

"Katherine, what's wrong?"

She almost fainted with relief at the sound of his voice.

"She's here, Dominic. Mother is here."

She took his hand and squeezed it tightly, pulling him into the pew beside her.

"Where?" he asked. "There's no one here except us. And what's that smell?"

"She was right behind me. She talked to me. It was her, Dominic."

"Are you certain? It's dark in here. Maybe it was someone who looked like her."

"No, no, no. It was her. I tell you, she talked to me. It was horrible. She still had the wire in her mouth, the one the undertaker said they put in. And her eyes . . ."

She started to shake again. Dominic put his arm around her shoulders and pulled her close.

"Dominic, help me," she moaned.

"Tell me about it, Katherine," he said in a gentle voice.

He stroked her hair until she stopped shaking. He pried the vomit-soaked handkerchief from her hand and placed it on the floor, under the kneeler.

"Whatever it was scared the daylights out of you," he said. "Tell me what happened."

While he held her and rocked her gently, she tried to explain what had happened. When she was finished, she couldn't tell if he believed her or not.

"It really happened," she insisted.

"She was right behind you? You're sure of that?"

"You don't believe me, do you?"

Without answering, he rose to examine the pew behind her. He ran his hand along the oak seat. He raised the kneeler and checked the floor.

"You think I'm being hysterical," she said.

He left her there, walking up the aisle to the vestibule of the church. She heard the outer doors open and close. Retracing his steps carefully, he came back to her.

"There's mud on the seat," he said. "There's no mud in the aisle or in the vestibule, no muddy footprints or pieces of loose dirt, but there's mud on the seat."

"That proves she was here," Katherine said.

"There's a little piece of fabric caught on the edge of the pew."

He held up a small piece of blue chiffon.

"It's part of her burial gown," Katherine explained.

Dominic held the fabric up to see it more clearly in the candlelight.

"Now we've got something to go on," he said. "Maybe now we can find out what this has to do with your mother."

"You still don't believe me?"

"I believe someone was here, yes. I don't understand why there's mud on the seat but none in the aisle. You'll probably try to tell me she just appeared in the seat, but I'm still not buying that coming-back-from-the-dead story."

"But you have evidence. That's proof, isn't it?"

He took some church collection envelopes from their rack in the pew and placed the piece of fabric in one of them. He scraped some of the mud from the seat into another.

"Not by itself," he said. "This is just evidence that somebody was here, in this seat. Since the mud hasn't dried, that means it was just a little while ago."

"While you were at the cementery," she said.

"That was convenient, wasn't it? A light in the cemetery that disappears when I follow it, and you see your mother while I'm on that wild-goose chase."

"But no one knew I'd be here. I didn't know it myself. It was your suggestion."

He frowned at her comment.

"That's true," he said. "I can't explain it. But before I'll believe it was your mother, we'll have to establish that this fabric really came from her burial gown, and that this mud came from her grave."

He left her in the pew while he went to find the lights. They flickered on, from the rear of the church forward. It was a harsh, overhead lighting that formed sinister pools of shadows throughout the church.

Katherine waited while Dominic searched.

He looked behind the altar, disappearing through a door that was hidden in the intricate woodwork, and reappearing from behind the side altar. He searched the nave of the church, and checked each of the pews. He opened the confessionals, and searched the crawl spaces behind the statues of Saint Theresa,

Saint Francis, the Blessed Virgin, and the Christ Child. She listened to the hollow sound of his steps as he went through the choir loft. At one point he stumbled against a chair, sending the clattering noise echoing through the empty church. She heard him go farther up the stairs, into the belfry, and downstairs, to the basement.

He found nothing.

She could have told him that at the beginning.

"You won't find Mother unless she wants you to see her," Katherine told him. "You're dealing with the supernatural now."

"Well, that may be true," Dominic said. "But there's nothing supernatural about those mud smears and that fabric."

They were interrupted by pounding on the side door.

"How dare you lock these doors?" the priest demanded when Dominic let him in. He looked at Katherine, who was still seated in the pew. "What's going on in here?"

His voice boomed through the church, his anger reverberating over the empty pews.

He was a heavy man, with powerful lungs developed over years of preaching. He wore a zippered black jacket and a white Roman collar.

Dominic stepped aside and allowed him to enter.

The priest strode to Katherine's pew. His face was florid. Up close, she could see the tiny red veins that decorated his bulbous nose. The smell of wine was on his breath.

"What are you doing here, young woman?"

Before Katherine could answer, Dominic spoke up.

"Father Malloy, this is Katherine Roshak. She's a professor from New York City."

"I asked the young woman a question, Dominic."

The priest kept his eyes locked on Katherine. She was trying to think of a way to explain what had happened, some rational way of describing it that wouldn't make him think she was crazy.

"You can see she's upset, Father," Dominic said.

"I can see she's been crying. I want to know why. And why are the lights on and the doors locked?"

"She was attacked," Dominic said.

Katherine lowered her eyes.

"Attacked? In church?"

The priest's voice was incredulous.

"It happens," Dominic said. "I dropped her off a half hour ago, and when I came back, she was hysterical. Someone came up behind her and attacked her."

He reached down and pulled out the handkerchief to display it for the priest.

"She was so frightened, she got sick, Father."

"Look at me, young woman," the priest commanded. "Is that true?"

Unwilling to trust her voice, Katherine nodded. It was true, as far as Dominic had chosen to explain it.

"Were you . . . hurt in any way?" Father Malloy asked. His voice was gentler now.

Katherine shook her head.

"She's still upset, Father. It's a good thing I got here in time."

"It's a terrible thing when a person isn't safe in church anymore," Father Malloy said. "I suppose now you'll be calling for a police investigation?"

"I'm not sure that will be necessary, Father. I've already searched the church. Whoever it is is gone. And I don't think Miss Roshak wants any publicity about this."

"I appreciate that, Dominic. It wouldn't be good for the church if this story got around. It would only frighten our parishioners."

Dominic held out his hand to Katherine. She rose slowly, still hesitant to face the priest.

"I'm dreadfully sorry this happened, young lady. I don't want it to give you the wrong impression of our church. It's just that the world we live in has changed so much. The influence of the Devil, probably."

"She'll be all right, Father. We won't tell anyone about this. And there's no need for the police to find out."

"I understand, Dominic. You can trust me. If you won't say anything, neither will I."

"Thank you, Father."

* * *

Halfway up the hill to the cemetery, Dominic turned off the headlights. He drove slowly past the gates, pulling onto the grassy shoulder farther up the hill. From there, they had a view of much of the graveyard.

"What are you going to do now?" Katherine asked.

"Nothing. Just wait."

"For what?"

"I don't know. See what happens."

"You're waiting for the light to appear again, aren't you?"

He raised a finger to his lips.

"Shhh. Your voice carries."

He lowered the window on the driver's side, enough to allow the cold air to enter the car and keep the windows from steaming up. The only sound from outside was the gentle rustle of dry leaves each time the wind started.

"This won't work," she whispered.

He didn't answer.

The moon was blacked out by heavy clouds. Once her eyes had adjusted to the dark, she could make out the pale images of the tombstones just inside the fence.

"This is a waste of time," she whispered.

From where they waited, she could look down and see the blanket of street lights that covered the floor of the valley. In the distance, the lights of Scranton reflected a soft glow against the low-hanging clouds.

"I still don't see anything," she whispered.

"Be patient, will you?"

"What sort of light was it?"

"It was just a light. It was over by your mother's grave, and it disappeared by the fence when I followed it."

"What did it look like? Was it floating? What color was it?"

Dominic rolled up the window.

"It was just a light, Katherine. Now you have to be quiet. You're going to keep talking, we might as well leave."

When he saw she was going to be quiet, he rolled the window back down.

They waited for nearly an hour. In the quiet of the night, Katherine kept imagining movements among the tombstones.

The harder she stared at them, the more they seemed to shift their positions. There was a noise in the bushes near the car. Katherine sat up straight, a shiver of fear making her suddenly alert.

Dominic took her hand.

"Raccoon," he whispered.

Katherine sat back against the seat and closed her eyes. The tension was giving her a headache. She was starting to doze off when she felt Dominic's grip tighten on her hand.

Her eyes opened instantly.

Across the cemetery, partially hidden by the trees and the monuments, a pale glow was visible. She couldn't see the source of the light, which was hidden below the crest of the hill, in the area of Mother's grave.

"Listen," Dominic whispered.

Katherine strained her ears until she could hear the blood rushing through her veins.

"What is it?"

"I thought I heard a noise. Scratching kind of sound."

She strained again, but still heard nothing.

"Maybe you'd better stay here," he said. "Keep the doors locked and you'll be safe."

She slid across the seat toward him.

"I'll be safer with you," she whispered.

"Don't kid yourself," he said.

That was when she remembered his gun had been stolen. He was unarmed. But that wouldn't make any difference. A gun wouldn't have any effect on Mother.

She followed him silently through the gates. They kept off the paved strip, walking on the grass to hide their footsteps. The glow ahead didn't move.

Dominic stopped before they reached the slope. She could hear it now. It was a scuffling sound. Dirt being thrown about. It could have been digging, she thought, except there was no sound of a shovel. It was more like an animal scratching.

While they listened, the noise stopped.

The glow disappeared.

Dominic swore under his breath.

123

He turned on a flashlight and hurried down the slope. Katherine ran after him, losing one of her shoes in the soft ground.

He stopped and ran the flashlight beam along the cemetery fence.

"Disappeared again," he said with frustration.

The white light reflected off the polished marble tombstones. It revealed the bony limbs of leafless bushes reaching through the wrought-iron fence.

"Just like before," he muttered.

He brought the beam to rest on her mother's gravesite, revealing a high mound of dirt.

"The chief had it filled in again," Dominic explained. "He's trying to keep this quiet."

He let out a low whistle as he approached the grave. Katherine took off her remaining shoe and walked on the cold ground. She had to pick her way through a strange scene. Clods of dirt were strewn madly about the neighboring graves. Splatters of fresh mud hung on the nearby tombstones. Fresh dirt was everywhere.

The source of the mess was her mother's refilled grave.

A hole had been dug nearly two feet into the fresh earth.

Dominic was already kneeling to examine the hole closely.

"It looks like finger marks," he said. "Somebody's been digging with their hands."

"Mother," she gasped. "It was Mother."

The marks of a woman's shoes were in the soil.

"Impossible," he murmured. "She can't be in two places at the same time."

"It's like she was trying to get back into her grave," Katherine said.

She reached down and tried to match her fingertips with the marks in the soil. Dominic pulled her back.

"That's what she was trying to do," she repeated. "They shouldn't have covered the grave."

She could visualize Mother frantically clawing and digging at the dirt, throwing it angrily about, desperately trying to return. Return to what?

"It doesn't make sense," Dominic said.

"It doesn't have to make sense," Katherine said, still stunned by the discovery. "The way she left me eight years ago didn't make any sense, so why should this?"

"Don't torture yourself," he said softly.

She felt his arm around her, reassuring her, lending her some of his strength.

"Don't let it get to you."

"They should dig the grave up again," she said. "They should leave it open for her."

"If she came out of the grave, why would she want to go back? I don't get it."

"Maybe that's why she appeared to me in church. Maybe that's what she was going to ask me. It sounded like she was going to ask me for something."

"You don't believe all this, do you?"

"I know what I saw. And I have a feeling that she's wandering around here, just out of sight."

She looked out into the darkness, beyond the range of Dominic's flashlight.

"Don't talk like that."

"She's cut off from her own grave. You've got to make them dig it up again."

"I'm not going to do anything," Dominic said. "Not until I get some mud samples checked out."

He moved around the gravesite, putting samples of dirt into envelopes he had brought from the church.

While she waited, Katherine continued searching the perimeter of the cemetery with the flashlight. She thought she saw a movement on the other side of the fence, but she couldn't be certain.

"Shouldn't we report this to the police?" she asked.

"What for? There hasn't been any crime committed."

He took the flashlight from her and helped her find her missing shoe.

"I don't know," she said. "It feels like something terrible is going to happen."

He looked up suddenly. They both listened, as if they had heard something in the bushes.

"Come on, let's get out of here," he whispered. "For how often I've been to Cara's grave, this is the first time I'm getting scared."

He drove her to the Scranton Medical and Forensic Laboratory. It was a square, bunkerlike building with no windows. A small TV camera was mounted over the front door. A sign warned that the building was under electronic surveillance.

The man who unlocked the door wore a white medical coat that was too tight, barely enclosing his enormous figure.

"What's so important I have to open up special for you on a Saturday night?" he asked Dominic.

Without waiting for an answer, he turned to Katherine.

"You're the professor. The one Dominic's been telling me about. From NYU, aren't you?"

He ushered them into the building, locking the door and setting a metal crossbar in place behind them.

"I almost went to NYU. That's when I was thinking of studying the law. I should have been a lawyer. From what I see in courtrooms, and I've testified in a lot of courtrooms, I could do better than seventy-five percent of the lawyers out there. Psychology professor, aren't you? I'm Johnny Henzes."

Her hand disappeared in his huge paw. He was a bearlike creature, with a deep rumbling voice, and thick patches of black hair on the backs of his hands.

"Dominic forgot how to introduce people," he said. "Interesting field, psychology. No definite answers. In my job, everything's definite. All based on the laws of science. Physics, biology, anatomy, that's all I ever testify about."

He took them down a long hallway. Doors on both sides wore "Biohazard" and "Radiation" warning signs. The entire building was brightly lit, yet there were no other people to be seen.

"When I'm here alone, I keep all the lights on," he explained. "A habit from childhood. You being in psychology, you'd know all about that."

The shelves and counters of his laboratory were cluttered with jars and boxes. A heavy smell of disinfectant irritated her nose. Two enormous microscopes waited under plastic covers. On the walls were tables of the elements, conversion charts, and a poster of a cat doing chin-ups. A stainless-steel refrigerator hummed in the corner.

The adjoining room was almost sterile by comparison. It was illuminated by a soft blue light. Inside was a multilevel cylinder half the size of a water heater. Four black knobs protruded from it. Below it was a camera fitting. To the side was a control table filled with knobs, gauges, and dials. Two amber TV screens waited in blank silence.

"My scanning electron microscope," Henzes said. "Ever seen one of these beauties?

"We'll have to dry out your samples first. They have to be perfectly dry, because the scope works on a vacuum chamber. Can't let any moisture get in there, or you'll ruin the equipment."

Dominic gave him the church envelopes. Henzes scraped a tiny amount of mud from each of them, labeled them on individual slides, and placed them in a small oven.

"While we're waiting, I'll show you what this baby can do. Been working on those samples you brought in the other day, Dominic. It's okay to show her, isn't it?" Without waiting for an answer, he turned to Katherine. "They came from your mother's coffin. But don't let that bother you, they're scientific samples and their job is to help us get at the truth."

Almost casually, he flicked a switch and turned a knob on the control panel. An image appeared on one of the amber screens.

"Look at that—you know what that is?"

Katherine shook her head.

"Go ahead, take a guess. How about you, Dominic? You know what it is?"

"It looks like a rope of some kind. Or a cord," Katherine said.

"Yeah, it looks like a rope." Henzes chuckled. "But it's a hair. A single human hair, magnified one thousand times. Look, you even see the ridges on it."

Fascinated, Katherine looked closer at the ropelike image.

"It's from the pillow in your mother's coffin," Henzes said.

Katherine recoiled from the screen. Suddenly, the image looked grotesque to her.

"Like I said, it's a scientific sample," Henzes quickly explained. "Don't take it personally. I found out she dyed her hair, your mother did. We can tell that from the optical microscope, but not from this one. This one only shows us the physical structure of specimens. Up to forty thousand times magnification."

He switched off the monitor and held out a stack of Polaroid prints.

"Some shots I took with the camera. It's got a built-in Polaroid. More stuff from the coffin. Look at this one, these are skin scales. Of course, they're eight years old, so they show a certain degree of decomposition."

"He likes to talk a lot," Dominic said. "This isn't a courtroom, Johnny. You don't have to give her all the intimate details."

"Without the details, you'd have no identification. It's hard to tell much from normal skin scales, because they all tend to look alike. Mine wouldn't be much different from yours. It's the decomposition rate and the other details that make them unique. You'll see that when we get to examining the rosary. That's what you need, detail enough to give you a matching standard that will stand up in court. I've done this kind of test before. And I always won the case."

"We're not going to court," Dominic said. "We're just looking for information we can use."

"From the tests I've done so far, the information you get is going to surprise you."

"Just do the examination, will you?"

Henzes removed the first mud sample from the oven. He inserted it into the viewing chamber, made a series of adjustments, and pushed a button on the console. An amber image appeared on the TV monitor.

What had been tiny grains of dried mud on a slide became complex structures riddled with caves and apertures.

"Fascinating, isn't it?" Henzes said. "Most people think the soil is dead, inert, just sitting there under the grass and trees. But it's alive. And it's beautiful. Look at these carboniferous crystals. Here in the Lackawanna Valley, the soil is rich with carbon. You'll find these crystalline formations literally everywhere, including the dust in the air you breathe. So this part of the sample doesn't do us much good, except to say it came from within a radius of about fifty-five miles."

He pressed a button to activate the Polaroid attachment. After removing the photograph of the sample, he adjusted one of the black knobs.

Katherine watched the image on the screen change, moving farther up the sample. A button on the console enlarged the image.

"We're now at one thousand power magnification. Here you begin to see organic matter mixed in with the minerals. Those spiderlike structures are rhizobia. They're a common bacteria, but they're fairly unique here in the valley. You see them more often in farms or on gardens, where they grow in proximity to leguminous plants. Beans and peas and that sort of crop. They convert the nitrogen from the air into nitrogen compounds for the plants. Basically, they all look alike. But when you find these rhizobia living in carboniferous soil, you start narrowing the field. Find them in identical quantities in two samples and that would say the samples are probably from the same site."

"So you've got a match," Dominic said.

"I said probably. So far what I showed you wouldn't stand up in court. A good lawyer would rip me apart if I tried to build a case around carbon crystals and rhizobia."

"What are those tiny filaments?" Katherine asked. "They look like fibers of some kind."

"Ah, you have the eye of a scientist, Professor."

He pressed a button on the console and zoomed in closer, until the filaments filled the screen.

"Those are the keys to what we're after. They're actinomycetes. Microorganisms whose main function is the decomposition of organic matter. They're living creatures that break down leaves and roots . . . anything that was once alive. When you turn over a garden or dig a hole, it's not the dirt that you smell. It's the actinomycetes at work."

Katherine tried to keep the smell of the gravesite out of her mind.

"They're between bacteria and fungi in size. They're hungry little buggers. They'll eat anything organic in the soil. As a result, they give us a kind of time slice of what's going on underground. The level of decomposition of organic matter, if you can match it in two samples, is one of the key elements in proving that one sample of mud came from exactly the same location as another. It'll even tell you how deep the dirt was, if you've got a sample to match from the lower depth."

He took a photograph of the sample, removed the slide, inserted another, and took another photograph. He laid the prints side by side.

"They look pretty much the same to me," Dominic said.

Henzes smiled and shook his head.

"You might have been a good policeman, but you're no scientist. Pretty much the same isn't good enough. Look at this."

He took a print from the earlier stack of photographs.

"That one matches perfectly," Katherine said.

"As close as I've ever seen," Henzes agreed.

"That means the sample from the pew is the same as the gravesite?" Dominic asked.

"Better than that," Henzes said. "I can place that sample inside the grave, not just on top. Right next to the coffin. Look at the level of actinomycete decomposition. That's a subsoil sample tagged from the six-foot level. Whoever you saw in church was down inside that grave."

"Let's not jump to that conclusion right away," Dominic said. "There are other tests you can make, aren't there?"

"You've got soil chemistry analysis, the basic pH series, at least a half dozen others. But based on what I see here, there won't be any contradiction of my findings. These two samples are identical. They both came from the same location, within inches of each other. I'd testify to that in court."

"I want you to run those tests anyway, just to be sure," Dominic said.

"But I already know the answer. Those tests are simply corroborative."

Henzes placed the soil samples in two large yellow envelopes,

130

on which he marked the tests yet to be done.

"You'll have to wait until Monday for those, when my full crew is in."

"Can't you do it now?"

"It's Saturday night, Dominic. I'm already doing you a favor just by coming in here. Besides, who's paying for all this? You're not with the police anymore." Without waiting for an answer, he chuckled. "Oh, what the hell, go get a bulletin board. We'll start constructing a chain of evidence here."

"The trouble with you is you think you're Quincy. You've been watching too much TV," Dominic muttered as he left the room.

"It's nice to hear him complaining again," Henzes said. "He hasn't been this interested in a case since Cara died. You're having a good effect on him, Professor."

Before she could protest, Dominic wheeled the bulletin board into the small room. Henzes pinned the two matching microphotographs at the top of the corkboard.

"I've already analyzed the samples you brought the other day. It was a woman in the coffin. An old woman, in her sixties."

"We already know that," Dominic said with a sigh. "I told you that when I brought the samples."

"Ah, but you had no proof. The body was missing. You didn't even know for certain if there was a body in the coffin to start with. You were pretty skeptical about the whole affair, as I recall."

Dominic shifted uneasily.

"That was two days ago," he said.

"In any event, the material you brought proves it was a woman in her sixties, dead more than five years. She had gray hair dyed brown. She liked to eat fish, bananas, and fried foods."

"That was Katherine's mother," Dominic reminded him.

"Of course. I'm sorry, Professor. But was I right about the fish, bananas, and fried foods? That was from an analysis of the protein content of hair strands taken from the coffin liner.

131

That's how they proved Napoleon died from arsenic poisoning, by analyzing the protein in a hundred-fifty-year-old strand of his hair."

"Let's get on with the testing," Dominic said.

"I could probably tell you what brand of hair dye she used, if that's important."

"It's not."

Henzes shrugged.

"I could tell through comparative analyis on the spectrometer. You never know what's important. The details. Cases are built on the details."

With surgical tweezers, he removed a single strand of thread from the fabric Dominic had found in the pew.

"We have a few threads from the coffin liner that we examined. Synthetic fiber, blue, with a crinkle weave that would indicate a chiffon-type fabric. This looks similar, but let's make sure."

He adjusted the microscope until the fiber showed up in sharp focus on the TV monitor. Holding a microphotograph for comparison, he increased the level of magnification until both threads were the same size.

"Like I said, a perfect match. The accumulation of evidence continues. The person in church wore the same garment as the person in the coffin. I assume you want a photograph of this?"

"Shoot it."

The Polaroids of the matching fibers went up on the bulletin board underneath the dirt samples.

Henzes scraped the remaining piece of fabric with a small knife, producing a small ball of lint. He placed the lint on a slide, and tapped the envelope over it.

"Don't sneeze," he cautioned them. "You'll blow away the evidence."

"It's just dust," Katherine said. "What do you expect to find there?"

"It'll tell us where this fabric has been. Every environment has its own unique characteristics. And it's deposited on us in dust. I don't mean just pollution, although that can be very helpful in identifying pieces of evidence. A high concentration

132

of hydrocarbons or fuel oils can identify a garment as being worn at an oil refinery, for example. In this case, we're looking to place this fabric in the coffin. We'll be looking for fibers from the silk liner, possibly formaldehyde crystallization, and, as I mentioned before, skin scales. A healthy person sheds about fifty million or so skin scales every day. A dead person sheds less, because you don't have your basic cell formation. But there's enough to go on."

He showed her a photomicrograph.

"Here's what we're looking for. This is a shot of the dust we found in the bottom of the coffin. That's a skin scale in the middle."

It resembled a saucer-shaped piece of frayed leather, surrounded by a tangle of magnified fibers and other objects.

"It's mixed in with some strands of hair, some of the chiffon, some silk filaments. The silk has that flat, irregular shape, where the chiffon is a manufactured synthetic, so it's more even. Those crystal shapes are cosmetic powder. Now that scale in the middle is more translucent than you'd expect. It's from an old person."

"It's from Mother," Katherine whispered.

"I didn't quite say that," Henzes corrected her. "To be perfectly accurate about it, that's a sample of skin from the body that was in that coffin the last eight years. My job is just to establish whether the fabric you found in church came from that coffin. It's up to someone else to establish whose body was in the coffin."

"Let's assume it was her mother, all right?" Dominic said. His voice sounded irritated.

"That's up to you," Henzes said, turning back to his microscope to examine the sample.

He adjusted the knobs until he reached the level of diffraction that allowed him to match the earlier photograph.

The image that appeared on the TV monitor was a dense thicket of platelike images and strands of fibers and hairs. She watched as Henzes made another adjustment and the TV image zoomed in to a portion of the sample. He adjusted for position until the leathery patch was centered on the screen.

"I think we've got a match," he said.

Dominic muttered something under his breath.

Henzes studied the image on the screen.

"A definite match," he repeated. "It's incredible."

"You're basing that on a piece of skin?" Dominic asked. "That wouldn't stand up in court."

"Well, it's like anything else," Henzes replied. "A single skin scale, when you consider the microscopic size, could give a lawyer something to attack. But look at the matrix it's in. On the left, you see two strands of hair. Gray hair, dyed brown. I could establish that that dye is the same brand as the one used in the coffin sample. Take a half hour to do it, that's all. On the right, you have a corrugated synthetic fiber from the fabric itself. Identical with the earlier sample. A few crystals of formaldehyde. White silk fibers with a reverse twist, matching the coffin liner. If you look closely, you can even see where *Dermatophagoides farinae*—that's a mite—has been nibbling at the edges of the scale, just as in the previous sample."

He stood back and folded his arms.

"Within this one sample, I can find thirty corresponding factors. At least thirty. If it was just the skin scale, I'd have to say no, it wouldn't stand up against a good lawyer. But with thirty corresponding factors, there's no way I could be wrong."

"Then it was Mother in church. It was. You've proven it."

"I still say it's impossible," Dominic insisted.

"You want to look at the shots I took of the rosary?" Henzes asked.

He pinned the dust-sample photographs on the bulletin board. Below it, without comment, he added another print.

"It's almost the same," Katherine said. "I can see the same types of fibers, skin scales, even the powder crystals."

"That's good. Now you know what to look for," Henzes said. "It does match. It has all the characteristics that we found in the coffin."

"Where is that sample from?" Dominic asked.

"I took that material from the beads of the rosary you brought."

Nine

"THEN THERE'S no doubt it was Mother," Katherine said. "All your evidence proves it."

Henzes held up his hands in protest.

"That's a conclusion for someone else to draw. My job is to examine the evidence. All I've done is compare samples. If asked to testify, all I can swear to is that the samples from the church and from the rosary came from your mother's coffin, where the corpse of an elderly woman had been decomposing over the years. Whether in fact it was your mother who appeared to you in church, I wasn't there, so I couldn't offer evidence. That would be just hearsay."

"One last question, Johnny," Dominic said. "Could anyone have set all this up to make it look like it was her mother?"

"You mean fake the evidence?"

"Yes. Could they do that?"

"Impossible. You're talking about evidence that's invisible to the naked eye. Just the question of collecting and preserving it, not to mention even knowing that it exists in the first place, would make it inconceivable. Even I would find it impossible to duplicate the matrix. You're talking about duplicating dust, Dominic. Dust!"

Dominic seemed preoccupied on the drive back to Dickson. Katherine stared out the car window at the passing side streets and alleys, half expecting to see a figure in blue chiffon in the shadows. It wasn't until they were back under the yellow mercury lights that lined the Main Street of Dickson that Dominic finally spoke.

"I might be able to arrange for a deputy outside your door tonight," he said.

The street in front of the Valley Inn was bathed in the red glow of the neon window signs. Cars were parked half on the sidewalk. The noise of the Saturday-night crowd spilled out through the doorway.

"What good will a guard do?" Katherine asked. "We're dealing with the supernatural."

"If you mean ghosts, you're wrong," he said. "Ghosts don't leave physical evidence behind."

He guided her around the back again.

"I'm not embarrassed to go in the front, Dominic. You don't have to be so careful of my sensibilities."

"The less people who know you're here, the easier it is to protect you."

"But how are you going to protect me? Mother's not afraid of you."

"Maybe not. But why does she show herself to you only when I'm not around?"

Before opening the door, Eddie turned on the porch light and lifted a slat in the venetian blind to peer at them.

"Come on, Eddie. What's the problem?" Dominic shouted.

136

Eddie opened the door just wide enough for them to slip inside.

"Dominic, am I glad you're back. You've got to come upstairs with me."

He quickly shut and locked the door behind them. The noise from the bar nearly drowned out his words.

"I didn't tell anybody about it, Dominic. I figured you might want to keep it quiet. I don't know what's happening. It's strange. Real strange."

"Calm down, Eddie. Just tell me what's going on."

"I knew you wouldn't want me to touch anything, so I left it just the way it was. Just like I found it."

He went ahead of them up the dim stairs to Katherine's room.

"I just went up to check the room, because I thought I heard a noise. You won't believe this, Dominic. Do you smell that?"

He stopped outside the room.

"You can smell it out here," he said, covering his nose with a handkerchief. "It smells like a dead animal in there."

Dominic raised his hand to his mouth and opened the door.

The stench assaulted them, as if it were waiting to attack whoever dared enter the room. Dominic coughed and drew back. He pulled out his handkerchief and waited for the air to clear. To Katherine, it was a familiar smell. It was stronger than the odor she remembered from the church. But it had the same sweet smell of decaying flesh, tinged with acrid odor of sulfur fumes.

She went into the room first, half expecting to find Mother waiting inside.

The room was empty.

The covers on the bed were pulled back.

Katherine stepped closer.

There was something on the bed sheet.

"I wanted to open the windows and let it air out," Eddie said from behind his handkerchief. "Except I figured you'd want to check out the smell yourself. No way I could ever describe it."

"You did the right thing," Dominic said.

Katherine tried to make out the image on the sheet.

"What do you figure that smell is?" Eddie asked. "Smells like something dead, but the room is empty."

"It's just a smell," Dominic said. "Just a stink, that's all. Maybe sewer gas backing up."

"There's no smell in the bathroom. Or downstairs. Just in this room. I don't get it."

"You can open the windows. It'll go away," Dominic said.

Katherine stared at the apparition, trying to make some sense out of it.

"I didn't touch the bed, either," Eddie said. "It was like that when I came in."

He waited by the door, apparently afraid to come closer.

"What do you think it is?" he asked.

"It looks like some sort of shadow," Katherine said.

She reached down to touch the imprint on the sheet. The image was brown, and rough to the touch. It crumbled slightly under her fingers. Dominic bent down to examine it.

"It's a scorch mark," he said. He sounded puzzled. "It's a scorch mark in the shape of a human figure."

"It's like a person was laying there," Eddie whispered.

She could tell he was frightened by how slowly he spoke.

"You can see the legs, and the head, and the shoulders."

Katherine followed his description of the figure.

"But there's no arms," he said.

Katherine touched the head of the image on the sheet.

"There's a whole body," Eddie said. "But where's the arms?"

"They're folded across her chest," Katherine said softly. "Just the way she was in the coffin."

Barely visible, scorched darker than the rest of the image, were two deeper burns where the arms were crossed.

"You're talking some weird stuff," Eddie said. "I don't know what's going on, but this is weird."

"Mother was here," Katherine said. "She was lying in this bed."

"The door was locked," Eddie protested. "No way she could have got in here."

"That's for sure," Dominic said. "Her mother's been dead and buried for eight years. No way she could get in here."

"Oh God, Jesus, Mary, and Joseph," Eddie let out a quick prayer. "How did I get into this? You said there wouldn't be any trouble. What's going on?"

"Don't worry," Dominic said. "This doesn't have anything to do with you."

He looked around the room.

"Do those smoke detectors work?"

There were two detectors, one over the doorway and one above the radiator.

"Sure, I check them every week. No use having smoke detectors if they don't work."

Dominic stood on a chair and lit a match by the unit closer to the bed. The heat of the match had no effect on it.

"Heat doesn't set it off," Eddie said. "It only works with smoke. Blow out the match and you'll see."

When he followed Eddie's advice, the tiny curl of smoke from the match triggered the alarm, setting off a high-pitched shriek that lasted until the smoke disappeared. Eddie held out a glass of water for the match.

"It's the smoldering fires that kill people," he said. "That's why I've got two alarms in every room. I'm not going to get trapped, not me."

He placed the glass back on the nightstand.

"The alarm didn't go off when the bed was scorched?" Dominic asked.

"I would have heard it if it did. I would have heard it all the way down in the bar. You know, when I bought these I tested them to see how far away I could hear them. No point in having alarms if you can't hear them."

He grunted as he tried to open the window.

"This window always sticks when people close it the wrong way," he said.

Unable to gain enough leverage with his dwarf arms, he had to step aside and let Dominic open it for him. The night air rushed into the room, sweeping away some of the smell.

"I did hear some moving around," he said. "But I figured it was the professor. If I could hear that, I sure would of heard the smoke detectors, wouldn't I?"

139

"How tall was your mother?" Dominic asked.

"Five feet three inches. Why?"

"Do you have a tape measure, Eddie?"

"You're wasting your time," Katherine said. "This image will be exactly five feet three inches."

Eddie disappeared while Dominic knelt down to examine the image. He ran his hand along the sheet, feeling for the difference between the scorched area and the untouched portion.

"Just checking," he said. "I like to be sure about things."

Shivering in the draft, Katherine watched him examine the sheet from different angles, as if he expected to find some clue, some sign that would explain how it had happened.

"All I could find was a yardstick," Eddie said from the doorway. It looked oversized in his small hands. He sniffed the air as he entered the room.

"At least the smell is going," he said. "I was afraid I'd have to close the bar if it spread downstairs. Can't serve drinks with a smell like that around."

Katherine watched Dominic measure the image on the sheet. His silence confirmed the length.

"Maybe she's trying to send me a message," Katherine said.

"What kind of message?" Dominic asked. "An image of a body is burned into a bed, what kind of message is that?"

"It's like the Shroud of Turin," Eddie said. "Ever see pictures of it? They had scientists from all over the world examine it, and they couldn't explain it."

"She's trying to tell me something," Katherine whispered, running her hand along the sheet. "I can feel it."

She straightened up and shivered in the cold draft from the window.

"I'm going to die," she said.

"Don't talk like that," Dominic said.

"That's what she's trying to tell me. That's not her image on the bed. I'm the same height. That image is supposed to be mine. She's trying to tell me I'm going to die."

"Don't let it get working on your mind like that. You're starting to imagine things."

"Did I imagine this bed sheet? She was here, Dominic. She was here for a reason. She's warning me."

140

A burst of cold air swept through the room. Dominic closed the window.

"I don't want you to sleep here tonight," he said. "I'll find you another place. Where you'll be safe."

"Safe?"

She laughed at the thought.

"Safe from what? From Mother? You can't stop her. She can go wherever she wants."

"If she doesn't know where you are, you'll be safe."

"I'm going to sleep right here. On this bed. This is where she wants me."

Dominic stepped between her and the bed.

"It's too dangerous," he said.

"Now look, it was your idea for me to stay here in the first place. You said you wanted to find Mother. You used me as the bait. Well, now she's here. And I intend to find out what she wants."

"I don't want any trouble," Eddie said from behind her. "That wasn't part of the deal when I took her in, Dominic."

"It doesn't have anything to do with you, Eddie. I told you that already," Dominic said.

She returned his stare without moving.

"You're a stubborn woman," he said. "Do you always insist on getting your way?"

"I'm here because of Mother. I want to know why she came back."

"It's not your mother. Not anymore. Now it's just a corpse that's been underground for eight years. It's just decomposing flesh."

"Don't say that!" she shouted. "Don't talk about her like that!"

"Decaying flesh, that's all it is. That's why it stinks so much when you see her. It's not human. It's not your mother."

"It is! It is! I saw her!"

When she tried to turn away, he grabbed her wrists and spun her around. His powerful fingers dug into her wrist until her hand went numb.

"There are five women dead already," he said. "Do you want to be next?"

"If that's what she wants, yes!"

"I won't let you!" he shouted. "I won't let you die!"

"You have no right to stop me from seeing Mother!"

Just as suddenly as he had grabbed her, he let her go. Katherine nearly stumbled backward at the release.

"I'm sorry," he said.

She rubbed the red marks his fingers had left on her wrist.

"I'm just trying to protect you," he mumbled.

He seemed too ashamed to look at her.

"I'm sorry."

She didn't know how to respond. All she could do was watch him as he removed the bed sheet.

"You don't want to sleep on this," he said. "It's evidence. Besides, it'll only give you nightmares."

He pulled the sheet out at the bottom and loosened the other sides, being careful not to tear the scorched section. He folded the sheet gently.

It bothered her that he was taking the sheet. Some twisted impulse within her wanted to sleep on the scorched image, to lie in the position Mother wanted. But she held her silence, afraid to tell him what she felt, embarrassed even to admit to herself the strange attraction the image had for her. Neurotic fixation, she told herself. But, even knowing that, there was nothing she could do to dismiss the idea from her mind.

Dominic ran his hand over the bare mattress.

"There's not a mark on it," he said in awe. "You'd think the burn would have penetrated through a single sheet. But there's not a mark on the mattress."

He turned to Eddie.

"You don't mind if I take the sheet. I'll drop it off with Henzes."

"Go ahead, I got plenty of sheets. I got sheets Phyllis bought that aren't even unpacked yet."

"I'll put a guard outside the door," Dominic said. "I think I can get Bednarek to do it as a personal favor to me."

"I don't need a guard," she said, finding her voice again. All she wanted was for them to leave her alone. She was tired of arguing, tired of trying to convince Dominic.

"It'll make me feel better," he said. "If you don't want it for yourself, okay. But I'm putting a guard out there. I just hope you won't need him."

He circled the room, checking the closet, the window, the hinges on the door. Ludicrously, she thought, he even looked under the bed. He must have realized how silly he looked.

"You never know," he explained with a shrug.

When he appeared satisfied that the room was secure, he asked Eddie to call Bednarek at the police station.

"I'll be outside the door myself until he shows up," Dominic told her.

"You're really serious about this, aren't you? You think you can have some effect on what's happening."

"I can try," he said.

"Aren't you going to check the locks? It's the only thing you forgot."

He laughed as he took a chair into the hallway.

"One thing I don't want is a locked door. If we hear trouble and have to bust in, we don't want to waste time busting down a locked door. If I had my druthers, I'd keep the door open a little, but you'll want your privacy."

Fortunately, the smell hadn't penetrated the closet where she kept her nightgown. After removing her makeup and showering, she found that Eddie had already remade the bed. It felt good to lie down with the fresh smell of clean cotton sheets next to her face.

In spite of her bravado in front of Dominic, Katherine was frightened of what awaited her. It took a long time before she could close her eyes. Knowing a guard was outside helped. But it didn't make it any easier to sleep. She kept waking and dozing in fits. Once she jumped up trembling, certain there was someone in the room with her. She listened until there was a ringing in her ears from the strain of trying to detect another sound.

Later she called out in her sleep. The deputy who had relieved Dominic burst in, gun in hand, and turned on the lights. The false alarm made her feel foolish, but safer, too. Despite her certainty that no one could prevent the appearance of her

143

mother, having another human being waiting in the night with her was comforting.

Finally, when the first gray signs of dawn were showing through the edges of the shade, she started to drop off into a deeper sleep.

In the last half-conscious twilight between dozing and dreaming, she was aware of the door opening.

She heard footsteps quietly enter the room and approach the bed.

Her eyelids were too heavy to open.

She slipped into a deep sleep, aware of a presence beside the bed, but unable or unwilling to react to it.

It was a car horn or a dog barking or a child's shout or one of hundreds of other morning noises that woke her up. The room was still shadowy, the window shade blocking the full force of the sunlight.

In the darkness beside the bed, a figure waited.

She remembered the sounds she had heard before falling asleep. She stared at the figure, at the smiling expression barely visible in the shadow of its face.

"How long have you been here?" Katherine asked.

"Not long. Just an hour or so."

"Isn't the guard still at the door?"

"He's asleep. Been asleep for hours."

"What do you want from me? Why do you keep coming into my room?"

"I don't mean any harm. I just wanted to look at you. You're so beautiful when you're sleeping, I could look at you for hours. I didn't mean to frighten you."

"It scares me to wake up and see you here."

"When you're asleep, it's the only time I can look at you without being ashamed of what I look like."

His voice quivered. She looked away, embarrassed, and pulled the sheet tightly against her chin, as if the fabric had some protective quality to it.

"See, there it is," he said. His voice suddenly had a bitter edge. "I can see the way you feel. You're not frightened that

I'm here. You're frightened of the way I look. It's my arms, isn't it?''

She tried hard not to look at his arms, at the short trunks that came down from his shoulders to meet the bottoms of his palms like someone who had been cut apart and put back together without the essential intermediate pieces. But she found herself unable to stop staring.

Nothing in her psychology studies had prepared her for this. It wasn't just another case study, or a student describing one of the hundreds of psychological deviations that had to be learned and understood before she would give a passing grade. She was watching paranoia reveal itself to her. Without having done anything to encourage it, she had become an object of infatuation, the center of his fixation, the focal point on which he projected his lonely fantasies.

"You'd better leave now," she said.

"I won't hurt you. I want to protect you, watch over you, like I did with Phyllis."

"I already have someone to protect me."

"Got a guard outside the door, but he's not doing a good job. Not if I could get in here this easy. You deserve better protection, a lonely woman like you. I can tell you're lonely, the way you look at Dominic. I'm lonely too. Why don't you let me help you?"

"By locking me up? Like you did yesterday?"

"That was a mistake on my part. I should have been gentler with you. That's what you women want, gentleness, don't you?"

Moving carefully, watching for any sudden move on his part, she slid to the far edge of the bed. Out of range of an outstretched arm, but still close enough for him to reach with a quick lunge, she thought.

"I can see you're scared. It bothers me to see you with that look on your face. It reminds me of Phyllis."

She was well out of reach now. Sliding off the bed, she kept the sheet wrapped around herself.

"I tried to help Phyllis, to take good care of her, because I thought she was different. Then I found out she just covered up her feelings about me better than the others. She made a fool of me, in front of my friends and customers. That's why I got rid of her."

His voice went flat, his eyes seemed to lose their focus as he spoke. The classic Krafft-Ebing description of homicidal sexual paranoia, she thought. She felt fear welling up inside her.

"When Phyllis brought that truck driver up here, to the room I fixed so nice for her, I couldn't take it anymore. I knew I had to get rid of her. It was right here, right in this bed, where she made a fool of me."

He laughed and shook his head at the memory.

"They all think she left town with that truck driver. But she never got out of the building."

He started coming around the bed.

Backed up to the window, Katherine yanked at the shade, sending it rolling up and flapping noisily around itself. Daylight flooded into the room. Eddie held up a hand to shield his eyes from the sudden flash of brightness.

The noise brought Bednarek rushing into the room, his gun drawn.

Seeing that it was only Eddie, he lowered his gun. His eyes remained cautious, however, alert for any surprise.

"I heard a noise," he said, glancing from one of them to the other.

Katherine let out a deep sigh.

"It's all right," she said.

She looked at Eddie, who stood motionless at the edge of the bed. He smiled, reverting back to his earlier friendly self. With his short arms, he didn't look threatening in the daylight.

"It's all right," she repeated. "Eddie just came in to see what I wanted for breakfast."

Officer Bednarek looked suspicious.

"How did you get in here?" he asked Eddie.

"You were asleep, Benny. I didn't want to wake you up."

"I was awake the whole time. You couldn't have gotten past me."

He looked around the room.

"Is there another way in?"

"You must have dozed off," Eddie insisted. "That happens. It's nothing to be ashamed of."

"I'm telling you I didn't."

Bednarek walked around the room, feeling the paneling for another entrance. He checked the inside of the closet.

"Don't worry," Eddie said. "I won't tell Dominic."

"I swear I was awake. I don't know how you got in here."

She heard him knocking against the walls in the closet. When he came out, he was shaking his head.

"Maybe you're right," he said. "Maybe I just blinked off for a minute."

"It happens," Eddie said. "We won't tell on you, will we?"

He turned to Katherine, who silently nodded agreement.

"I'll finish with you later, Professor," Eddie said before disappearing through the doorway.

It was almost noon when Dominic returned. Katherine was dressed and watching from the window when he pulled up in his rusted car. She heard him argue with Bednarek about payment outside the door. He forced a smile when he entered. She smiled back, a warm smile to make up for arguing with him yesterday.

"I couldn't get Henzes to open up last night," he said, explaining the delay. "I had to wait until this morning."

"Do you always do that?" she asked. "Try to get people to work at night?"

"It makes Henzes feel important, getting called out of restaurants like a big shot. You had a little trouble with Eddie, according to Bednarek."

She shrugged. "Not really."

"He's got some peculiar ways, but I think he's basically harmless. If he gives you any trouble, let me know."

She quickly changed the subject.

"Did Henzes find anything?"

"Nothing much. The sheets were a cotton-and-polyester blend. Brand new, according to Johnny. Never washed. The scorching was mostly on the nap of the fabric. That's a nice sweater you've got on."

"Thanks."

The psychology professor part of her made a mental note that he was showing greater interest in his surroundings. That was one of the first signs of recovery from withdrawal.

The female part of her was flattered. It was a white Irish knit sweater, one of her favorites. She had picked it this morning to lift her spirits.

"Now that we're getting along again, are you ready to take a trip with me?" he asked.

"Where to?"

"Your favorite place, New York. There's a man I have to see. And bring the keys to your condo."

He ushered her out the back way. She was glad she didn't have to face Eddie on the way out. She still wasn't sure she should tell Dominic what Eddie had privately confessed. It was a question of ethics she still had to work out.

They headed east on Route 81, into the foggy Poconos.

"According to Henzes, it was a short burst of intense heat that made the image on the sheet."

"That's what the arson squad said about my bathroom. A short burst of intense heat."

"Henzes said it didn't come from any object lying on the bed. Put something that hot on a sheet and it's going to burn through to the other side. The pressure and weight will force the heat right through. Also, the sheets were new, so there were still fold marks running across them. If any weight was applied to the heat, the fold marks would be ironed out."

The road ahead disappeared into the fog. Dominic put on the headlights, driving slowly and watching for the cars that materialized out of the whiteness ahead of them. Occasionally one would appear in the middle of the road, heading directly at them, forcing Dominic onto the gravel shoulder.

"That proves it was a message, doesn't it?" she said.

"All it proves is what I said. Anything else is just pure speculation."

"You don't have any other answer, do you?"

"No. Not yet."

"Then it's just like I said yesterday. It was put there as a

148

message for me. Mother's trying to communicate with me."

"I'll agree with part of that," he said. "The image was there for a reason. But that doesn't mean there's anything supernatural about it."

"How do you explain the fact that it was exactly my height?"

"I can't explain that."

"And how could anybody get in that room without Eddie knowing it? The door was locked, supposedly."

"Are you trying to tell me your mother . . . how do you say it, materialized? She materialized in that room?"

"There's no other explanation," she said.

At the higher elevation, moisture in the fog condensed on the windows, smearing the sides with water and making it doubly impossible to see. They drove slowly, creeping along the white line at the edge of the road.

"I go for the simple solutions," Dominic said. "You claim your mother is running around doing all these things. You think she's some kind of zombie, back from the dead and trying to get even with you. Well, I don't believe in zombies. That only happens in the movies, not in real life."

"It's not just Mother. What about those other empty graves in New York?"

"I don't know the connection between what happened in New York and what's happening in Dickson. But if your mother had to claw her way out of the grave, then she doesn't have the power to materialize inside a locked room."

"But it happened. She made that image on the bed."

"Henzes didn't find anything on that sheet other than the mark. Nothing. Just normal room dust. If your mother's corpse was around he would have found traces on the sheet, just as he did in the church and coffin samples. You saw how he works. But all he found were the scorch marks."

"And you have no explanation for that."

"No. Not yet."

"You haven't believed me from the start. Every piece of evidence we find, you reject. When you don't have any explanation, you act as if it didn't happen. You're a master at reality rejection."

"Don't give me that psychology stuff."

"Why? Does it make you feel inferior?"

"Are you kidding? You're the one that believes in ghosts, not me."

"Why can't you accept that this is really happening?"

"And why do you like to argue so much? It's hard to talk to you without you turning it into an argument. What's the problem?"

Katherine slumped against the seat.

"I'm sorry," she said.

Ahead of them, the Delaware River Bridge appeared out of the fog. Rumble strips in the highway vibrated against the wheels, warning Dominic to slow down. The fog was thicker along the river. It was a while before she spoke again.

"I don't know why I argue like that. Sometimes I wish I could change. I know all about psychology, but I don't know about people. I look at other women and they have husbands and lovers and friends. Not me. You think it's because I argue too much?"

"Everybody has friends," Dominic said. "Even Eddie has friends."

"Not me. The only people I know are the ones I work with. I guess in that respect, I'm really my mother's child."

She laughed bitterly at herself.

"That's not exactly true, Katherine," Dominic said. "You've got me. I wouldn't be doing any of this if I didn't like you."

She sighed and shook her head. She wished she could believe him. But she knew from the literature on dysthymic disorders that a replacement relationship was a common way of working through melancholia.

"Who's the man you want to see in New York?" she asked in an effort to change the subject.

"An undertaker named Angelo Brescia. I found out all those missing bodies in New York were buried by him."

Ten

THE BRESCIA FUNERAL HOME was on a narrow street squeezed between the massive gray slabs of New York's municipal buildings and the expanded shops of an overcrowded Chinatown. It was one of the last Italian businesses left behind when the Little Italy district shrank to the north.

"The old families are moving out," explained Angelo Brescia. "The young ones are going to New Jersey and Long Island, where they can live better than here."

Angelo Brescia had lost an enormous amount of weight recently. His skin hung loosely from the sides of his face, collecting in lumpy bags of flesh below his chin. His old brown suit sagged at the shoulders and hung in oversized folds around his waist. Only his shoes seemed to fit, heavy wing-tips that curled up at the toes.

"The old people that were left still came to me," he said. "They wanted to be buried by someone who knows the family. It's a very personal business, you understand."

It was dark inside the narrow building. The front windows were covered with blue-and-red plastic sheeting, giving the surviving light a churchlike quality. The interior smelled of candle wax. The ceiling was darkened by the soot of decades of burning tapers.

"The old people are dying off, and the young ones, you lose touch with them after a while. Oh, they still know me and they try to be nice when they come back to visit their folks, but they've got their own ways too. They don't want to drive all the way from Jersey for a funeral."

It was hard to tell what color the carpeting had once been. A statue of Christ, pointing to his exposed and bleeding heart, stood beside the entrance to the darkened Slumber Room. Katherine was relieved to see that the Slumber Room was empty.

He ushered them into his office, a windowless square filled with leather-cushioned chairs and an old oak desk. The smell of stale cigar smoke hung in the air.

"I'm just trying to hang on for a few more years," he said. "That's all I need is a few more years. This property is going up in value forty percent every year. It's the last good site on this side of Chinatown. They can't expand any farther to the west, because they run into the government buildings. The amount of money coming in from Hong Kong, I could get three million for this property, if I can hold on to it for a couple of years."

The leather cushion sighed under Brescia when he settled into his chair. He folded his hands on the desk and studied Dominic.

"You're Italian, aren't you?" he asked.

152

"Second generation," Dominic said. "My grandfather came from Palermo."

"*Ah, Siciliano, eh?*"

"*Si.*"

"*Sono Napolitano.*"

"*Gli Italiani in mezzogiorno alla stessi, non è vero?*" Dominic said.

"*Certo!*" Brescia agreed.

After grunting his acceptance of Dominic as a *paisan*, Brescia slipped back into English.

"It's a terrible business, this stealing of the corpses," he said.

"Why do you think they're being stolen?"

The old man sighed and shook his head.

"So many crazies in this city," he said. "More crazies than any place in the world. Drug addicts with their brains burned out. Satanists. People who cut the legs off cats just to see them try to crawl. The crazies are all on the streets now, instead of being locked up like they used to be."

"The five corpses that are missing. You buried them all, didn't you?"

Angelo Brescia nodded his head.

"It's a terrible thing," he repeated. "The word gets around. These old people don't like it. They think it's my fault somehow. They blame me. You know, there's two people died in Little Italy last week. I should have had the funerals, but they went to another place up on Fourteenth Street. They're superstitious, these old people."

"You knew the families of the people you buried?" Dominic asked.

"Of course I knew them. It's my business to know them. Being an undertaker is like being a politician. You have to know everybody and get along with everybody. The more you know about their personal history, the more support you can give them in their time of bereavement."

"What about the families?" Dominic asked. "Tell me about the families that were left behind."

"That's the real tragedy," Brescia said. "Some crazies open

153

the graves, that's bad enough. But the real tragedy is what it did to the widows and the families."

"What do you mean?"

"You know how superstitious these old people are. They come to America with all these beliefs from the old country. The evil eye, and omens and hauntings, they all believe in it."

Katherine shifted uncomfortably in her seat.

"I can understand that," Dominic said. "A missing corpse makes people upset."

"It's not just the missing corpse," Brescia said. "The word got around that the corpses came back from the grave. They came back to haunt the survivors. To make them pay for their sins."

Katherine was going to say something, but an almost imperceptible movement of Dominic's eyes cautioned her to be silent.

"How do rumors like that get started?" he asked in a casual tone.

"You take an old woman who's living alone in a small apartment and afraid to go out in the street for fear of being mugged or raped or murdered, all she can do is think about her poor dead husband who disappeared from his grave. It eats away at the mind. People like that, with nothing else to think about, all they do is focus on death. You see them in church every Sunday, wearing their black dresses and veils. First thing you know, the old lady thinks her dead husband pays her a visit. After a while, the mind snaps."

"Suicide?" Dominic asked.

"The last one was two days ago. Mrs. Canaglia hanged herself in the cemetery. And you know, they wouldn't let me bury her. I offered to do it for free, just to reestablish my reputation, but the family wouldn't let me touch her."

"I heard about that. She hanged herself over the empty grave," Dominic said.

"You're not going to accuse me, like the old people do?" Brescia asked.

"I'm not superstitious," Dominic said.

"What about her?" Brescia asked, without looking at Katherine. "She's not a reporter, is she? If this gets in the papers, I might as well close up and sell out."

"*Non,*" Dominic said. "I don't like reporters any more than you do. I told you on the phone we have a similar case in Pennsylvania. I thought maybe you could help."

"Well, I'd say watch out for the next of kin. They're the ones to worry about, not the dead."

"But you said there were sightings of the dead," Katherine interrupted, unable to keep quiet any longer.

"That's just old and lonely people talking," Brescia answered. "Crazy stories. Bodies don't come back to life."

"Did anyone call the police?"

"Are you kidding? This is Little Italy. They don't want the police around here. I don't either. First thing you know, they'll be accusing me of stealing from the bodies. These old-timers, they still bury their dead with wedding rings and jewelry, just like the Egyptians used to. They always check to make sure it's all there before we close the coffin."

"What about the next of kin? Surely they call the police."

"I don't know. What would the police do anyway? With all the crime in this city, they're not going to hold some old lady's hand because she thinks she saw a ghost."

"I already found that out," Katherine said.

Angelo Brescia looked at her with sudden suspicion. He drew back from the desk, as if trying to distance himself from her.

"It's one of your relatives, isn't it?" he said. "You're involved in the case he was telling me about, aren't you?"

He turned to Dominic, agitated now.

"Why did you bring her here? You trying to say I had something to do with this case of yours? I never saw this woman in my life."

Suddenly nervous, he reached into the drawer for a cigar. His hand was trembling as he lit it.

"You said I should protect the next of kin," Dominic responded. "That's why I brought her with me."

"She claims she saw a ghost?"

"It's not a ghost," Katherine said. "It's really Mother. We

155

have evidence. Physical evidence that's already been examined by qualified people."

A series of quick puffs by the undertaker filled the room with cigar smoke. Katherine tried to suppress a cough. The smoke irritated her throat and gave a stale taste to her mouth.

"I don't believe any of it," Angelo Brescia said from behind the protective shield of smoke. "It's all superstition. It's against the laws of physics. I'm a religious man, you know. But once I finish with a body, there's no way it's going to come back to life until Judgment Day. And even then it's going to be tough."

He poked the cigar at a fat brown ashtray, dislodging the ash at the tip.

"We know all about that part of it," Katherine said, not wanting to hear any of the details.

"Did you work on the bodies yourself?" Dominic asked.

Brescia continued to puff, filling the room with thicker smoke. Katherine decided it was a defense mechanism, his way of shortening unpleasant meetings.

"What does that have to do with it? What does it matter who worked on the bodies? They were dead. I've got copies of the death certificates on file. You want to see them?"

"No," Dominic said. "I just want to know if you worked on the bodies yourself."

"I never cared much for that part of the business, fixing up the bodies, if you know what I mean."

He rolled the tip of the cigar against the edge of the ash tray again, sculptured the glowing tip until it had a sharp point.

"Most people get used to it after a while. Me, I never did. That's why I always had assistants whenever I could afford them. They'd do all that part of it, while I handled the administrative work and the selling part of it."

"Then you didn't work on the bodies?"

"None of the ones that are missing. I checked that in my files. If there was anything wrong with the preparation of those bodies, it wasn't my fault. But you can't explain that to the old people."

"I guess not," Dominic said. "Can I talk to your assistant?"

"Oh, he's been gone for at least three years now. These

young people, they're too impatient. Business goes off a little and they leave. Not like the old days, is it?"

"Nothing's like the old days," Dominic said. "Do you know where I can find him?"

The undertaker leaned back in his chair, apparently pleased that he had diverted suspicion from himself.

"Look for a busy funeral parlor," he said. "You find the busiest funeral parlor in New York and he's probably there."

"What do you mean?"

"Just a joke." Brescia smiled. "I used to kid him about it a lot, that he was the happiest when he had a stiff to work on. I'm sorry, miss, but that kid really loved working with those dead bodies. He was an artist of the flesh, that's what he was. He could take a guy run over by a subway train and make him look like he just dozed off."

He paused, relishing the memory.

"The kid showed up about ten years ago, maybe eleven years, with his diploma from mortuary school. Someplace down south, Knoxville, I think. Yeah, that was it, Knoxville, Tennessee. I was glad to see him, because I was running two funerals at a time. The funeral business goes in waves, you know. Sometimes you get three, four years in a row when it seems like every family has somebody dying. Just constant. And then it stops. I can't explain it, but it comes in waves. Maybe it has something to do with the weather cycles, I don't know."

They waited while he took another long puff on his cigar, exhaling the smoke more slowly now. He seemed relaxed. The smoke was having its effect on him, along with the memories of more prosperous times.

"Anyway, when he showed up, it was right at the peak of one of those cycles. And he turned out to be the best cosmetologist I ever had. Why, we used to take pictures of the remains, before-and-after pictures, like we were plastic surgeons. I wanted to send those pictures to *Sunnyside and Service* magazine, I was that proud of the work he did. But he wouldn't let me. He wanted the pictures for his scrapbook. Probably used them to get his next job, and I can't say I blame him for that. It's like a résumé, you know. Otherwise, the body's buried and

157

you got nothing to show on your job interview."

He forgot about his cigar for a moment, caught up in his memories.

"Now the old people, they really go for cosmetics. They like their women to look younger and their men to look stronger when they're laid out. Some old lady dies of cancer, she's all shriveled up and the pain lines are deep in her face, the family doesn't like to look at that."

Katherine glanced at Dominic. He kept his face blank. If Brescia's comment bothered him, he was masking it well.

"When word got around about the quality of restoration we were doing, that's when business really picked up. We were even getting business from families I didn't know. Everybody would comment on how healthy our corpses looked." He laughed softly. "Even me. I couldn't get over it. But then, with the young families moving away and taking their parents with them, business started slowing down. It didn't matter how good a job we did on the corpses, or how many clubs I joined or weddings I went to, there wasn't anything I could do about it. It was just a question of geography and the city changing, that's all it was."

The warmth disappeared from his voice.

"That was the beginning of the hard times," he said. "Business slowed down, and as soon as that happened, the kid left. Just disappeared. Never even waited for his last paycheck. I thought that was strange. I guess he wanted to go someplace where there were more bodies coming in. He really had a love for working on the bodies."

"And you don't have any idea where he is?" Dominic asked.

The undertaker shook his head and picked up his cigar again. Hiding behind the smoke again, Katherine thought.

"No. I don't know anything about him. I don't know why he came here in the first place, why he picked me to work for, and I don't know where he went. He just came and left. That's all."

"You must have a name, a Social Security number. Something for me to go on."

"I don't see how that can help you. Those people are dead.

158

So the kid made them look good before we buried them. So what? That's his job, making them look good. That's why they send corpses to funeral parlors."

"You never know what can turn up," Dominic said. "Maybe there's something in the way they were embalmed."

Angelo Brescia laughed. The heavy flesh under his chin quivered.

"What do you think this is, the movies? You're looking for zombies? I'm telling you, it's just a bunch of crazies stealing those corpses."

"That's probably true," Dominic said. "But still, you didn't work on the bodies yourself."

"So what?"

"That's the same thing that happened in Pennsylvania. The undertaker up there didn't work on the corpse that came back."

"Came back? From the dead? I thought you cops deal with facts, not fairy tales."

"We have evidence," Katherine interrupted.

"I didn't believe it any more than you," Dominic agreed. "But we have samples of soil, skin cells, hair, fabric, even mold. They all match with samples we took from the casket. Katherine claims she saw her mother. And it looks like we can prove she did."

"Not to me. You can't prove it to me. I don't believe in ghost stories. If you were around dead people as long as me, you wouldn't either. It's just dead meat, folks. Dead meat. Like the hamburger you buy in a store. When that spirit, or soul, or life force, or whatever you want to call it, is extinguished, the body is just dead meat. It even smells different."

A murky cloud of smoke nearly obscured his face as he started puffing more furiously. Short, intense bursts of smoke without inhaling.

"I never could stand that smell," he said. "That's why I started smoking these. It gets the odor out of my nose. I don't like the smell of flowers, either. I don't even know what I'm doing, still in the business. I can't wait to sell and get out. It's not just the stiffs you got to put up with, it's the old people, too. You got to hang around the old people and be nice to them,

159

or you won't get their business. That's why I won't retire to Florida. Too many old people."

"The funeral director in Pennsylvania told us the assistant he had eight years ago was named Effenbeck."

The name caught Brescia in the middle of inhaling a deep breath of smoke. He stopped, coughed, sputtered, tried to catch his breath, and turned red as he choked on the cigar smoke.

Eyes bulging, he pounded at the desk with his fist. Dominic jumped up and hit him on the back.

The force of the blow knocked the undertaker against the edge of the desk. With a tremendous gasp, he was able to suck in some oxygen. He leaned back in his chair, waving his hand to indicate he was all right.

Dominic picked up the cigar from the floor and stubbed it out before depositing it in the ashtray.

Katherine opened the small window, letting in some fresh air and the sounds of the street.

Brescia was leaning back, slowly sucking in and exhaling deep drafts of air in a regular rhythm. His face returned to its normal color.

"Are you all right?" Dominic asked.

Brescia took a few more breaths before answering.

"It can't be him," he said. "It must be someone else with the same name."

"What do you mean?"

"You have to excuse me for coughing like that, but it was such a coincidence, I had to catch my breath."

He had to stop again before continuing. His breath still came heavily.

"Effenbeck. That's what surprised me. You said the name of that assistant in Pennsylvania was Effenbeck."

"That's right," Dominic said.

"For a minute there, you really took me by surprise."

"What's the problem?" Dominic asked.

Instinctively, the undertaker reached for the cigar. Even though it was no longer lit, he put it in the corner of his mouth. Its presence seemed to relax him.

"The kid that worked for me was named Effenbeck, too," Brescia explained.

160

"It's him," Katherine said. "It's the same one."

She shivered, whether from the sudden draft blowing in through the window or the mention of the assistant's name, she didn't know.

"It couldn't of been the same kid," Brescia said. "The Effenbeck worked for me was blond and had one of those little Dutch-boy haircuts. The kind that looks like it was cut with a bowl. He had blue eyes and he was just about your height, lady."

Katherine turned to Dominic. Not a muscle on his face made a flicker. Why wasn't he surprised?

"Effenbeck's not a common name," he said.

"That's why you·shook me up," Brescia said. "For a minute I thought we were talking about the same guy. But it has to be another Effenbeck, doesn't it?"

"Do you have his Social Security number?" Dominic asked.

Still breathing heavily, Angelo Brescia steadied himself with a hand on the desk as he rose and turned to the wooden file cabinet. He grunted as he leaned over to the bottom drawer. Thumbing through a stack of papers, he found a yellow file folder. Inside was a W-2 form.

With a trembling hand, he passed it to Dominic. Having accomplished this simple act with great effort, he slumped back into his seat and took a deep breath. Katherine worried that he might be having a heart attack. Psychosomatic reaction, probably.

Katherine turned to look for some sign in Dominic's face. As usual when he was confused, his expression was frozen.

"It's him, isn't it?" she asked.

Dominic compared the Social Security number with the number Walter Kuranda had given him over the phone. He looked puzzled.

"It is," she whispered. "But what does he have to do with Mother?"

"The numbers match," Dominic agreed. "It's the same Social Security number. But it can't be the same person."

"Why not?"

"According to the dates, he'd have to have been working in New York City and in Pennsylvania at the same time."

"That's impossible," Brescia said, sounded relieved that there was a way to refute this possibility. "He was working six, seven days a week. That was during the busiest years we ever had. I told you he was a workaholic. He never took any time off."

"But how can it all match?" Dominic asked. "The name, the description, the Social Security number, even the mortuary school. The other Effenbeck went to Knoxville, too."

"I don't know," Brescia said. "But he couldn't be in two places at one time."

"Do you have a photograph of him?"

Brescia shook his head.

"I have nothing. Nothing except those records. He always had me convert his paycheck to cash, without even signing it. I don't even have a signature on file, except for the W-2."

"You said you took before-and-after pictures of his work."

"He wouldn't let me take his picture. And I don't have any of the others. Like I told you, it was for his own scrapbook."

"What about the address of that school in Knoxville? Can you help me with that?"

"Of course. I have a directory of professional mortuary sources."

He spun around in his chair and took a red volume from a shelf.

"It's an old book," he apologized as he thumbed through the pages. "I don't keep up with the trade like I used to."

He found the page he was looking for.

"Of course, that school has been there for more than a hundred years. The address wouldn't change."

He wrote out the address and telephone number for Dominic.

"This isn't going to mean trouble for me, is it?" he asked. "I have enough problems now. I don't want the state to take away my license."

Dominic had no answer for him. Brescia shrugged in helpless resignation.

"Maybe it's just as well," he said. "All these problems are making the decision for me. It's about time I got out of this business. The only funeral I had in the last three weeks was some guy with AIDS. I didn't even know the family. Nobody else would take him. I had to charge extra for the hazards involved. But that's it. The Chinese? They've got their own rituals. So without the Italians, I'm finished. Unless I want to specialize in AIDS victims."

He walked them to the door.

"I don't know why I got into this business in the first place. I told my father I didn't like it. When my time comes, I left instructions to cremate me. I don't want anybody pumping my body full of chemicals."

"I feel sorry for him," Katherine said as they slowly made their way uptown in the afternoon traffic. The FDR Drive jammed up with northbound traffic near the UN, so she told Dominic to turn off at Forty-second and take Madison Avenue north. She could tell from his reaction to the traffic that the meeting with Brescia troubled him. Instead of the calm, withdrawn personality she had observed the past week, he was swearing under his breath at the buses and taxicabs that pulled out in front of him.

When they reached her building, Dominic parked in the restricted zone right in front of the canopy. The security guard stared at them through the glass doors. He made them wait at the outer door while he talked on the telephone. Casually, making no attempt to hide his attitude, he slowly reached over to press the buzzer, allowing them to enter.

"Real busy, aren't you?" Dominic said in an angry tone.

"That's a no-parking zone out there," the guard said. "You read the sign?"

"Did the electric company leave anything for me?"

"That car stays there more than five minutes, I'll call the towing company. We've got a contract with them. They'll be here in ten minutes."

Dominic suddenly reached over the console and grabbed the guard by the collar. He pulled him halfway over the console, as if he were a helpless manikin. With his left hand, he pinned the guard's arm to the console, preventing him from reaching for his nightstick. The entire action took place as casually as if

Dominic had reached out to greet an old friend.

"I asked you a question, shithead, and I'm not going to repeat it."

"Assault. This is assault," the security guard said. "I'll call the police. I'll press charges, you can be damn sure of that."

"I am the police," Dominic said. "I'm here working on a case, and you're obstructing justice."

"You didn't show me any badge."

"I don't have to. Just take my word for it."

"I don't believe you. I'll call the police. You better not hurt me or it'll go hard for you."

"You know what the New York police will say?"

Dominic shook the security guard by the neck when he didn't answer.

"They'll say, where's your witness? Well, you don't have a witness, shithead, and I do. This lady will say you attacked me when she brought me into the building as a guest. You want her to make a formal complaint to the building management?"

The security guard looked at Katherine. She nodded agreement. As shocked as she was at Dominic's sudden anger, there was nothing else she could do.

"All right, they were here this morning," the guard said. "The envelope is in the top drawer."

Dominic motioned to Katherine to retrieve the envelope.

"What is it?" she asked.

He released the security guard, who slumped against the console.

"You keep your mouth shut about all this," he told him. "Otherwise, I'll be back for you."

The guard didn't respond. Dominic opened the envelope and let out a low whistle.

"They sure hit you for electricity in this town," he said.

"What is it?" she asked again.

"Just an electric bill," Dominic said.

He folded the envelope and put it in his pocket. The guard rubbed his neck and watched in suppressed anger as Dominic took Katherine by the arm and hurried her out.

By the time they reached the George Washington Bridge,

they were in the peak rush-hour traffic. One lane on the upper deck was closed for repair work. It took two hours to get from the ramp at the top of the Harlem River Drive to the express lanes of Route 80 in New Jersey.

The fog that had settled over New Jersey for the entire week was growing thicker, fueled by the smoke from thousands of small piles of burning leaves. The low yellow beams of the special fog lights on Dominic's car weren't much help. He used the taillights of a semitrailer as a beacon to lead them through the dark hills of New Jersey to the Delaware River. When the trailer turned south toward Easton, they were left to creep slowly through the mountains. The divided highway eliminated the need to worry about oncoming traffic, but it was hard to stay on the road.

In front of them, the fog took on shifting shapes. It reminded Katherine of watching clouds as a child, the way they formed into recognizable silhouettes, dissolved and spread and reformed into others. The fog was so thick in places, it seemed to resemble human shapes. It was just a trick of the mind, she knew. The eye sent impulses to the brain, where the ophthalmic nerve sought out patterns in even the most meaningless random gatherings of visual data and tried to fit them into some rational framework.

She tried to ignore what her eyes claimed to see. But it was harder to ignore what she had heard.

"It defies logic, doesn't it?" she asked.

"I didn't expect that business about Effenbeck," he said. He twisted the wheel violently to avoid another car.

"That's why you got so upset with the security guard," she said. "You didn't have to take it out on him."

"Just when I thought I was starting to figure things out, I run into another thing I can't explain."

"That's because you're looking for logical answers."

"What other kind of answer is there?"

"The paranormal. The supernatural. There are things in the world that can't be explained."

"It's got to be a coincidence," he insisted. "Just two people with the same name."

"Effenbeck isn't an ordinary name," she said.

"In some parts of the country it is. The Pennsylvania Dutch, they've got a lot of German names like that. Kutztown is just fifty miles from here."

"The physical description is the same," she said.

"A lot of people look alike."

"The school in Knoxville. That's a triple coincidence."

"But it's possible."

"And the same Social Security number?"

"I can check that out with my buddy who works for the Social Security office."

"You're a classic case of denial," she said. "Deep down you know it's the same person, but you refuse to admit it, because it doesn't fit with your concept of reality."

"One person can't be in two places at the same time," he said. "If you're trying to say I'm crazy for thinking that, you're right."

"We're dealing with something that defies natural laws. You were looking for a connection, and you found one. Now you refuse to accept it, in spite of the evidence."

"Scraps of paper, that's all," he answered. "Just names and numbers on paper. That's not hard evidence."

"You have testimony from two witnesses. They both said the same man worked for them at the same time."

"They could have been mistaken."

"Why are you so obstinate, Dominic? Why won't you accept the facts?"

"Because it's against everything I believe in. Every day since you showed up, something happens that I can't explain. The empty grave. The burning car. The bathroom fire. The apparitions. And now this. One man who's supposed to be in two different places at the same time. Not just for a day. But for years. It goes against the laws of nature, against the laws of logic, against everything that makes any kind of sense to me."

It was suddenly clear to her, the reason for his denial, the reason he kept dismissing her answers, the reason he was unwilling to accept what she saw as the obvious truth.

"You're afraid, aren't you?" she said.

"Afraid?" He laughed. "What's there to be afraid of? Ghosts? Zombies? That's for the movies. Fiction. It's all in your mind. These things don't happen. There's got to be a logical explanation."

"And if there isn't?"

"Everything has an explanation," he said. "Take my word for it. I've been on screwy cases before. Never this weird, I've got to admit, but there's always been an explanation."

"You'll never solve this one until you accept it for what it is."

"What's there to solve?" he almost shouted with frustration. "What's the crime? Stealing a body? That's not a major crime. Scaring you? That's not a crime. I've already spent five days and two trips to New York on this. And for what? Maybe those New York cops are right not to waste any time on cemetery vandals."

"It has something to do with Cara, doesn't it?"

"Don't bring her name into this. You have no business talking about Cara, God rest her soul."

"You're afraid she might come back, aren't you?" Katherine said. "You want to prove Mother didn't come back, so you can be sure your wife doesn't come back."

"Cara is dead. She won't come back."

"You're guilty about her death, aren't you? I can tell the signs. What's bothering you?"

"That's what I get for being nice," he said. "I tried to help you, and all you do in return is insult me."

"I'm sorry," she said. "I can't help it. It's the psychologist in me. I'm always analyzing."

He stared straight ahead, his jaw quivering with anger.

"Yeah, well, you can start analyzing yourself now, because I'm finished trying to protect you. I'll drop you off with Eddie and you can solve your own problems."

He drove in silence over the tops of the Poconos. A rain squall washed some of the fog from the air. She wanted to apologize again, but she was afraid to re-open the conversation. She knew the symptoms. Hostility, sudden flashes of anger, playing the injured party, and another attempt at withdrawal. It was guilt suppression. But what sort of guilt?

"I know what you're doing," he suddenly said. "You're trying to analyze me, figure out what's wrong with me. But you should be thinking about your own problems, not mine. I cried over my wife. I kissed her good-bye when the last breath was leaving her mouth. I mourned, I grieved, I couldn't let go for months. I spent hours at the cemetery every day. That's why they think I'm crazy. But I let her go. She's dead, and she's not coming back. I know that."

His voice quivered. She could see the reflection of tears forming in his eyes as he swallowed, trying to control his emotions.

"You're the one who never grieved," he said. "You're still confused. You're a psychology professor and you don't even know how to deal with death. That's your problem. That's why you think your mother is back from the dead. You never let her be dead in the first place."

It was nearly midnight when they arrived in Dickson. In his anger, Dominic took her in through the front of the bar. The last few customers were leaning over their drinks. Eddie was nowhere in sight. The bartender told them he had gone upstairs a few hours ago.

"Probably doing some cleaning," he said. "You know Eddie."

Dominic ran up the stairs two at a time. By the time she climbed the stairs, he had already thrown open the doors to all the rooms upstairs except hers.

He pounded on the door.

There was no response.

"I don't remember locking it," she said as she fished the key from her purse.

The room was dark and silent.

"Eddie?" Dominic called.

Nothing moved in the room.

A sense of foreboding swept over Katherine.

There was someone in the room, she was certain. A sweet smell hung in the air. It reminded her of what the two undertakers had said. It was very vague. A wisp of an odor.

She was certain it was the smell of death.

Eleven

EDDIE ELBOWS was sprawled across her bed, his short arms desperately tangled in the sheets. His body was swollen smooth, the skin bursting in places, his face and arms the deep red color of second-degree burns. The heat from his body radiated from the bed.

"What in God's name happened to him?" Dominic whispered in awe.

He reached out to feel for the vein in Eddie's neck, but pulled his hand away, rubbing his fingers.

"Feels like he's been in an oven," Dominic said.

He wiped his fingers against the sheet. Looking closer, Katherine could see fluids crusting on Eddie's skin. Not just perspiration, but bodily fluids forced through his pores by the intense heat of the body.

"God rest his soul," Dominic said, blessing himself quickly.

Katherine found herself staring at Eddie's fingers, swollen by the heat into shiny links attached to palms that were ballooned out of shape.

"Like he was cooked alive," Dominic said in a voice that was on the verge of breaking.

Katherine raised a hand to her nose to blot out the odor the body was beginning to exude. A warm, meaty smell.

"Mother," she whispered. "Mother was here."

Except for the swollen body on the bed, the rest of the room seemed untouched. Nothing appeared burned in any way. Even the glass of water Eddie kept for an ashtray was still on the dresser, although there were beads of condensation on the sides of the glass. Dominic felt the glass, stared at it for a moment, and then checked the bucket of water Eddie kept near the radiator.

"It was meant for me," Katherine said.

"We don't even know what happened here, never mind who it was meant for," Dominic said.

"It's another manifestation. There was the fire in my bathroom, the burning car, the scorched bed sheet, and now this. Four manifestations of heat, all aimed at me."

"Don't talk like that when the police get here," he warned her. "Way the chief feels about us, he'll send you to the psychiatric ward at the state hospital. Wouldn't look good for a psychology professor, would it?"

She followed his advice and stayed quiet when Bednarek showed up. The chief was on his way, he explained, from a fishing trip at Lake Wallenpaupack, about an hour away. Bednarek secured the area, asked Dominic questions about the discovery of the body, and took photographs with the Polaroid.

The coroner, when he arrived, was stunned.

"It must have happened somewhere else," he said. "It

couldn't have happened here. Not in an ordinary room like this."

"It was here," Dominic said. "The door was locked. There were no signs of dragging across the rug, and the bar downstairs was full earlier, along with a few people in the back room. There are three witnesses who saw Eddie go up the stairs to the bedroom. He couldn't have been taken from here, killed, and then brought back. It wouldn't make any sense, besides its being impossible to transport the body past all those people downstairs."

The coroner pulled back an eyelid. The eyeball was milky, like the eye of a steamed fish. Katherine tried to hold back the urge to vomit.

"This doesn't make any sense either," the coroner said. "It's impossible. It looks like he was cooked to death."

"The body temperature was a hundred and twenty when I got here," Bednarek said.

The coroner looked up in surprise.

"I put a thermometer in his mouth," the deputy explained. "I thought you'd want to know that fact. It must have been higher before I got here."

"Very good, Bednarek," said a familiar voice from the doorway behind them. It was Johnny Henzes, from the Scranton Medical and Forensic Laboratory. The huge bear of a man filled the doorframe. He wore a raincoat that was too tight for him. Beneath it was a dark blue suit, white shirt, and blue striped tie. He looked as if he just been called out from a dinner engagement. Henzes nodded to Katherine and Dominic as he shambled into the room.

"Brain death occurs at about one hundred twelve degrees," he said. "Having achieved terminal temperature, the question I'd ask is why was the temperature elevated so far beyond that necessary to accomplish the objective."

"I'm sure glad you're here," Dominic said.

Henzes shook hands with the man from the coroner's office, who didn't seem too pleased to see him. He brushed past the deputy to study the body.

"A hundred and twenty degrees, you say? How long ago was that?"

"About a half hour," Bednarek said.

"That would put the time of death between one to two hours earlier," Henzes said. "Cracks in the skin tissue are caused by the swelling of the epithelial cells, which would indicate a body temperature of at least one hundred forty degrees. Given a slow cooling, that temperature must have been reached quite some time ago."

He touched the reddened flesh.

"Still hot," he said. "You're right about him dying here, Dominic. He's got that sheet in what we'd call a 'dead man's grip.' He grabbed the sheets in agony and locked his fingers so powerfully, they stayed in that position through rigor mortis."

He rose and shook his head.

"It was a very agonizing death. It's a lot less painful to die by freezing than by burning."

"There are no signs of a struggle," Dominic said.

"Probably caught him by surprise," Henzes said. "Probably didn't know what was going on. Your body heat starts elevating, first thing goes through your mind at our age is a heart attack. Symptoms would be the same. Flushed feeling, shortness of breath, sweating. He probably didn't have any idea until the pain got real bad."

"But what could have caused it?" Dominic asked. "What makes a man's body temperature shoot up without him knowing what's causing it?"

Henzes shrugged.

"An unexplained source caused it," he said. "That's what I'd testify if you put me on the stand right now. If I get the chance to sit in on the autopsy, I might find out a little more about how the human body reacts to heat. But I don't think even that would help me explain how it happened. Look around, like you already did if I know you. Nothing else in the room seems to have been exposed to the same massive dose of heat that killed your friend."

"There's something else," the man from the coroner's office said. "The very slow cooling of the body would indicate that these aren't surface burns. The high temperature must permeate the trunk and vital organs."

"That's true," Henzes said. He turned to Dominic. "He means the body's cooked all the way through."

"And that's really impossible," the coroner's man said. "How do you heat a body like that without leaving burn marks on the sheet?"

Katherine sucked in her breath.

"We had burn marks yesterday," she said.

"That's right." Henzes nodded. "Burn marks yesterday, but no body. A burned body today, but no burn marks on the sheets. It's beyond me."

"But it happened," Dominic said. "And if it happened, there has to be an explanation."

The body continued to exude its warmth, along with the sweetish odor of the dead flesh.

"It's a warning to me," Katherine said.

They turned to her. Dominic shook his head, cautioning her to be quiet.

"It's a supernatural manifestation," she said. "There isn't any explanation, not any human explanation. Mother is back from the dead, to take revenge on me."

She let out a deep agonized sigh that rattled in her throat as it escaped.

"No one can help," Katherine moaned. "That's what she told me, no one can help."

Dominic tried to take her in his arms, but she pulled away from him.

"I thought I told you to go back to New York," came a voice from behind them.

It was the chief, returned from his fishing trip. He wore one-piece army coveralls, dirty and faded and muddy at the knees. He didn't look happy at being called back from his trip. Remembering Dominic's warning, Katherine fell silent. The chief grunted and pushed past her to the bed.

"What kind of problem we got here, Bednarek?" he asked, staring down at the swollen body.

"Looks like a homicide, Chief."

"You can't call it a homicide," Henzes corrected him. "Not until you explain the manner in which death was administered."

"You said he died from being heated up."

"But we don't know how the heat was applied."

"Then it's a probable homicide," Bednarek said.

"All you've got so far is death from unnatural causes," Henzes said.

"We'll decide what we've got," the chief said. "Who invited you here anyway, Henzes? We've already got the coroner's office represented."

"Dominic asked me to come."

"Then you better send your bill to Dominic. We're not paying any bills for services we didn't order."

He turned to the man from the coroner's office.

"What's the story?" he asked.

The coroner's representative cleared his throat before answering.

"Probable cause of death was heat. The body was heated to about a hundred forty degrees. Brain death normally occurs at about a hundred ten. Basically the guy was cooked to death."

"How?" the chief asked.

"Can't say. No localized burn marks readily visible. Nothing to indicate he was killed elsewhere and brought here."

"What about electricity? Could he have been wired?"

"No scorch marks. At least none that we can see. Maybe we'll find something at the autopsy."

The chief turned away and frowned.

"It's starting to smell," he said. "Somebody open a window. And let's get the body out of here."

The man from the coroner's office motioned to two men who were waiting in the hallway. They unfolded the accordion legs on a wheeled stretcher and lined it up with the height of the bed. They put on rubber gloves to keep the body fluids off their hands while they transferred Eddie to the stretcher.

Bednarek struggled with the window, which was jammed. He had to hit it with the end of his nightstick to break it loose and allow the fresh air to cleanse the room.

"What did you have to do with this?" the chief asked Dominic.

"Eddie was my friend," Dominic said.

"That's not what I asked."

"We weren't even in town when it happened," Dominic said. "We were in New York today. We found him like this when we got back."

"How long ago was that?"

"About an hour ago."

"You called Bednarek first?"

"That's right. He called the coroner's office."

"I suppose you can prove it, that you were in New York when this happened?"

"You won't take my word for it?"

"Don't play games, Dominic. I'm not in the mood for any of your arguments. A man is dead, and I'm asking you if you can prove where you were."

"Yes, I can. We went to see Angelo Brescia, an undertaker in Manhattan. We spent over an hour with him. You can call him and check it out."

The chief looked at Katherine.

"The girl was with you?"

"The whole time. After we left Brescia, we stopped at her condo to pick up an envelope."

"Anybody see you there?"

"The security guard in the lobby."

"They already gave me that information, Chief," said Bednarek. "I've got the telephone numbers and addresses."

The chief grunted his acknowledgment.

"You can be damn sure we'll check it out," he told Dominic. "I'd take you in on suspicion right now, but your buddy Henzes is right. We don't have a homicide case . . . yet."

Dominic took a cigarette from the same crumpled pack of Camels he had been using since she had first met him. He didn't seem to be a smoker in the normal sense. He used the cigarettes only when he was puzzled, when he appeared to be stalling for time to allow his mind to sort through events. He ignored the chief for a moment while he carefully smoothed out one of the cigarettes. He lit it, took a long puff, and exhaled slowly.

"So now at last we have a crime," he said.

"You sound like you were looking forward to it," the chief said in a suspicious voice.

Dominic took another slow puff before responding.

"Until now all we had was an empty grave, a burning car, nothing of any serious criminal nature. But now we have a dead man."

"It's not a homicide. Not yet," the chief reminded him.

"But he's dead. Dead by unknown means. That's worse than a straightforward murder," Dominic said. "If he was stabbed or shot or strangled, at least you'd know how it happened."

"We'll find out. It's just a matter of time. The autopsy will tell us more," the chief said.

"A man is cooked alive in a locked room without any sign of struggle, and you think an autopsy is going to help you?"

He smiled. He seemed to be making fun of them, Katherine thought.

"We've got a lady who's been telling us that her mother is back from the dead," Dominic went on. "Nobody wants to take her seriously, because it defies every logical explanation."

He took another puff on the cigarette. The room was silent. Everyone was watching him.

"Well, Eddie's death defies every logical explanation too. But it's murder. That's what it is. Whether Eddie was killed by someone alive or dead, it was murder."

"If it's a murder, we'll solve it," the chief said.

"And how do you plan to do that? You haven't got any idea of what you're dealing with."

"And I suppose you do?" Bednarek said with a sneer. "You're going to tell us about ghosts, just like the professor? You're two of a kind," he said.

The chief put a hand on Bednarek's arm to silence him.

"If you have any information about Eddie's death, you'd better turn it over, Dominic. You're not a policeman now, remember. Withholding evidence is a crime."

"All I have is a theory. A theory isn't evidence. If you're not going to arrest us, we're going to leave now."

He turned to Katherine.

"You'll have to stay with me. They won't let you stay here, even if you wanted to, because this is a crime scene. They might not even let you take any of your clothes with you. The chief might think you're taking evidence."

After some discussion, they let Katherine leave with a small suitcase filled with enough clothing for two days.

"I don't think I should stay with you," she said when they were in the car.

"It's for your own protection," he said.

"I know you're trying, Dominic. But there's nothing you can do. Mother's after me. She's angry with me. What she did to Eddie was just a warning. You'll be next, if you don't let me face her myself."

"I can't do that. We'll find a way to fight this together."

"You shouldn't get mixed up with my problems."

"I already am."

"There's a psychological term for what you're doing. It's called transference. I think you're getting me mixed up with Cara, transferring your feelings and emotions from her to me."

"The trouble with you is you psychoanalyze everybody except yourself. Why do you keep fighting me when I'm trying to help you?"

"I don't know," she said. She slumped back against the car seat. "I used to think I knew everything, but now I don't even know if I'm sane anymore."

"Well, that makes two of us," Dominic said. "The chief thinks we're both crazy. And maybe that's why I like you. At least we've got something in common."

She had to laugh at that.

"I've got one stop to make before we go to my place," Dominic said. "I hope you don't mind."

He pulled up in front of a darkened church on a small side street in the town of Olyphant.

"You want to pray at this hour? Can't that wait until tomorrow?"

"I don't want to pray," he said. "I want to talk."

"At this hour? It's after midnight, Dominic."

"This priest doesn't have office hours."

He sat in the car staring at the church, as if trying to summon up his courage. The broad granite steps of the church disappeared in the darkness between huge columns that supported the roof. It was an older church than the one in Dickson. Beside it was the rectory. A dim light illuminated a single side window.

"I called Father Ambrose before I called Henzes," Dominic explained. "He said he'd wait up for us."

"Well, if talking to a priest makes you feel better, I guess you should get it over with. It's a catharsis, isn't it?"

"Don't give me that psychology stuff again. We should have talked about your mother with a priest right at the start."

"Your Father Malloy in Dickson wasn't much help."

"He's still young, still into politics and procedures and appearances. It takes thirty, forty years for a priest to get all that out of his system. Father Ambrose is from the old school. He still makes cemetery rounds, like the immigrant priests used to do. He prays over the graves every day. The other priests don't like that. They call him the Cemetery Priest and try to make him out to be senile. But the bishop's office can't remove him, because the old people in the valley always call him for the last rites. They don't trust the younger priests. They know the younger priests won't pray for them after they're buried. They believe in Father Ambrose."

"You sound like you believe in him too."

"If it wasn't for him, I never would have recovered from Cara's death. The first two weeks, I actually slept in the cemetery, on the grass by her grave. Father Ambrose found me there one morning when he was making his rounds. He came back and stayed with me that night, just talking about death and what it really means, in the spiritual sense."

"And that resolved your separation pain, talking it through?"

Dominic took a deep breath and sighed his disappointment.

"You sound like a textbook. You try to convert it all into buzz words you use in your classroom."

"It's a classic psychological approach," she said in her own defense. "He just happens to be a priest, but he's using psychological techniques."

"I'm talking about a priest who goes alone every day to the cemetery to pray for dead people. He kneels down in the grass and prays over corpses that can't see him or hear him or pay for office visits. That's not psychiatry. That's religion. And when he puts oil on the eyelids of a ninety-year-old man who's dying because his kidneys gave up and his body is filling with urine, that's not psychiatry. That's religion. We're talking about a priest who believes that dead people are put into the hands of God and his job is to intercede for them. So don't insult him by spouting your psychological bullshit in front of him."

A small woman with a Polish accent greeted them at the door. She led them down a hallway lined with dark wood, a reminder of the immigrant craftsmen who had put up the church and rectory.

Dominic knocked softly at the door.

"Enter," came a command from inside.

The only light in the room was an old butterfly reading lamp beside a red leather wing chair. It barely illuminated the room, filled from floor to ceiling with shelves of books. Stacks of books on the floor receded into the shadows. In the bright center of the light's focus sat the priest. The width of his shoulders under the black cassock indicated that he had once been a powerful man. Now his head was bent forward from the effects of osteoporosis. A small hump was visible at the base of his neck. Age had drained his body of muscle, leaving behind a thin layer of skin that was stretched taut over the bones of his face. His hair and eyebrows, still bushy, were a brilliant white. He looked at them with dark eyes that were still clear.

He nodded his greeting without rising from the wing chair.

"Father Ambrose, this is Professor Katherine Roshak, the woman I told you about."

Unsmiling, the priest studied her face.

"Are you a baptized Catholic?" he suddenly asked.

His voice had an aggressive edge that surprised her.

"Does that matter?" she asked.

She felt Dominic touch her arm in warning.

Father Ambrose smiled at her response and waved away any further explanation.

"Only a Catholic would answer like that," he said. "Most other people are afraid of us."

"She's been through a difficult time, Father," Dominic said.

"It's just a point of information." Father Ambrose smiled. "I always like to know a person's religious affiliation."

A book lay open on the priest's lap. When he saw her interest in it, he held it out to her. The text was densely printed, in what seemed to be Latin.

"Summa Contra Gentiles by Thomas Aquinas," he said. "In the original Latin. It's better to go to the original text for clarity and precise meanings, rather than rely on someone else's translation."

"I'm sorry that we have to bother you this late at night, Father," Dominic said.

"It's no bother," Father Ambrose said. "I don't sleep much anymore. Once you get to my age, the body requires less sleep. I find it quite helpful. It allows more time for meditation and prayer as death approaches."

He placed the book, still open, on the table beside him.

"How can I help you, Dominic?"

"First, I have to tell you, Father, I'm no longer a policeman. I was dismissed from the force."

"All the more reason for me to help you."

"I appreciate that, Father. I have some questions to ask you about a crime that was committed."

"I am no detective."

"But there are things you know, Father. Things that might help."

"You're not referring to information from the confessional, I hope. You know the sanctity of what is said in the sacrament of confession."

Dominic shook his head.

"No, no, Father. I don't mean anything like that. It does have to do with religion, though. At least, I think it does."

The priest raised his white eyebrows in surprise.

"You're not investigating a priest?"

"I wish it were that simple," Dominic said. "It's easy to keep track of a priest's comings and goings."

As he spoke, Dominic studied the titles of some of the older books on the shelves.

"It has to do with faith, I think. And with some of the things you spend a lot of time studying. You have a lot of books on the occult." He read off some of the titles. *"The Satanic Bible, Demonolatry, Ritual Magic.* Isn't it unusual for a priest to read books like this?"

Father Ambrose smiled. "It pays to know the enemy."

"Do you believe in all this?"

"If you believe there is a God, then you must surely believe there is a Devil," Father Ambrose said.

"What about ghosts, Father? Do you believe in ghosts?"

"I believe in life after death."

Dominic suddenly sat down on the ottoman in front of the priest and leaned forward, his eyes as intent as those of the old man.

"I mean ghosts, Father Ambrose. People coming back from the dead, coming out of their graves to haunt the living."

Father Ambrose stiffened. His eyes narrowed.

"You're quite serious about this, aren't you?" he asked.

"Yes, I am. And I've already talked to undertakers, other police, and Johnny Henzes down at the crime lab. Nobody has an explanation. That's why I'm asking you, Father. Can a dead body rise from the grave?"

The priest leaned back in his chair.

"You're talking about two different concepts, Dominic. A ghost would be considered an apparition, the disembodied spirit or soul of a dead person. The popular literature describes them as moving through walls and appearing and disappearing without a trace. A dead body rising from the grave is another matter entirely. The soma has physical substance, and would be subject to the same laws of physics as a living body. That is, gravity, visibility, impermeability, corruptibility, and all the rest."

He paused, apparently hesitant to continue.

"Does this have something to do with Cara?" he asked. He blessed himself at the mention of her name. "God rest her soul," he murmured.

"No," Dominic said. "At least, I hope not. But it's important for me to know whether you believe a person can rise from the dead."

"Of course I believe that. The resurrection of the dead is the most basic tenet of Christian religions. The entire basis for our religion rests on the Resurrection of Christ."

"Yes, I know that, Father. And I know all about the dead rising from their graves on Judgment Day."

"The Book of the Apocalypse," the priest said.

"But what about now? Today?" Dominic asked. "Is it possible for someone to rise from the dead today? For their body to come out of the grave?"

The priest's voice became guarded.

"Not unless we were approaching the Day of Judgment. The warning signs of the approach of the end of the world are spelled out very clearly in the Bible. I haven't seen those signs yet. At least, no more than two of them."

"But then it's really true?" Katherine asked. "You really believe that the dead will be resurrected?"

"How could I doubt it and still be a priest? The resurrection of the body is attested to by the Apostles' Creed, the Nicene-Constantinopolitan Creed, the Athanasian Creed, the Fourth Lateran Council, the Second Council of Lyons, and Constantine's Benedictus Deus, and reaffirmed by the Second Vatican Council in its Dogmatic Constitution on the Church, and most recently in the Vatican Letter on Certain Questions Concerning Eschatology."

He paused and smiled.

"You seem surprised," he said. "I take my priesthood very seriously. As my own death approaches, I've become even more interested in eschatology, which is the branch of theology that deals with the final things. Most of the younger priests think it's morbid of me. But after all, our religion is really a preparation for death."

"And you do believe the physical body of a dead person can rise from the grave?"

"To answer that, I'm afraid we have to get into a semantic discussion. The actual mechanics of resurrection are still open to question. Scriptural references carefully straddle both sides of the fence. For every reference in John or Revelations about the dead hearing the trumpet and rising from their tombs, there are other readings such as Corinthians in which we are told a natural body is put down and a spiritual body comes up. If you think in physiological terms of the body as the corpse that rests in the casket, the corruptible flesh, then most modern theologians would have problems with the concept. But if you think of the body as the soma, which is the literal description in the New Testament, and describe it as the entire personal history, the same self, the identical reality, then even radical theologians would feel comfortable with the concept."

Dominic took out another of his crumpled cigarettes.

"Do you mind, Father?"

It was the first time she had heard him ask permission of anyone to smoke.

"I quit, but I still enjoy the smell of tobacco," Father Ambrose said.

Dominic smoothed out the cigarette before lighting it.

"I was hoping to get an answer that would help me," he said after slowly exhaling. "I came here because I figured you were a real expert in these kind of things."

"I'm sorry I can't be more help, but I'm afraid we'll never know the real answer until the time comes. All we can do until then is argue over the meaning of words."

Dominic smoked quietly for a few moments. She knew he was thinking, using the cigarette as a crutch. Apparently, so did Father Ambrose. He waited for Dominic to speak.

"I didn't believe it at first, Father," he said at last. "When Katherine came to Dickson and said her mother came back

183

from the grave, I didn't want to believe it."

He lost himself in his cigarette again. The priest waited patiently.

"You see, I figured if her mother really did come back from the dead, then Cara . . ."

He stopped and tried to hide his emotions by drawing on the cigarette again. He coughed on the smoke. When he cleared his throat, he stubbed out the cigarette.

"I just couldn't handle that, Father. You know, at the end I was wishing she would . . . I was thinking it would be better for her . . . I just wanted her to stop suffering."

He took a deep breath and turned away from them.

"I think she knew that. She sensed it. I could never hide anything from Cara. I've felt guilty about it ever since. When Cara died, she knew what I was thinking. I'm sure of it."

He sat down on the ottoman again and leaned closer to Father Ambrose, lowering his voice as if he were in the confessional.

"Is that a sin, Father? Wishing for someone to die when they're in such pain? Just wanting to get it over with so you don't have to watch them suffer?"

The priest reached out and took Dominic's hands in his.

"You had nothing to do with her death, Dominic. Only the Lord decides when our days on earth are over. Cara knows how much you loved her. I'm sure she's looking down at you now with even greater love than when she was alive. You have nothing to fear from Cara, or from the Lord, Dominic. You were a good husband. You stayed with her and gave her your love until the last breath left her body, and even after she was buried."

He squeezed Dominic's hands between his.

"It's time to put that behind you, Dominic. It's time to embrace life again. Put the guilt behind you. Cara wouldn't want you to torture yourself any longer."

They sat locked at the hands, staring at each other. Katherine felt like an intruder. Dominic lowered his head. Father Ambrose put a hand to Dominic's head, stroking his hair gently, the way an adult would comfort a child.

When Dominic looked up, the haunted expression was gone from his eyes.

"Thank you, Father," he said.

Katherine shivered at the power that appeared to move between the two of them. What she had witnessed wasn't covered by any of the classic works of psychotherapy. It had taken less than a few minutes. But Dominic's guilt was gone.

Father Ambrose turned to Katherine.

"Now tell me about your mother," he said. "You think she's been resurrected from the dead?"

"I saw her in New York City last week," Katherine said. "Twice. The first time, I thought I made a mistake. But when she came to one of the classes I was teaching, I knew I couldn't be wrong. That's why I came here. To visit her grave."

"Had you been to visit her grave before?" the priest asked.

"No," Katherine answered, feeling embarrassed. "The only time I saw her grave before was the day of the funeral, about eight years ago."

She expected the priest to make some gesture of disapproval, but he didn't.

"The grave was disturbed," she continued. "It looked like it had been opened. So I went to the police."

"I didn't believe her," Dominic said. "But when I had the grave opened, the coffin was empty."

He handed Father Ambrose the Polaroid photographs he had taken at the cemetery that night.

"The coffin was open and empty under six feet of dirt."

"Are you certain she was properly buried?"

"I talked to the undertaker and to the priest who officiated at the funeral. The body was there when they sealed the coffin. We took samples from the empty coffin and had them tested at the crime lab in Scranton. The tests indicate a woman's body was in the coffin for a period of years. The body had already undergone a certain degree of decomposition."

Father Ambrose handed the photographs back to Dominic.

"I'm surprised you didn't hear about it, Father," Dominic said. "Didn't the gravediggers tell you about it?"

"It's been a few weeks since I last made the cemetery rounds, Dominic. My heart's been giving me trouble, and the doctor doesn't want me straining it climbing those hills."

"I'm sorry," Dominic went on. "Anyway, this isn't the only empty grave. We found others. Five of them in one cemetery in New York City. There are probably more we don't know about."

"It could be vandalism," the priest said. "With the rise of interest in occultism and Satanism, cemeteries and churches have become targets for all sorts of strange rites."

"We're told people saw the corpses from those other empty graves. Just as Katherine did."

"It could be hallucinations," Father Ambrose said in a cautious tone. "Wishful thinking. You know how these things happen, Dominic. You went through it yourself. People see what they want to see. I'm sure if you talk to them, you'll agree with me."

"Those people are all dead, Father. Every one of them who claimed they saw a corpse is dead. Committed suicide, according to the New York police."

Father Ambrose gasped and quickly murmured a quiet prayer.

"Tell him about the manifestations," Katherine said.

The priest looked up with sudden interest. Dominic sounded uncomfortable when he started to explain what she meant.

"A series of strange things happened since we opened the grave."

"Manifestations?" the priest said, testing the word out loud. "Why do you call them manifestations?"

"That's her word," Dominic said. "She's a professor. She likes fancy words."

"I mean a manifestation in the supernatural sense," Katherine said. "No one can explain how they happened, so they must be manifestations of some unknown power."

Father Ambrose frowned, apparently not liking her reference to the supernatural.

"Whatever you want to call them, they started right after we opened the grave," Dominic said. "Her car was parked in front of the police station while we were at the cemetery. The next morning, it erupted in flames, for no apparent reason."

"A brand-new car, parked right in front of the police station," Katherine said for extra emphasis. "It wasn't even running when the fire started."

"That's when I got kicked off the force," Dominic said in a sheepish voice. "The chief blamed me for it."

"When I went back to my condo in New York, I found the bathroom was burned out. Absolutely charred."

"The arson squad said it took a tremendously intense source of heat to cause the damage, yet there wasn't any sign of the source of the heat. There wasn't enough flammable stuff in the bathroom to cause more than a smoldering fire. They couldn't explain it."

"It had to be a sign from Mother," Katherine said. "There was a message on the mirror, in what looked like her handwriting. It said 'No one can help.' That was the same message they found eight years ago."

"Her mother committed suicide," Dominic explained. "They found her in a motel bathroom up on the highway by the drive-in. She wrote the same four words on the bathroom mirror before she killed herself."

"What do those words mean?" Katherine asked.

"Maybe she wants you to pray for her," Father Ambrose suggested.

"But when I went to church in Dickson, Mother was there, too."

In the darkness of the room, the priest's eyes took on an intensity that was almost hypnotic.

"You're certain it wasn't a hallucination?" he asked.

"That's what I thought it was," Dominic said. "But there were bits of dirt and fabric left in the pew. They matched up at the crime lab with samples we took from her mother's coffin."

"What else?" he asked, growing impatient. "What other manifestations?"

"There was a figure scorched on the bed sheet in the room where Katherine was staying. There was no sign of fire. The smoke detectors hadn't gone off, but the sheet was clearly scorched."

"Was it your mother's figure?" Father Ambrose asked.

"I don't know. It was either Mother or me. We're the same height." She turned to Dominic. "You didn't tell him about the rosary."

"Sorry, I forgot," he apologized. "I thought I saw a figure across the street from Katherine's room one night. She was staying in a spare room at the Valley Inn. When I went to investigate, I found the rosary her mother was buried with."

"It was the same one," Katherine said. "She must have been out there, watching me."

"What else?" Father Ambrose asked, eager now to hear more. "There must be something else, or you wouldn't have come here at this hour of the night. I know you too well, Dominic."

Dominic took a deep breath. He turned to Katherine first, as if seeking psychic support from her.

"Is it that serious?" the priest asked.

Dominic nodded. He exhaled slowly.

"Well, what is it?"

"Just a few hours ago, Eddie Elbows was murdered."

"God rest his soul," Father Ambrose said, blessing himself. He prayed silently for a minute. Dominic closed his eyes and joined him in prayer. Uncertain what to do, Katherine lowered her head and tried to remember how to pray.

"Why do you think Eddie's death was connected to the empty grave?"

"It was the way he was killed. I never saw anything like it, Father. And I've seen my share of dead people. We found him in the bed in Katherine's room. His body temperature was so high, he cooked in his own blood."

"Dear God," Father Ambrose sighed. "You're certain it couldn't have been an accident?"

"Father, I don't even know how it could have happened if it was planned, never mind happen by accident. Eddie was cooked alive. And nothing else in the room was touched or burned."

Father Ambrose turned to Katherine.

"When you saw your mother in church, what did she look like? Was there a glow around her?"

"I didn't notice. I was so frightened by her, the way she looked after all those years in the coffin. I'll never forget it, Father."

The priest closed his eyes. He frowned as if he were trying to dredge up some fact that would help him understand the puzzle they had brought him.

"Some of the old writings talk about the odor of corruption," he said.

Katherine frowned as the smell came back into her consciousness. She could almost feel it in her nostrils, that peculiar odor of decay, but with something else mixed in, something that didn't belong.

"It was a stench," she recalled. "A terrible odor. It made me vomit."

"There was a strange smell in the room when the bed sheets were scorched," Dominic added. "We had to open the windows."

"It was in the grave, too," Katherine said. "A faint odor, but the same one."

Father Ambrose stiffened in the chair. His hands gripped the armrests until his knuckles went white. His voice trembled when he spoke.

"Did it have the odor of sulfur about it? The smell of stale fires? Did you smell that along with the odor of corruption?"

Frightened by the priest's sudden reaction, Katherine took a step backward.

"Yes," she said. "That's what was so strange. It was almost as if she had been burning."

Father Ambrose rose slowly from the chair, his eyes growing wider, as if he were seeing something she had forgotten to describe. He towered over her, a surprisingly big man. For a moment, he seemed to ignore their presence.

"The stench of the Devil," he said in a hoarse whisper. "What you smelled were the fires of hell. The Devil is among us."

Twelve

"**Y**OU MUST BE joking," Dominic said.

Father Ambrose spun around. His eyes had taken on a new life, a hot, burning intensity that made Katherine draw farther away from him.

"It's the Devil himself," Father Ambrose said, in a voice so low, he seemed afraid he might be overhead. He looked nervously from the door to the window, with fear in his eyes. "He announces his coming with fire. Every one of those manifestations you described was heat, flame, fire. He does it to evoke fear in those who don't believe in his evil presence."

"But it was Mother I saw in church," Katherine insisted.

"Saint Athanasius described how easy it is for the Devil to create apparitions and appearances of characters that look real. But the stench of fire and corruption is impossible for him to hide, no matter what appearance his phantasm takes on."

He searched the bookshelves until he found an old leather-bound volume.

"Tell me," he said. "Did the apparition make any sound? Any noise at all?"

"She spoke to me," Katherine said. "The same words that were on the mirror. She said, 'No one can help.'"

He flipped through the pages until he found the reference he sought.

"What did it sound like?" he asked. "The voice, what was it like? Can you remember that?"

Katherine closed her eyes, trying to reconstruct the terrifying details.

"It didn't sound like Mother. Not like I remember her voice. It was hard to understand, almost like it was being blocked. Like something was in the way."

Father Ambrose snapped the book shut.

"Yes!" he said in triumph. "Yes, it's the Devil. *De Praestigiis Daemonum* describes his voice that way."

He waved the book at them.

"It says the Devil takes on a harsh voice when he speaks. It's described as muffled, sounding as if it comes from behind a mask."

"That's it," said Katherine. "That's exactly how she sounded. Hollow and muffled, like it was coming from behind something, almost as if it wasn't connected to her face."

"Now wait a minute," Dominic said. "Hold on before you get carried away. I came because I had a hard time believing a person could come back from the dead. But now you're talking about devils. Do you mean the Devil? Like in the Bible?"

The priest's eyes glowed.

"The Devil, Beelzebub, Satan, Lucifer, all one and the same. Who else could make a man boil in his own blood?"

Dominic took a deep breath. He appeared hesitant to argue with Father Ambrose.

"There might still be another explanation," he said.

"This is the only explanation," Father Ambrose insisted. "Why else would graves be opening? Corpses disappearing and reappearing? Do you have any other explanation for the manifestations?"

"I don't have any proof, if that's what you mean."

"If it's true, if it really is the Devil," Katherine interrupted before Dominic could continue, "then why is he after me? Why me?"

Father Ambrose kept looking around the room, as if he expected the Devil himself to appear out of the shadows behind them.

"Satan is a creature of incredible cunning," the priest said. "He has a malicious and infinite hatred toward the human race. That's why I doubt that he is after you alone. The literature describes him as veiling the most pernicious plans under incredible artifices and disguises. You may be merely caught up in one of his evil schemes."

Dominic made another attempt to dissuade Father Ambrose from his belief.

"But, Father, all those things you're saying. Didn't the business of the Devil go out after the Vatican Council?"

"You haven't kept up with your religion, Dominic. The Pope himself referred just recently to the invisible presence of an obscure enemy, the Demon, a live being, as a terrible reality. The Devil has always been among us. Even the most sophisticated theologians will attribute Hitler's work to the Devil's influence. And they say it without apology, as just one example of Satan's ability to infiltrate our minds. If you believe in God, you must believe in the Devil."

Dominic seemed to give up trying to dissuade him.

"I've never even dealt with the Mafia, let alone the Devil," Dominic said. "What are we supposed to do in a situation like this? How do we fight the Devil?"

"There are many superstitions and stories about dealing with

Satan. Legends have people defeating him by appealing to his vanity, by tricking him with offers of their souls, even by capturing him with mirrors. But separating superstition from fact is difficult."

"Then there's nothing that can be done," Katherine asked.

"The Devil's powers are second only to God's. The only way to defeat the Devil is to ally yourself with the Lord. To wrap yourself totally in God's strength. You must pray, and never let your mind open to Satan's powers."

"I'm not very good at praying," Katherine said.

"Satan is already trying to infiltrate your mind. That's the purpose of these apparitions, I'm convinced. When he enters your mind, then and only then can he work his powers. If you concentrate your mind on God, on love for your fellow man, that will be your best protection."

He opened a desk drawer and removed two packets. Each contained two rectangles of cloth, connected by two red strings. Each of the cloth rectangles displayed a religious picture on the front and a prayer on the back.

"These are scapulars," Father Ambrose said.

He placed one around Katherine's neck.

"They'll offer some protection."

Dominic was going to put his in a pocket, but the priest insisted on putting it around his neck.

He led them down the hallway to a dark room. A single candle provided the only illumination. It was the rectory's chapel, a private prayer room for the priests. There were four kneelers, each with room enough for two people.

Following Father Ambrose's directions, they knelt down and bowed their heads to the small altar. Father Ambrose prayed silently for a few moments before leaving them alone in the room. Katherine turned to Dominic, who shrugged his shoulders to indicate that he was as bewildered as she.

When the priest returned, he carried a silver bucket. He dipped his fingers in the water and sprinkled them both. Cool drops of water struck Katherine's forehead as she listened to Father Ambrose praying over them in Latin.

When he was finished, he put his hands on her head and blessed her. He repeated his action with Dominic.

"I hope my blessings will help," he said when he was finished. "They're the blessings of an old priest, so I hope they still carry some weight with the Lord."

"I'm sure they do, Father," Dominic said, in an obvious attempt to humor the old priest. "I'm sure the Lord knows you pretty well by now."

Father Ambrose smiled.

"I hope so," he said. "Because I think I'll be seeing him soon."

He led them back down the hallway to the front door.

"One last caution," he said. "It would be wise for you to stay with her, Dominic. A lonely mind is easy prey for the Devil."

"Do you believe that?" Katherine said when they were back in the car. "For a minute there, he really had me believing in the Devil."

"That's Father Ambrose," Dominic said. "He takes his religion very seriously."

"It sounds pretty farfetched to me." She giggled nervously. "The Devil. He actually called him Beelzebub. I haven't heard that word since I don't know when."

But Dominic wasn't laughing. "If you don't believe it, take off your scapular," he said.

Katherine touched the fabric that rested around her neck. "You didn't tell him about Effenbeck," she said. "Why not?"

"That would have only proved his Devil theory even more," Dominic said. "Someone being in two different cities at the same time, he'd say that was one of the Devil's tricks."

"Aha, then you don't believe him either."

"Tell you truth, I came here because I still didn't want to believe your theories. I expected him to poke holes in your so-called manifestations. Resurrection? I expected him to laugh at it. I wasn't ready for this business about the Devil."

"You're still fighting it, after all that's happened, aren't you?"

They stopped at the traffic light on the other side of the

Olyphant bridge. It was after one in the morning. There were no other cars on the street. But Dominic patiently waited for the light to change.

"What about you?" he asked. "You sound like you don't believe him."

"I'm not a religious person," she said.

"That's not what I asked."

"He makes a very convincing presentation."

"You're still wearing the scapular he gave you."

"It can't hurt," she said.

"Well, one thing I know he's right about is not leaving you alone. Whether it's the Devil or your mother or the Creature from the Black Lagoon, I'm not going to let you out of my sight until this is over."

Katherine wanted to tell him that was the one good thing that was coming out of all this. She wanted to tell him how grateful she was for his help. How good it felt to have him here to protect her and take care of her. How close she was starting to feel to him. How he was filling a void that had existed ever since her father died.

But of course she didn't.

The moment passed irretrievably, and they drove in silence to Dominic's house.

They stopped at a narrow, two-story wooden frame house with steps leading up to a small porch. It was identical to the other wooden houses that passed in front of their headlights. They were company houses, he explained, built by the coal companies for the miners who populated the valley in the early part of the century.

The rooms inside were small boxes filled with furniture and stale air. The front door opened directly into the living room. With its Early American couch and end tables, hooked rug and lace curtains, it had the dusty look of a room he no longer used. She saw a framed photograph of a woman in a wedding dress on the low table in front of the couch.

The dining room was where Dominic apparently did his living. Old newspapers and magazines were stacked on one of the chairs. Beer cans and a dirty plate sat on the table. A portable TV faced the table. On top of the TV, an ashtray was badly in need of emptying. The smell of it filled the room.

Katherine threw off her coat, opened a window, and started cleaning off the table.

"Hold on," Dominic said. "I'll clean up. You're my guest."

"Get me a sponge, and get rid of that ashtray," she said.

One of the beer cans was still half filled. She gave it to him to empty in the sink.

"Do you realize what time it is?" he asked. "Why don't we wait until morning?"

"When I come downstairs to make breakfast, I want a clean kitchen," she said.

"I didn't bring you here to cook for me," he said as he handed her a sponge. "I mean, you're my guest."

She took it without looking at him, and began to rub at the dried rings the beer cans had left on the table.

"With all you're doing for me, the least I can do is cook for you," she said. "I'll be cooking breakfast anyway."

"You're just keeping busy to take your mind off things," he said.

When she didn't answer, he turned and went back to the kitchen. She smiled when she heard the water running in the sink and plates and silverware clattering. When the living room was clean, she joined him in the kitchen, drying the dishes as he washed. Domestic work was good therapy. The mindless rituals of cleaning and washing and rubbing countertops until they shined was a lot easier than talking about problems. There was something else, too. It seemed so natural to be working with him in the kitchen. It gave her an odd feeling when she thought of how many times he had performed this same ritual with Cara. Supper on the table, maybe a little TV, and then wash the dishes together before going to bed.

Of course, she wasn't going to bed with him tonight. But she had given herself to his protection. And here she was playing the role of helpmate. And enjoying it. The way she analyzed the situation, with his psychological need to establish a replacement relationship and her growing dependency on him, the moment was fraught with emotional dynamite. But she made no attempt to leave his side.

It was a revolving blue light that shattered the moment for her.

Dominic froze when the light came through the window. It disappeared and returned, disappeared and returned, a bright blue light that announced the presence of the police even before they heard the knock on the door.

There were two of them: the chief and Bednarek.

She was thinking it must be important for the chief to be here at this hour of the morning. She watched and listened from the doorway in the dining room.

"I'm afraid we're going to have to take you in, Dom," said Bednarek in a sympathetic voice.

"Read him his rights," the chief said.

"I know my rights," Dominic said. "But I already told you, I was in New York when Eddie died. You can't charge me with that. I have a witness."

"Afraid not, Dom," Bednarek said.

"Angelo Brescia is dead," the chief said. "He died in a fire that started just about the time you said you were there."

"Brescia's dead? Are you sure?"

"They recovered his body an hour ago," Bednarek said. "When we couldn't get through to his number, the telephone company told us about the fire. We talked to a Lieutenant Coleman at NYPD. He said it was arson."

Katherine was stunned.

It was so simple and easy the way they discussed it. A few words to mark the end of another life. A man in a loose brown suit who liked cigars would never lean back in his office to surround himself with the aroma of his favorite addiction again. What was happening? What terrible motive could be causing Mother to do this?

"That makes you the prime suspect," the chief said. "You were the last person to see Angelo Brescia alive. And the first person to see Eddie Elbows dead. Except for your lady friend back there."

He nodded in Katherine's direction. Instinctively, she pulled back from his stare.

"That's two dead people in one day," the chief said. "You've been pretty busy today."

"You're making wild charges," Dominic said. "All you have is proximity, not probable cause. You don't have any evidence."

"We'll get the evidence," the chief said. "We'll get the evidence while you're in jail."

"I know the law as well as you do," Dominic said. "You can't arrest me just because I found a body."

"We're taking you in, Dominic," the chief said. "Sorry to break up the evening you've got planned with your lady friend, but you're going to jail."

"On what charge?"

"Impersonating an officer and assault. That security guard you roughed up in New York says he's going to teach you a lesson. And Lieutenant Coleman is pissed off, too."

"I never told Coleman I was still on the force."

"We've got you on the two counts," the chief said, the satisfaction obvious in his voice. "We'll hold you on the out-of-state charges until they extradite. All the paperwork, that'll take at least a week. By then we'll have the evidence we need on the two murders. I hate to say it, Dominic, but you should have taken my advice. You and your lady friend both."

"You don't have anything on her. Leave her out of it."

There he was, protecting her again.

"Can't leave her out of murder charges," the chief said. "She comes here from New York with that story about her mother coming back from the dead. You know what I think? I think that was just a cover. In case she wants to plead insanity later."

Dominic started for the chief, but Bednarek stepped between the two of them, blocking his way.

"Don't make it any worse on yourself, Dom."

"You see the way it looks?" the chief asked, ignoring the anger on Dominic's face. "She takes you to New York, and now the man you went to see is dead. She brings you back to Dickson, and what do you find? Another dead man. Now I'm not

199

going to ask her anything about Brescia until we place charges. When we do come back for her, I want to make sure we do it all by the book. No inadmissible statements."

"What about the empty graves in that New York cemetery?" Katherine asked. "Didn't Lieutenant Coleman tell you about them?"

The chief smiled at her.

"The way I figure it, you knew about those graves before you came here. Probably where you got the idea in the first place. You're a psychology professor, the way I remember it. Maybe this time you outsmarted yourself."

An answer for everything, it seemed.

"And what am I supposed to do, just wait to be arrested?"

"Nothing else you can do, Professor. You're a material witness in an ongoing investigation. You make any move to leave town, we'll arrest you. I could get a court order to keep you here, but that's just extra paperwork. I think you get my message, don't you?" he said with an exaggerated wink.

"It can be dangerous for her to stay here alone," Dominic said. "There's something out there killing people. She might be next."

"You're going to give me those ghost stories again?"

"We just left Father Ambrose," Katherine interrupted. "Maybe you should talk to him if you don't believe us."

The chief laughed aloud.

"Another of Dominic's friends from the cemetery. They've been trying to retire that old priest for years. He's another one that sees spooks under every chair."

"The least you can do is detail Bednarek to watch the house tonight."

"He's the only officer on duty tonight. I take him off patrol, I'd have to call in Panko or Babinsky. And it's not just time and a half, it's double time at this hour. Besides, what's there to worry about?"

"Somebody or something is out there killing people," Dominic repeated. "They're after Katherine."

"Nice try, Dom," the chief said. "But the way I figure it, I'm putting one of those somebodies in jail. There aren't going to be any more problems tonight."

Seeing the lingering concern in Dominic's face, she stepped forward and touched his arm, then impulsively kissed him on the cheek.

"I'll be all right," she told him. "It's just a few hours. First thing in the morning, I'll find a lawyer and have you released."

They put handcuffs on Dominic and led him out to the car. She watched from the porch. Before they put him in the back seat, Dominic stopped for one last look at her. She waved to him, feeling foolish, schoolgirlish, but wanting to give him some signal of affection to remember.

Bednarek put a hand on Dominic's head and guided him into the car. Katherine watched until the revolving blue lights disappeared around the corner.

She was alone now.

Alone for the first time since the fire at her condo.

What she felt now was more than fear. More than the tingling sensation of vulnerability, the lurking thought that someone was watching her. It was a surprising emptiness. The one person who had shown any concern for her was gone. The psychologically impaired (why did she insist on thinking of him that way?) ex-policeman who was her only protection had been taken from her side. Ex-policeman because of her.

In the silence of the house, she began to realize that her loneliness was stronger than her fears.

She took her Hartmann suitcase up to his bedroom.

First door at the top of the steps.

It was a colonial-style bedroom, with patterned wallpaper and an oversized double bed whose four heavy oak posts almost overpowered the room. The bed was unmade, just the way Dominic had left it in the morning. The feather tick was rolled back. The pillow still had the indentation of his head.

Draped over a chair was the white shirt he had worn yesterday. His pajamas hung from a doorknob, and his scent hovered in the room. A musky, masculine smell. She inhaled deeply, relishing the intimacy of it.

She was trespassing, she knew. There was probably a second bedroom where he expected her to sleep. But once inside this sanctuary of his, she was unable to leave.

She felt safe here.

Protected by the symbols of Dominic's masculinity, as if they were amulets that could ward off any evil.

In a silver frame beside the bed was a picture of Cara and Dominic in front of the house. It was a black-and-white photograph, Dominic looking heavier, happier, his cheeks puffed out in a wide smile. He was wearing a white shirt, tieless, open at the neck, sleeves rolled up, and dark slacks. She smiled at the stiff, old-fashioned pose.

Beside him, Cara looked vulnerable, almost bashful as she hid herself in the crook of his arm. Even then, he was protective. Eddie was right about Cara's beauty. Dark hair, pale skin, aquiline nose, and a small petal of a mouth above a perfect chin. Subconsciously, Katherine raised a hand to her own face. Cara was a classic Italian beauty. And obviously in love with Dominic. It was funny how you could tell that from a single photograph. Was it the way their bodies touched? Or the way they smiled at each other?

She wiped her fingerprints from the silver frame and placed it carefully back on the table.

She knew that what she was about to do was neurotic, but the combination of loneliness and fear overpowered her inhibitions. And she desperately wanted to feel closer to Dominic. She put the scapular on the dresser.

Instead of her own nightgown, she slipped into his pajamas. They were wrinkled from use, and smelled of his body. She shivered with a strange sensation. Neurotic, perhaps, but enjoyable nevertheless. She had to roll up the sleeves and tighten the waist cord to move comfortably. The bed was far more spacious than the one in her condo. It was a bed for two people, she thought, trying to imagine how much room Dominic would take if he were beside her.

The last thing she saw before turning out the light was Dominic smiling at her from the photograph. She smiled and sank into the delicious hollow his head had left in the pillow.

But she couldn't sleep.

As soon as the lights were out, her fears returned. The darkness frightened her pleasant fantasies away. She lay in bed with her eyes wide open. She could barely make out the ceiling. Her ears strained at the stillness. The sounds of the furnace, the hot air vents expanding and contracting, a dog suddenly barking in the next yard all kept her awake. At any moment, she expected something to appear in the room.

Her mind raced from the strange warnings of Father Ambrose to the frightening tableaux of the past week: the cemetery scenes, the undertaker's gleaming body tables, the image of Mother's mouth straining to speak.

And slowly, she became convinced she could smell the odor of corruption here in Dominic's bedroom.

She recognized it from the earlier occurrences. A putrid odor laced with the smell of sulfur. And something else. What was it Father Ambrose had said? The odor of stale fires, that was it.

The smell started as a faint wisp. At first she thought it was her imagination. But it grew and grew until it irritated her nose and made breathing difficult. There was no mistaking it. It filled her nose and mouth and lungs with its filthy, greasy presence. She wanted to vomit, but the fear of what was coming overpowered her nausea. She stuffed a bunched-up section of bed sheet protectively against her mouth and waited.

She was too frightened to move.

There was nowhere to run.

All she could do was wait for the bedroom door to open.

Slowly, quietly, the door handle started to turn.

The light from the hallway illuminated the angle of the door as it opened. Accustomed to the low level of light, she could make out the figure in the doorway.

Mother. It was Mother.

She stood in the doorway in her long burial dress.

"Katherine . . ."

The voice was a moan for help.

Thirteen

Hᴇʀ ᴠᴏɪᴄᴇ ᴡᴀs strained and hollow. It seemed to emanate from somewhere behind her face. Just the way Father Ambrose had described it: behind a mask.

At her feet, barely visible in the backlight, there seemed to be a cloud, a fog of some sort that was blowing into the room. The smell was becoming grotesque.

Katherine whimpered with fright and bit into the sheet that she held against her mouth.

Stiff-legged, the figure in the doorway came into the room. The light from downstairs provided just enough illumination for Katherine to recognize the face before her.

Why hadn't she followed Father Ambrose's advice? The scapular was on the dresser, out of reach as Mother came closer.

"Don't hurt me," Katherine pleaded in a quivering voice. "Don't, please don't."

"No . . . one . . . can . . . help . . ."

Again that gasping voice, as if the words were being painfully formed. Each syllable was expelled with a rush of air that seemed to flow through stiffened passageways to form its sound. Katherine cowered in fright, holding up the sheet as if it could protect her.

She blessed herself and began to pray, words she thought she had forgotten long ago.

"Our Father, Who art in Heaven, hallowed be Thy name. Thy Kingdom come, Thy will be done . . ."

Tears formed in her eyes as she stared at the figure coming closer. The skin hung open on the cheek, where it had been struck with something. No blood came out. The eyes were gray and opaque. Lifeless. Unseeing.

". . . on earth as it is heaven. Give us this day . . ."

"Praying . . . won't . . . help . . ."

". . . our daily bread, and forgive us our trespasses, as we forgive those . . ."

She let out a scream as a hand reached for her. The arm didn't bend at the elbow. The fingers were stiff and distorted.

Mother kept coming closer. The prayers didn't stop her. The scapular didn't stop her. Father Ambrose's blessing seemed useless.

"Please, Mother," she whimpered. "Go back."

"I . . . can't . . ."

Again the heavy sighing. In the dim light, Katherine couldn't see her lips move as she spoke. The wire that protruded from her mouth glinted menacingly.

"Don't hurt me," Katherine moaned.

She scrambled to the head of the bed, putting the last few feet of distance between them. She forgot about the odor as Mother came closer.

"No . . . one . . . can . . . help . . ."

Each word seemed unconnected to the next. It was an agonizing sound. Each word seemed to be torn from a rusted, unused throat.

". . . except . . . you."

Katherine let out a low moan and began to sob. She pressed her back against the headboard, wrapping herself in the sheet until it was impossible to move any farther.

"I . . . want . . . to . . . go . . . back . . ."

Katherine's body began to shake uncontrollably.

". . . help . . . me . . ."

"Oh, Mother, please God this can't be happening."

Katherine was on the edge of hysteria. She turned her face to the headboard and started to cry. She couldn't look at the decomposing flesh any longer. Behind her, she sensed the figure coming closer.

"Help . . . me . . ." sighed the voice.

"Anything, Mother, anything, just tell me how." Her own words came in an uncontrolled rush.

"Destroy . . . it . . ."

"Yes, yes, I will," Katherine said, willing to agree to anything in her panic.

"The . . . money . . ."

"Yes, the money."

"Destroy . . . it . . ."

"Yes, yes, I hear you, destroy the money."

She was sobbing freely now, pressing her face against the board as if trying to force her way through the wall to escape the creature whom she was afraid to call Mother any longer.

"Burn . . . it . . . evil . . . destroy . . . it . . ."

"Yes, yes, the money is evil, but what money?"

"Evil . . . Father . . . left . . . evil . . . money . . ."

"Yes, I'll burn it all, destroy it, whatever you say."

"Burn . . . it . . . in . . . my . . . grave . . ."

"Your grave, that's where I'll burn the money, in your grave."

"At . . . the . . . hour . . . of . . . my . . . death . . ."

Katherine could only whimper as she pressed harder against the headboard. She'd do anything, anything that was necessary to put an end to all this.

"Then . . . I . . . can . . . rest . . ."

They were the last words she heard.

She waited, but the only sound in the room was her own tortured sobbing. She slumped against the headboard and cried until she had no tears left.

When she finally opened her eyes, the figure was gone. The bedroom door was open. There was no sound from downstairs. The dog in the next yard had stopped barking.

In the silence, Katherine suddenly became aware of the stench that was left behind. With her fear gone, revulsion overcame her. She felt her stomach start to surge. The acid taste of bile rose up in her throat. She lurched violently as the vomit poured out. Once, twice, filling the bed sheets around her.

She crawled out of the mess and lay on the uncarpeted floor until she recovered her strength.

The silence in the house soon became ominous. Her fear pushed her into a corner of the room, into a small space where she cowered behind the dresser. She expected the figure to return at any moment.

She was trapped.

She was too terrified to stay in the house alone, yet also too frightened to venture out into the night. All she could do was hide. Press herself into the corner and hide. She was afraid to move. Afraid to go out into the light of the hallway. Afraid of what might await her at the bottom of the stairs.

She jumped each time the slightest sound broke the silence. The creaking of the wooden house became a foot on the steps. The wind outside became heavy breathing. The sound of the furnace became a moan.

Curled up in her hiding place, the psychology professor within her knew what was happening. Extreme anxiety, excessive excitability, sensory disturbances: she was suffering the classic symptoms of hysteria. She tried to force her mind to reassert control over the irrational fear. If she let the symptoms grow stronger, the end result would be total collapse.

She had to focus on something else. To divert her mind from the triggers that were sending out the signals of synthetic fear to the synapses of the brain. She had to find some way to jar her central nervous system, disrupt its fixation and return it to a more normal processing of information.

But how?

How do you apply therapy to yourself when you feel your own rational thought processes slipping away from you?

It had to be quick. She felt her body start to tremble in psychogenic disorder. She wasn't far from a total breakdown, she knew.

Pain.

Physical pain.

That was the only way to override the growing storm in her mind.

She pulled back the pajama sleeve, wet now with her perspiration, and felt her forearm for the most tender and sensitive part of her flesh. She found it just below the elbow, on the inner portion of the arm where pale flesh is smooth and hairless.

She raised her arm and bit it.

The first sharp flash of pain wasn't enough. She had to bite harder and deeper to obliterate the thought of anything else from her mind. Harder and deeper until she felt the skin break under her teeth. She tasted the sweet warm juice of her own blood.

The stinging, burning, intense pain of the bite overwhelmed her. Sinking back against the wall, she moaned and squeezed her arm to stop the flow of blood. All she cared about now was the throbbing pain in her arm. The damage to her arm was being converted into nerve impulses and sent along the neural pathways to the central cortex of her brain, where signals arrived in such volume that they overwhelmed the capacity of the hypothalamus and surrounding limbic system to continue generating hypercharged emotions.

The pain gave her mind time to regroup.

In control of her thought processes again, she rose and turned on the room lights. There was no longer anything to fear in

Dominic's bedroom. All she felt now was pain and shame. The bed was filled with the wet evidence of her nausea. That would be hard to explain to Dominic. Pressing her bleeding arm against her body, she stripped the dirty sheets from the bed and piled them in a corner.

She worked methodically. She cleaned her arm and took a shower, forcing herself to endure the the cold water until her entire body was quivering. At one point, she wondered whether she was really helping herself with these physical shocks or had actually gone over the edge and was acting out some strange form of paranoia.

But when she was done, she felt refreshed. Her mind was clearer than it had been in days. She knew exactly what she had to do.

Father Ambrose disagreed.

"Cooperating with the Devil won't save you," he said when she explained what she was going to do.

The old priest was surrounded by a fresh stack of books. Some of the titles were in Latin, some in French, and some in languages she didn't recognize.

"I've been doing some research since you called," he said. "I can find nothing that indicates Satan has ever expressed interest in material possessions himself, except as a means to tempt others. Perhaps he intends the money for some other, deeper scheme. I'd suggest you don't attempt to deal with him."

"All I want is a safe place to get a few hours' sleep. I have to drive to New York when it's light. I don't want to drive through the mountains when it's dark."

Father Ambrose closed a book and put it on the table beside him. He rubbed his eyes in an effort to wipe away the fatigue of a night spent poring over old books and old languages.

"Do you realize what you're doing?" he asked without looking up at her. "The consequences it might have? This is not an ordinary request you're dealing with. In all the histories of the Devil's dealings with man, in all the books on the occult, not once has Satan ever asked a human for money. He has always *offered* money, wealth, beauty, fame. Why is he asking you for something he can produce himself?"

"You said you had a room for me, Father."

"If you do as he asks, if you do his bidding now, you'll be taking the first step to putting yourself under his power."

She shifted uneasily in his gaze.

"It's been a long night, Father."

"That's how he works, you know. It's all documented, as much as such things ever are. He starts out with simple requests. They're really tests, because he can't force you to do his bidding. You have to do it of your own free will. And once you start, it's almost impossible to stop."

"I'm really very tired," she said.

Father Ambrose sighed and rose from his chair to summon the housekeeper.

"You don't believe me, do you?" he asked. "All my talk about the Devil, you must think I'm just a crazy old priest, as everyone else does."

"All I want to do is get some sleep, Father."

She tried to sound as pleasant as she could, feeling sympathy for the old man.

"You don't believe me," he said with a smile. "Yet something inside you, some little voice, tells you that by coming here you'll be safe for the night."

"I didn't want to stay in that house alone. I thought I'd be safer with someone around to watch. You're the only other person I know here, that's why I came."

Father Ambrose held out his arms. The hands were thin and bony. The muscles had long ago withered away.

"Look at me, Katherine. I'm eighty-two years old. Do you think I can protect you? The only thing I'm good for is reading and praying."

"Then pray for me, Father. I'll need it tomorrow."

His shoulders sagged in defeat. He slumped back down in his chair.

"I guess I'm not even good at preaching anymore," he said. "I can't even convince you of the danger you're in."

The housekeeper appeared in the doorway. She was too small to help Katherine with the oversized Hartmann suitcase.

"What about Dominic?" Father Ambrose said. "Will you be taking him with you?"

"He'll only try to stop me," Katherine said. "And I'm afraid I might listen to him."

"You're going to leave him in jail?" the priest said in a disapproving tone. "After all he did to help you?"

Katherine lifted her suitcase. She wasn't going to let Father Ambrose change her mind.

"As long as he's in jail, he'll be safe. I want to put a stop to all of this before any harm comes to him."

"You're deluding yourself, Katherine. The Devil isn't going to be bought off that easily."

She hesitated in the doorway. The housekeeper was already out in the hall.

"Promise me you won't say anything to Dominic about this," she said to the priest.

"I've known Dominic since he was an altar boy."

"I'm not asking you to lie to him. I'm just asking you to give me until tomorrow night before you tell him about this."

"I wish there was some way I could offer you protection. Perhaps I could accompany you."

"With all due respect, Father, your protection didn't help me at Dominic's house."

She picked up her suitcase and started out the door.

"Perhaps it did," the priest said behind her. "You're still alive."

Katherine hurried up the steps behind the housekeeper.

She spent the night in a small room that was bare except for a single cot, a dresser, and a crucifix on the wall. A bare bulb on the ceiling gave a harsh glare to the room. The window was a small frosted glass pane high up on the wall. It was too small for anyone to enter, she noted with relief. Surrounded by sleeping priests on the upper floor, Katherine slept soundly for the first time since the apparitions had started.

Like a jail matron, the housekeeper was back in the morning, rapping on the door until Katherine opened it. She stood guard outside the bathroom until Katherine was done showering and blow-drying her hair. She watched impassively while Katherine applied her eyebrow pencil, blush, and lipstick. And finally, when Katherine was fully dressed, she escorted her down to breakfast. The woman was obviously determined not to let Katherine wander the halls of the priests' residence alone.

Three priests were at the breakfast table. The youngest of them looked up at her with puzzled curiosity. The oldest, probably the pastor, frowned his disapproval. The third tried to ignore her. She was dressed for her visit to New York City, not for breakfast with three strange priests.

She hesitated at the entrance, as uncomfortable at her own appearance as they were at seeing her.

"Is Father Ambrose here?" she asked.

The two younger priests deferred to the pastor.

"He doesn't eat breakfast anymore," the older man said. His voice had the sepulchral resonance of a man who enjoyed preaching. But he seemed unable to make small talk.

The housekeeper set out an extra plate on the table for Katherine, followed by a glass of orange juice and a coffee cup. Katherine sat down with the three men in black. She felt out of place, a made-up woman in a red dress among these somber men with the pallor that came from spending their days in churches and hospitals.

"Is he still asleep?" she asked.

"He doesn't sleep much anymore," the pastor said.

The priests were careful not to look up from their food.

"He belongs in a nursing home, not a rectory," the youngest priest said.

"They've been telling me that for years," said Father Ambrose from the doorway.

Katherine rose to help the old priest, but he waved her away. The housekeeper automatically brought him a cup of black coffee.

"Of all the nursing homes I've seen, the worst, the absolute worst, are the nursing homes for priests," he said. "Look how dismal it is right here, just having breakfast with us. Why would I want to go to a nursing home, where all the priests are as old as me?"

Katherine ate her bacon and eggs in silence, not wanting to get involved in what must be a long-standing argument.

"I'm not planning to die in a wheelchair," Father Ambrose declared. "I'm like an old horse. I want to die in harness, either in front of the altar . . ."

He paused to allow the pastor to shake his head in distaste at the thought.

". . . or doing the Lord's work helping those who need me."

"You're too old for any of that," the pastor said. "Why don't you admit it? All you're good for now is reading and praying. You've said so yourself. You can do that as well in a nursing home as you can here."

"But then I'd be leaving the people who need me."

The pastor finished his breakfast and handed his plate to the housekeeper. He dabbed at his mouth with his napkin.

"What people need you?" he asked. "You're flattering yourself, Ambrose. The parish existed before you came here, and it'll continue long after you're gone."

"That's the difference between us," Father Ambrose said. "You deal with parishes, and I deal with people."

The pastor threw down his napkin in irritation.

"I suppose allowing a woman to spend the night in the rectory is your idea of helping people?"

Katherine looked down at her plate, embarrassed by the turn in the conversation.

"It's totally inappropriate for a single woman to stay in the rectory overnight," the pastor said.

The housekeeper was standing near the open kitchen door, close enough to hear the conversation.

"But she had nowhere else to go," Father Ambrose said.

"This is not a motel," the pastor replied.

"It sends the wrong signal to the parish," the younger priest joined in.

"Exactly," the pastor said. "The bishop won't like this."

He rose, and the other two priests followed his cue. They left

214

their breakfasts unfinished in their eagerness to follow the pastor's lead.

When they were gone, Katherine apologized to Father Ambrose.

"I shouldn't have come here," she said. "I seem to bring trouble wherever I go."

The old priest waved her explanation away.

"Appearances, that's all they care about," he said.

He drained his coffee cup and held it up for a refill. The housekeeper maintained her impassive expression as she came out with the last of the coffee. She ignored Katherine's empty cup.

"There's a different kind of priest today," Father Ambrose said. "Maybe it's because they grew up during Vietnam, I don't know. But they're more interested in politics and foreign affairs and how the bishop looked on TV last night."

He made a sour face as he drained the cup.

"I guess it's more glamorous than sitting in a dark confessional for hours listening to people's problems. They don't even call it confession anymore. Now it's reconciliation. And nobody wants to talk about sin, much less the Devil. They wouldn't ever understand what you're going through, Katherine. They'd tell you to go see a psychiatrist."

He let out a deep sigh. His shoulders sagged. In the morning light, he looked frail and worn.

"They laugh at my books," he said. "To them, the Devil is a theological concept, something to discuss in the abstract. But I've spent my life fighting Satan and his evil works. I'd give anything to confront him once, before I die. Anything."

The old priest's voice grew hoarse. He squeezed her hand with the little strength he had left in his aging muscles. Under his heavy white eyebrows, the dark eyes began to gleam.

"I want to help you, Katherine. I want to help you turn back the hand of Satan. There'll come a time when you need me. A time when you think all hope is gone. Don't ever allow yourself to surrender."

He was looking deep into her, his eyes focusing at some point inside her head, as if forcing her to remember what he said.

"When that time comes, you must call on me. No matter how impossible it seems, I'll be there. I give you my vow as a priest. Wherever you are, I'll hear you."

Stunned by his intensity, Katherine took a deep breath before answering. She covered his hand with hers.

"I will, Father. I promise you I will."

She called City Trust from the rectory. Collect, to avoid giving the pastor any further reason to criticize Father Ambrose.

Herman Braithwaite was horrified.

"You just can't liquidate a trust fund on such short notice," he said in his Boston accent. "There are forms to be signed, legalities to follow. And what about the restrictions?"

"All the restrictions ended on my twenty-eighth birthday, Herman. You know that as well as I."

"Even if you were serious about it, an orderly liquidation of assets would take a certain length of time. To maximize return, you don't just dump securities on the market. There are questions of timing."

"I want it all sold and converted to cash."

"The tax consequences alone are enormous. Your father set up the trust fund when the stock market was much lower than it is today. Your IBM shares alone have gone from twenty-two to one thirty-five, and split twice. I really have to insist that you talk to your tax attorney."

"Hundred-dollar bills will be fine."

Braithwaite started to talk faster. His voice had a defensive sound to it.

"I think we've done an outstanding job on your trust assets, Katherine. The annualized rate of return has averaged . . ."

He paused, and she could hear the soft click of the keyboard as he typed instructions into his desktop computer.

". . . over the last five years, it's averaged twenty-six percent. That's five points better than the average annual increase in the Dow Jones and seven points better than the Standard and Poor's. You're not going to be able to beat those figures at any other trust department. We're right in the upper tier of investment firms."

"Don't get so defensive, Herman. I'm not moving the funds to another firm. Anyway, I wouldn't need cash if I wanted to do that."

"Then why do you need all this money? I'd be irresponsible if I didn't advise you not to liquidate this quickly. About a third of your trust fund is invested in municipal bonds for the tax advantages. With interest rates where they are now, the bonds are selling at discounts. You'll be taking substantial losses if you sell them off now."

"I'll be at your office in about two hours. I need the cash then."

"Even assuming we closed out all your positions, converting to cash that fast is impossible. The settlement time on stock transactions is five business days. That means the funds won't be available to you until about a week after we sell all your stocks."

"That's too late. I need the money today."

"I'm sorry, Katherine. If you'd given us more advance warning, perhaps we could have arranged something. Why don't you come in and talk about it, anyway?"

"You don't understand, Herman. It's absolutely essential that I get the money. Lives depend on it."

"Are you all right, Katherine? You sound strange. Where are you calling from?"

"Pennsylvania. I can't explain this to you, but I've got to have that money today."

"If you're in some sort of trouble, maybe you should go to the police. I mean, if it's that serious . . . well, frankly, I'd be very suspicious of any deal that had to be consummated with cash."

"I've been to the police," she said in a pleading voice. "There's nothing they can do. I need that money, Herman."

"Do you know how much money you're talking about? You know, in this whole conversation you've never once asked what the current value of your trust fund is?"

"I don't care. I mean, yes I care, but all I want is the money my father left me, whatever it's worth today."

"We're talking two million eight hundred thirty-one thousand five hundred forty-two dollars, at current asset value."

The figure stunned her into momentary silence.

"That much?" she said in a weak voice.

"It's like I said, the rate of growth has been twenty-six percent per annum over the last five years. Of course, there were a few years in which losses were incurred, but those were recession years, in which every investment lost value."

"I didn't realize it was that much."

"Well, you were never interested in the principal. It would be more money except that we've been sending you interest checks from the income portion of the account, and dipping into capital for expenses like your BMW and the condo. By the way, how's the BMW running? This is the first long trip you took with it."

"Well, actually, I had a little accident with it."

"Oh?"

"Nothing to worry about," she hurried to explain. She didn't want to arouse his suspicions any further. "The insurance will take care of it."

"You weren't hurt, I hope."

"No, nothing to worry about."

"Good, good."

"About the money, Herman . . ."

"There are problems coming up with the cash that fast, Katherine. But I've been thinking here while we're talking."

His voice lost its defensive quality. He started calculating again. She waited to hear what his offer would be.

"Everything I've said is true," he said. "I mean, there's no way we could convert your holdings to cash in less than three days. That's the way these things work. And of course, you would have to take a loss on your municipals. Liquidating today . . . let me run it through my PC. . . . that would reduce your net by about forty-two thousand, making it two million seven hundred ninety thousand. Of course, there'd be brokerage commissions involved . . ."

Of course, she thought.

"This is all very unorthodox, folding a trust fund this quickly, but I'm taking into account the fact that we've handled this account for a number of years, and your father was a substantial customer . . ."

Meaning you made a lot of money over the years, she thought.

"And, as you say, you're not simply transferring the funds to another money manager. That is true, isn't it?"

"Yes, it is."

"Well then, considering all that, I think I have a solution that will meet your immediate needs for cash. What we can do is provide you with a short-term bridge loan, secured by your assets, with the interest discounted in advance. We'd calculate the interest for a week and deduct it from the amount you'd get. Clean and simple, and you'd have your money today."

He couldn't let her get away without one last nibble at the trust fund, she thought.

"Why are you charging interest for a week?" she asked. "You said the settlement was three days."

"Technically, it is three days. But normally the funds are delayed for one reason or another. It isn't unusual for a two- or three-day delay, and then the checks have to clear. Since you'll be closing out your account, the company has to protect itself, by adopting a worst-case scenario. If the settlement takes place in three days, we'll credit the balance. I don't think you'd have to worry about that."

"And the interest rate?"

She knew there was nothing she could do about it. She just wanted to know how much they were taking advantage of her.

"Given the circumstances, I'd say two points over prime would be equitable."

"I'm in no position to argue, am I?"

"And, of course, there'd be a special handling fee, because we'll have to expedite the paperwork."

"Of course."

"But you did say you wanted the cash today. If it wasn't for that, you wouldn't have to pay any of these fees."

She could almost hear him smiling at the other end of the line. Smiling at the figures that were coming up on his desktop computer. Well, what did it matter? The money was going to be destroyed at 4:32. That was the hour of Mother's death. Realistically, she didn't have much time. Two hours to New York, two hours back, an hour or so fighting traffic in the city. That gave her only two hours' turnaround to sign the papers and do the other things she planned.

Such as convincing the security guard at her condo to drop the charges against Dominic.

"Why should I?" the security guard said.

He seemed insulted that she would even ask. Katherine had stopped at the condo before going to the trust company. The security guard looked past her to the rusted Riviera she had parked out front. When he was certain Dominic wasn't waiting outside, he turned back to her.

"He comes in here acting like a big shot, roughing me up. I don't have to take that from anybody. I wouldn't have let him get away with it, except he was pretending to be a cop. That's what held me back."

"Why don't you just let it drop?" she said. "He didn't really hurt you."

"A guy like him shouldn't be allowed to walk the streets. That police chief talked to me, he said your friend is already in trouble, even without me. Said something about a guy getting killed in Pennsylvania."

She could see she wasn't going to make any progress with the security guard.

"How much do you want?" she asked.

"What do you mean?"

"You don't look like the kind of man who wants revenge," she said, trying to flatter him. "You just want satisfaction, don't you?"

"Yeah, that's what I want. Satisfaction."

He seemed to enjoy the term.

"One way to get satisfaction is to see him in jail," she said. "You've already got that satisfaction. The other way is to get paid for your trouble."

"Are you trying to bribe me?"

"I'm just trying to see that you get satisfaction," she said.

"Would five hundred dollars satisfy you?"

He looked at her with sudden interest.

"Is this his money or yours?" the security guard asked.

"It doesn't matter," she said. "I'll make that one thousand dollars, but you're going to have to call Pennsylvania and tell them you're dropping the charges."

A broad smile came over the security guard's face.

"You'd pay me that just for one phone call?"

"It's a very important telephone call to me."

"You must really like this guy, to come up with that kind of money."

"He's a good friend. He was trying to help me."

The security guard tilted his head at an angle and studied her.

"I think he's more than a friend. Guy like that, I can see where a woman could go for him. Big macho type, likes to throw his weight around."

"Please," she said. "Will you drop the charges?"

He shrugged.

"What the hell, why not? Like you say, I already made my point. He's sitting in the cooler and he knows he's there because of me. Just tell him not to show his face around here anymore."

Katherine took out her checkbook.

"Hey, wait a minute," the security guard said. His voice turned suspicious. "What are you trying to do? You trying to get me in a corner, aren't you?"

Katherine looked up from the checkbook.

"I thought you agreed. I thought it was okay."

"I didn't agree to any check. You're trying to pull a fast one, aren't you? Get me to cash the check and then you call the police, claim I was trying to shake you down. No way. No checks on this deal. It's cash only. Period. End of discussion."

"I don't have that much cash on me. But I'll get it and be back here in an hour."

"I'll be waiting."

"But just one more thing," she said. "I don't want you to make that call yet."

"No way I'm going to make any call until I get that cash in my hand."

"Good. Because I don't want you to officially drop those charges until tomorrow morning. There are still a few things I have to take care of first."

"You get the cash, and we'll talk about it then," the security guard said.

At the bank, she had to sign the bridge loan agreement before Herman would even let her see the money.

"It's still in the vault," he explained. "They get very nervous about having that amount of money out here on the floor."

The room where she sat was high-ceilinged, dark-wood-paneled, with about two dozen classic wooden desks, each occupied by a man or woman dressed in the same conservative clothing as Herman. Although they were all vice-presidents, according to the nameplates on their desks, none of them had a private office. Around the perimeter of the room, behind the wood paneling, were client offices in which the vice-presidents could discuss the private financial and personal affairs of the beneficiaries of the trusts.

Herman took her to one of these offices, where he spread out a series of documents. They were the usual printed forms that banks have a preference for, with her name and the date typed in neatly among the much smaller legal printing. Some documents had paragraphs deleted with broad diagonal pen strokes. Others had typewritten paragraphs added.

The first document was the dissolution of trust, which she had to sign in two places, on three separate copies.

The second document was an authorization to liquidate assets "at market."

"Normally you wouldn't have to sign this one," he said. "Verbal authorizations are all we require under ordinary circumstances. But given the losses involved in selling the municipal bonds, and certain of the stocks, they wanted it all to be very legal."

"I understand," she said, and signed quickly.

The third document was the loan agreement. Neatly typed in at the top was the amount of the loan, after deductions for interest. The amount was less than he had quoted her earlier.

"Both the bond market and the stock market were off today," he quickly explained. "And as I mentioned, we discounted the interest in advance."

"That's all right," she said.

He seemed delighted when she signed without any further comment. Delighted but puzzled.

"Don't you have any questions?" he asked.

"None," she said. "When do I get the cash?"

He checked the signatures on the forms and arranged them in sequence in a blue folder.

"After twenty-eight years, a few more minutes shouldn't make much difference," he said with a grin.

He was probably trying to be humorous, but she was beginning to dislike his manner.

"I have a meeting in Pennsylvania at four-thirty," she said. "I've got a two-hour drive ahead of me."

"Patience, patience," he said. "This all has to be done correctly, to protect both of us."

He spread out two more forms. The first was a Xerox copy of a typewritten statement.

"Did you speak to your tax attorney?" he asked.

"Yes," she lied, not wanting to create any further delay.

She glanced at her wristwatch. It was already one-thirty.

"Then he's already explained that you'll be liable for capital gains and income taxes on the money you're withdrawing from the trust."

She nodded silently.

"This statement says we've advised you of the tax consequences, that you've consulted your attorney, and you hold us blameless for any assessments."

She signed on the line indicated.

"The final document is your withholding waiver. Without your signature here, we'd have to deduct twenty percent of the principal and forward it to the IRS."

She signed the final paper and pushed it across the table.

Ever careful, he checked the signature before putting it in the folder. He gave the folder to a secretary and asked her to call the vault room.

"I'm looking forward to this myself," he said with a grin.

"Tell you the truth, I've never seen that much cash. Really. I just deal with numbers on computers. Nine, ten, twenty million a day goes over my desk, but it's all just numbers. After a while, you forget you're dealing with real money."

When she didn't answer, he fell into an uncomfortable silence that lasted until a thin little man and two bank guards came into the conference room.

The little man ignored Herman. He studied Katherine through bottle-thick eyeglasses that magnified the pupils of his eyes.

"Miss Katherine Roshak?" he asked.

She felt the need to rise at his formal approach.

"That's me."

He lifted a brown Samsonite two-suiter onto the table. Flipping the metal latches on the sides, he raised the lid of the suitcase. Inside were three rows of one-hundred-dollar bills, with twelve stacks of bills in each row.

"Two million seven hundred twelve thousand eight hundred and ninety-two dollars, as you requested."

It was unbelievable. She was afraid to touch it, afraid the guards would step forward and stop her.

It was like one of those scenes from the ten o'clock news, where the police make a drug raid and find suitcases filled with money. Braithwaite was right. Up until now, through all the formalities, it was just numbers. Move a decimal point here, add a zero, what did it matter?

But this was different. This was cash. Row after row of Benjamin Franklin portraits stared up at her from the suitcase, each topping off a thick stack. She could smell the ink of the bill. This was the legacy of her father. The money that would have provided her with financial independence for the rest of her life. Travel. Clothing. A place in the country. Security.

"Somehow I thought it would be more," Braithwaite said when he recovered from the shock. "I mean a bigger pile. Is that all of it?"

"You want a pile, it'll make a stack eleven feet high if you take it out of the suitcase," the little man said. "It's been counted three times, twice at the Federal Reserve. Getting this many hundred-dollar bills isn't easy on short notice."

He reached in and took out one of the stacks of bills. A heavy rubber band held together smaller, half-inch stacks wrapped with paper.

"Each of the small stacks is ten thousand dollars, a hundred hundreds. Ten of those in each stack, nine stacks in each row, three rows deep, plus one partial stack. That's two point seven million in the rows and twelve thousand eight hundred ninety-two in the partial. I'll wait here while you count it."

"That's all right," Katherine said. "I'll take your word for it."

Behind the thick lenses, the custodian's eyes registered surprise. He recovered quickly.

"That's up to you, as long as you sign the receipt."

Another form.

The two guards accompanied her to the parking lot across the street. They stayed with her until the money was safely locked in the trunk, the suitcase jammed in among Dominic's booster cables, spare tire, and scattered tools.

She paid off the condo security guard with hundred-dollar bills and made him promise again to call Pennsylvania in the morning.

When she finally arrived back in Dickson, it was nearly four o'clock.

Dominic jumped up from his cot when Bednarek led her to the cell. He hesitated when he saw that no one was with her.

"What happened to the lawyer you were supposed to get?" he asked.

"You'll be safer here," she said.

"It's not me I'm worried about."

"I know," she said. "But you've done enough already. It's time for me to do my part."

He thrust his arms through the bars. She moved closer to him until his hands touched hers. From the open doorway Bednarek watched.

"Katherine, you can't do it yourself," he said.

"Too many people are getting hurt," she said.

She wanted to let him pull her against the bars, squeeze her against the harsh metal just so she could feel his strength. That

225

was what she needed now, but as usual she was afraid to admit it. Instead, she kept her voice cool and rational.

"I'm going to see Mother," she said.

"Katherine . . ."

His eyes reflected his anguish. His hands tightened on hers. ". . . don't."

"I know what she wants, Dominic. I talked to her last night."

"You're making a mistake."

"I'm going to settle things with her, so she can rest in peace."

"Katherine . . ." His voice was pleading. "It can't be your mother."

"We've already been through that. Only Mother would know the things she knew. It's her. And I'm going to do what she wants."

"Katherine . . . you're being used. I don't know exactly how, but you're being used. It's all a hoax. It has to be."

She decided not to tell him about the money. It would only complicate matters, and she had to be leaving soon.

"You'll be all right," she said. "I've arranged for the charges to be dropped against you."

"I don't want you hurt . . ." he said.

"By the time you're free, it'll all be over," she said.

"I don't want to lose you, too . . ."

She saw what looked like tears in his eyes.

At that moment, she would gladly have thrown herself at him, in spite of Bednarek watching. This man, sitting in jail thinking only of her. He needed her as much as she needed him. But this was not the time to give in to her emotions.

She pulled away from him.

She needed her strength to face Mother. And it had to be alone. In the end, whatever happened to her, she knew Dominic would be safe. And right now his safety was all that mattered to her.

She wanted to tell him that, but the words wouldn't come.

All the years of denying the truth about Mother had built up a wall inside her that prevented her from saying what she felt. Her jaw trembled as she tried to speak and hold back her tears at the same time. She turned away, afraid to reveal anything more, afraid he would say something that would stop her.

"Katherine . . . ," he called as she walked away.

Bednarek stepped aside to allow her through the door.

"Katherine!"

His shout was cut off when Bednarek closed the door.

She ran out to the old Riviera.

Blinded by her tears, she nearly crashed into another car when she pulled out.

It was already 4:15.

Mother's time of death was 4:32.

She sped through the small town, wiping the tears from her eyes. Past the Valley Inn, a black wreath hanging on its front door. Past the Visitation of Mary Church, and up the steep hill to the old cemetery.

She slowed the car as she entered the wrought-iron gate. The cemetery appeared empty, as on all her previous visits. If anyone came to visit the graves, they never lingered when darkness approached. She parked the car at the edge of the paved lane, behind the *Pietà*. The stark surroundings were familiar now. The white tombstones, the black marble slabs, the rows of markers that followed the curve of the hill were ready to guide her to Mother's grave.

She left the car running and the door open, as on the first visit. It seemed so long ago. It could have been happening to a different person.

She took the Samsonite bag from the trunk. Two million dollars in tight stacks made it as heavy as a suitcase filled with textbooks.

Once again, she realized she was wearing the wrong shoes for a cemetery. As soon as she stepped off the paved strip onto the dead grass, her heels sank into the soil. Combined with the weight of the suitcase, it made walking difficult. Every step became an effort. She had to pick her way slowly among the old graves. She kept watching for some sign of movement ahead. But the hundreds of marble markers offered too many hiding places. She smelled the air, but the only odor was the decaying smell that came from the surrounding woods.

She checked her watch.

It was 4:32.

The time of Mother's death.

That was the final proof Dominic was wrong.

It couldn't be a hoax, because the death certificate never specified the exact time of death. That was a fact Katherine had deduced from the broken wristwatch they gave her before Mother's burial. The crystal was smashed from striking the floor when Mother fell. Even the police paid no attention to it. The precise time was a fact that only Katherine knew.

And Mother.

As she reached the final row of graves, a fresh mound of brown earth awaited her.

She stopped for a moment, and a surge of fear washed over her.

The grave was supposed to be covered.

She had seen it herself that night with Dominic.

But now it was open again.

She looked around. In the deepening gloom, no one was visible. The only sound she heard was the pounding of her own heart. There were no squirrels. No birds. Not even a leaf stirred in the breeze. The stillness seemed unnatural, as if the very earth itself were holding its breath in anticipation.

More slowly now, much more slowly, she started to walk toward the open grave. With each step, the opening was more visible. A dark, silent hole beside the huge mound of dirt.

Every fiber in her body wanted her to stop, to turn and panic and run as fast as she could back to the car. The fight-or-flight phenomenon. She wouldn't allow it to take control of her mind.

With each step, she could see deeper into the grave.

She could make out the top of the coffin.

Why was it open again?

And what was that inside?

Forgetting her fear, she stepped up to the edge of the grave, trying to make out the awkward lump in the coffin. A familiar smell came from the grave. Not as powerful as she remembered, and mingled with another, sweeter odor. An odor she remembered from the embalming room.

228

The air around her seemed suddenly to grow cold. So cold she felt her skin go numb. She gasped for breath, but her lungs didn't want to work. She felt the blood drain from her head. She started to sway at the edge of the grave as her mind refused to admit what she was seeing.

In the coffin, skin blackened from decomposition, Mother waited for her.

She was only partially clothed. Her body was smaller and thinner than Katherine remembered. Small and vulnerable. And totally motionless.

Katherine dropped the suitcase and stared, trying to make sense out of what she saw.

Gray hair came out of the dark skin of Mother's forehead. The cheeks were sunken. The lips were pulled back from the teeth in a hideous smile.

There was a sudden movement in the grass, a thrust at her back, and Katherine felt herself falling into the grave.

Falling toward Mother.

The body in the coffin made a soft crunch when she hit. She could feel the breaking of old bones beneath her.

The aged padding of the coffin provided little cushioning effect. Her head slammed against it, dazing her.

She was vaguely aware of a sudden darkness. The top of the coffin slammed shut.

She felt herself slipping into unconsciousness.

She tried to struggle, to force herself awake, but the blow to her head was working its deadening force.

The last thing she remembered was a sound like hailstones striking the roof.

Again.

And again.

But it wasn't hailstones, she realized with her last rational thought.

It was earth striking the coffin.

The grave was being closed over her.

Fourteen

SHE HAD NO way of knowing how long she had been unconscious.

When she awoke, she was enveloped in blackness. Her nostrils burned from breathing foul air.

Above her was silence.

The shoveling of dirt had stopped, or the dirt had become so
deep that fresh dirt no longer made a sound when it hit.

It couldn't be possible that she was trapped in a coffin underground. It had to be a dream. She had to be coming awake in
a black, airless room. Certainly not a coffin, her mind told her.

She was afraid to move. Afraid that the slightest movement might cause her to touch something that would reveal the truth of what her mind was desperately trying to deny.

The air was growing heavy. It was getting harder to breathe. And her back was getting sore from the object that occupied the same space. She tried to tell herself it must be a blanket that had gotten twisted in bed beneath her.

When she finally did move, she felt a bone pushing against her ribs.

A blanket?

Come on, Katherine, admit it, she thought.

You can't deny it anymore.

It's Mother. And she's dead. Dead and buried and decomposing and stinking and filled with formaldehyde and the flesh falling off her bones and she was here in the coffin with her and there was no way to get out, oh Dominic, Father Ambrose, dear God in Heaven, help me help help . . .

"Help!" she screamed. "Help! Help! Help! Help!"

The sound of her voice bounced back in her ears, unable to penetrate the metal coffin and the thick covering of earth above. She pounded against the lid of the coffin. Her elbows scraped against Mother's body beneath her. The coffin offered little room for movement. She tried pushing against the lid of the coffin, but that only pushed her tighter against the decomposing body.

She started to whimper.

She scratched at the padding above her. She ripped off the silk covering and tore at the cotton batting. It fell over her face and into her mouth. She felt her fingernails breaking as she broke through the last of the padding to the metal lid.

She cried and screamed and scratched until she could feel the slippery warmth of blood pouring from her fingertips.

It was getting harder to breathe.

She pounded against the bare metal above her, knowing as she did it how useless the action was. She pounded and screamed and whimpered until the difficulty of breathing sapped her energy. This was how it was going to end, she thought, fighting for breath until her lungs ached with the struggle and filled with the foul taste of putrefying flesh. It was the same way Mother had died. Struggling for her last breath in the smoke of the hotel bathroom. It must have been Mother's plan from the beginning.

The two of them, together in death.

There was no point in fighting anymore.

Mother was dead.

And now it was her turn.

Father Ambrose, dear God, please help.

Slowly she felt around the lumpy mass beneath her until she located Mother's hand. The desiccated flesh was cool and rubbery to the touch. She held Mother's hand, the way she had done when she was a child.

The pain in her lungs grew sharper. Her head ached. Her ears began to ring. And she became aware of another change.

The panic was disappearing.

In its place, she experienced a growing sense of calm. An incredible feeling of peacefulness suffused her. She felt warm, mellow, and euphoric. It was just as Moody and Kübler-Ross described it in their works on near-death experiences. She felt herself floating into a dark tunnel, with a brilliant light at the end. Now that she was experiencing it herself, her professional curiosity was aroused.

Did those psychologists really understand the process? Was this really a movement into another life? Or was it merely a deadening of the reticular formation? The lack of oxygen was closing down the systems. The diffuse network of brain fibers that monitored information from the body's sense receptors was being cut off, numbing her emotional responses.

In the last moments of available oxygen, she turned her thoughts to Dominic. In the final moments before the golden light enveloped her, she felt the stirring of resistance. She wanted to shout, but didn't have the strength.

She didn't want to leave Dominic behind.

She tried desperately to hang on.

Her head began to throb with strange sounds. She felt her body start to shake.

And suddenly the warm, euphoric feeling was gone. She felt

she had been suddenly transported into a different climate.

It was cold.

A chill wind was blowing over her.

Her lungs filled with a sweetness, a delicious sensation that brought a moan to her lips.

"Katherine?"

She opened her eyes and looked up at a dark silhouette with the stars and moon behind it.

The silhouette reached down and slipped a hand behind her head. Drawing her limp shoulders forward, he pressed her to his chest.

"Thanks be to God," the silhouette said.

She recognized the voice.

The cold fresh air revived her quickly.

"Father Ambrose . . ." she murmured as he helped her to her feet.

"Hurry," he said. "Dominic is in danger."

Somehow he got out of the grave and pulled her up behind him. She was still too confused to understand how he did it.

In the moonlight, his eyes gleamed brightly.

She looked around at the huge mound of dirt and the old priest who stood before her. He looked stronger than he had in the rectory. He stood erect, without the osteoporotic slump she remembered.

"Go to Dominic," he said before she could ask the question on her mind.

"The funeral parlor," he answered before she could ask the next question.

"His life is in danger," he said, taking her by the arm and starting her on the way to the car.

She ran in her stockinged feet through the rows of tombstones to the waiting car. When she reached the Riviera, Father Ambrose wasn't with her. She turned to look, but he was nowhere to be seen. The moon gave a harsh light to the cemetery, enough to see there was no movement among the tombstones.

The key was still in the car. She turned on the headlights, bathing the entire area with the high beams.

Father Ambrose was gone.

The cemetery was silent.

She thought of the suitcase with the money, lying out there beyond the range of the headlights. She put the car in reverse and backed out of the cemetery. No way would she go back to that grave in the darkness. If Mother wanted to destroy the money, she could do it herself. Or Father Ambrose could return it. Thank God for Father Ambrose and his cemetery rounds.

There were two cars in the parking lot at the Kuranda Funeral Home. One of them was an old Cadillac hearse with New York license plates. The other had WK-1 vanity plates from Pennsylvania, identifying it as Walter Kuranda's.

She felt foolish walking across the parking lot in her stockinged feet. Her fingers ached, and her blood spattered her clothing. She could still smell the odor of Mother's remains about her. She didn't know who was inside. It was going to be embarrassing to be seen in this condition. But Father Ambrose had said Dominic was in danger.

She hoped the old priest was mistaken. Dominic was supposed to be in jail until morning.

The side entrance to the building was locked. She went around the back, to the kitchen entrance, which led to Kuranda's living quarters. Through the curtains she could make out a light in the room beyond. The kitchen door was unlocked. She opened it gently, her mind already making excuses to use when the funeral director discovered her.

She carefully made her way through the darkened kitchen. There was no sound from the room beyond. Her stockinged feet enabled her to creep up to the doorway in silence. Ever so slowly, she peered around the edge of the doorway.

The room was empty.

A chair was tipped over.

A lamp lay shattered on the floor.

The carpet was wedged against the far door, as if something had been dragged across it. Beyond the door, she knew from her earlier visit, the stairs descended to the embalming room.

She padded softly across the room.

From downstairs, she heard a hollow dripping sound. She hesitated at the top of the stairs, straining her ears to hear any sound of movement.

The sound she heard came from behind her.

It was a sharp, metallic sound. She had heard it once before, when Dominic was demonstrating how to use his pistol.

"Turn around," said a voice. "Very slowly."

She followed his instructions.

He was a small man, about her height, with blue eyes, cupid lips, and a Dutch-boy haircut. He had Dominic's pistol in his hand. She recognized him immediately.

"I didn't expect to see you here, Professor Roshak."

"You remember me?"

"Of course I remember you," said David Effenbeck. "I consoled you in your time of grief. Can I be of any assistance to you now?"

"I'm looking for Dominic Delaserra."

She stared down at the gun in his hand. The last time she had seen it was when she slid it under her pillow four nights ago.

Effenbeck curled his thin lips back in an artificial smile.

"I'm so glad that I can help you," he said. "Dominic came here looking for you. And now you can be together."

He motioned with the gun for her to go downstairs. She stepped over the carpet and started down, afraid of what she would find. The dripping sound grew louder. Effenbeck followed her down the steps, keeping a careful distance between them.

They passed through the darkened display room, empty coffins filling the shadows on both sides. Ahead, the door to the embalming room was open. The operating-room lights flooded the entrance with their harsh glare. The dripping sound came from the room ahead.

She didn't want to see what was waiting in there. She turned back, ready to plead with Effenbeck. He raised the gun and pointed it toward her head, nodding for her to continue.

Katherine was trembling by the time she reached the door. When she saw the figures on the embalming table, she had to hold on to the door for support.

On the first stainless-steel table, carefully positioned within the gutters that were still coated with the remains of his blood, was the nude figure of Walter Kuranda. His body looked thin and pathetic. Drained of its blood, it seemed to have been partially deflated. At the foot of the table, the last drops of the dark red liquid were dripping into a plastic container. It was the sound she had heard from the stairs. His hands were trussed together over his head with a wire that ran under the table, looped once around a metal brace to keep it from slipping, and ended up around his ankles. It would have been impossible for him to do more than turn his head.

On the second table, similarly bound and nude, was Dominic.

His eyes were closed. Unlike Kuranda's body, Dominic's wasn't yet surrounded by his blood.

"Is he . . . ?" She couldn't finish the question.

"Deceased?" Effenbeck asked. "No, not yet, but his time draws near."

Dominic opened his eyes. He blinked twice, trying to focus.

She started for the table, but Effenbeck barked a command to stop.

"You were supposed to be in jail," Katherine said with tears in her eyes. "You were supposed to be safe."

He wet his lips before forming the answer. That was when she noticed the blue lump on the side of his face. He hadn't yet seen Kuranda's body. He nodded toward Effenbeck.

"He came for me," Dominic said. "He bailed me out and told me you were waiting for me."

"Didn't you recognize him?" she asked. "He's the one who embalmed Mother. The one who worked for Brescia in New York."

Dominic closed his eyes.

"Stupid," he murmured. "How could I be that stupid?"

Effenbeck motioned her to the far side of the room, putting the maximum amount of distance between her and the table on which Dominic was stretched. She kept moving backward at his direction until she was wedged into a space between the glass sterilization case and the aspirator.

"Now my question to you, Professor," he said, "is, why are you still alive? I thought you had joined your mother for eternity."

"It was you in the cemetery," she said. "You were the one who pushed me into the grave."

"Me? Hardly. How could I be in two places at the same time? Unless I had supernatural powers, of course."

He let out a high-pitched giggle.

Dominic struggled with the wire that bound him. Effenbeck watched until Dominic stopped. He shook his head.

"Pathetic, isn't it?" he said. "The human body is a pathetic sight without clothing. You all think you're so special, so strong, so beautiful. But stripped of your clothing, stripped of your makeup and your artificial beauty, you're nothing but meat, to be drained of blood and look even more pathetic."

He giggled again, as if enjoying some inner joke.

Katherine noted the inappropriate laughter. It was a symptom of schizophrenia. Given the bizarre circumstances and his odd humor, he was probably the hebephrenic type.

"How did you get here?" he said suddenly. "How did you get out of the grave?"

"Then it *was* you," she said. "You were the one who pushed me."

He giggled again.

"Yes, it was me, and it wasn't me," he said. "I was here the whole time, taking care of your friends. But yes, I was at the cemetery, too, taking care of you. It's part of my powers to be in two places at one time."

"I don't understand," Katherine said.

"He's crazy," Dominic said. "It doesn't take a psychology professor to see that."

"I'm not bound by your ordinary human ways," Effenbeck said, ignoring the insult.

"Then why do you need a gun?" Katherine asked, intrigued by the pathology of his delusive disorder.

"Because I'm in this body now, while my other form approaches."

"Your what?"

238

"Soon I'll be two spirits, two bodies, two minds in one being. Mere humans like you will never understand."

Katherine felt a chill. She thought of Father Ambrose and his warnings. She was still wearing the scapular. She pulled it out from her blouse and held it where Effenbeck could see it.

It had no effect on him.

He sat, grinning at them, breaking into occasional laughter at some private joke.

"How long are you going to keep us here?" she asked.

"Until your mother arrives," he said, breaking into the high-pitched giggle again.

"Mother is dead," she said.

Upstairs, the door slammed shut and the deadbolt slid into place. Effenbeck continued grinning. The noise upstairs didn't disturb him.

"So now you think she's dead?" he taunted her. "All those years you pretended she was just resting. You said she was just asleep."

"How did you know that?" she asked.

"I know all about you," he said. "You have no secrets from me."

"He's trying to make it sound like more than it is," Dominic said. "You must have poured out your heart to him at the funeral, when he was supposed to be comforting you. He probably knows your whole life history."

The stairway door closed softly, just loud enough for her to hear. It was followed by a squeaking noise on the steps.

Katherine watched the open doorway behind Effenbeck. The display room was dark and shadowed. She thought she saw a movement, but couldn't be sure. Someone was there. But doing what? Why the hesitation?

"But how could your mother be dead if you saw her all those times?" Effenbeck asked. He seemed to be leading her on.

"I don't know," she said. "It must have been a delusion. A hallucination. Stress-induced, probably."

"That's the psychological explanation," he said. "But are you prepared for the reality of it?"

239

"The reality is that she's dead," Katherine said. "I know that for a fact. I can accept that now."

Effenbeck let out his high-pitched giggle again, rolling his head back in pleasure.

Behind him, there was a movement.

A stiff, hesitant movement. A small figure. It waited in the shadows, forcing Katherine to squint to make out the face.

She heard Dominic let out a gasp. From his angle, he could see the figure more clearly.

"Katherine . . ."

It was the muffled voice, harsh with the sound of pain and stiffness.

Katherine felt her knees grow weak. She sagged against the sterilizing cabinet for support.

The figure entered the room.

It was impossible.

She had left Mother in the coffin in the cemetery, a collection of brittle bones and darkened flesh that permeated her clothing with its smell.

"Your mother's not dead," Effenbeck said. "She was just resting."

He had a shrill laugh of someone enjoying the sight of her fear.

Katherine's breath came in shallow gasps that didn't deliver enough oxygen to her lungs. She started to feel dizzy.

Mother's face was dark and broken open in places. The skin was pulled back over her teeth in the hideous expression Katherine remembered from the coffin. The embalmer's wire protruded from a hole in the cheek.

"Katherine . . ."

She walked stiff-legged toward Katherine. Dominic stared in open-mouthed horror as she passed the table.

"No . . . one . . . can . . . help . . . ," came the strangled voice from her throat.

A slender, blackened hand reached out to touch Katherine's cheek. The stench from the flesh was overpowering.

The room went dark before Katherine's eyes and she felt herself sliding against the sterilizing case, felt the wooden sides giving way, heard the smash of glass, and over it all, coming not just from Effenbeck, but someone else too, a shrill, high-pitched, hysterical laughter.

She awoke in a pool of her own blood.

She started to whimper, feeling the pain of dozens of sharp pieces of glass sticking in her arms and legs.

"Now do you believe?" Effenbeck asked.

Katherine rose unsteadily to her feet. Effenbeck motioned with his gun for her to step back against the wall, to her former position. She pulled splinters of glass from her arms. Some were daggerlike in length, hanging from her dress where their points had so easily penetrated. She was lucky none had found an artery or other vital spot.

She watched in horror as Mother raised a hand to her own cheek, gouging her fingers into the soft tissue. She ripped at herself, tearing the cheek forward, ripping the lips away from her teeth. Katherine felt a wave of nausea as she watched the dead tissue hit the floor. It landed with a sticky sound. There was no blood. After eight years of decomposition, the tissue was the consistency of thick paste.

Katherine drew back from the blackened tissue at her feet, arching her back against the wall. The shreds of glass that were stuck in her arms and dress were forgotten.

In a sudden frenzy, Mother began ripping at her face with both hands. Huge chunks of tissue were torn away. Lumps of gray hair, still attached to tissue, joined the obscene pile on the floor.

Hideous laughter streamed from Mother's throat. She ripped away the front of her chin and part of her nose. The places where all the dark tissue was torn away revealed a clean, creamy surface.

Katherine thought it was the skull being revealed. It was smooth and clean and pale, except for those areas where bits of blackened tissue clung stubbornly.

Mother continued to tear at her face and throat in the strange frenzy, faster and faster, ripping and rubbing and gouging the crumbling, puttylike flesh.

As Mother's face disappeared under her attack, another face was emerging from beneath.

It had delicate features, with small cupid lips, narrow eyes,

241

and a receding chin. Yellow hair in a Dutch-boy cut appeared.

She remembered Father Ambrose's warning. The Devil could assume any form, take on any visage to serve his evil needs.

She stared at what had been her Mother's face just a few minutes before.

Now it was the face of David Effenbeck.

The young man's head had replaced Mother's head on the figure before her.

The creature grinned.

Katherine looked across the room. David Effenbeck was holding the pistol and grinning too.

She must be hallucinating. She closed her eyes and shook her head, trying to fight back the dizziness that came from the cortex of her brain rejecting the visual images her optic nerve was sensing.

When she opened her eyes again, David Effenbeck's head was still in two places. The expressions were identical. A wide grin ended in small dimples on each head. Pale blue eyes were set behind long lashes. And both heads broke into laughter again at the same time.

It was the bizzare, almost hysterical laughter of schizophrenic disorder.

She stared in disbelief.

The head with the gun started a sentence.

"Is your mother dead . . ."

The second head finished the sentence.

". . . or is she just sleeping?"

Both heads tilted with a quizzical expression, waiting for her response.

She couldn't find any words. The heads appeared to move in unison.

"If you treated your mother better . . . ," the first head said.

". . . she might still be alive," the second head finished.

Both heads of David Effenbeck frowned.

"For that . . ."

". . . you must die."

Both heads of David Effenbeck looked at her with hatred in their eyes. As if guided by the same mind, the same reflexes, each head licked its lips in nervous anticipation.

Fifteen

"**T**HAT'S HOW he was in two places at the same time," Dominic said.

Instead of being frightened, he sounded almost relieved.

"They're twins," Dominic said. "Identical twins. That's the part I couldn't figure out. But it's so simple. That's how they were able to work for Kuranda and Brescia at the same time. And how they stayed a step ahead of us, whether we were here or in New York."

The two heads turned to him with identical expressions of dismay.

"We're not twins . . ."

". . . we're the same person . . ."

". . . the same mind . . ."

". . . in two bodies."

"That's why they killed Brescia," Dominic said. "And why they killed Kuranda. When we went to see Brescia, they realized the two funeral directors were telling us all we needed to understand what was really happening. Identical twins, using the same name, the same Social Security number. It's the only way one person can be in two places at one time. It was the simple answer, and I didn't see it. I was starting to believe that business about ghosts."

Katherine stared at the two faces. They were exact mirror images of each other. Monozygotic twins. Their reactions to Dominic's explanation was identical. They snickered from the same sides of their mouths.

"Stupid . . ."

". . . that's what you are."

"Stupid . . ."

". . . just like all the others."

Their speech patterns, their cadences, even their thought processes were identical. True identical twins with the uncanny ability to know what each other was thinking. After years of study and lecturing about pathological parallelism in identical twins, this was the first time Katherine had ever been able to abserve a truly disturbed pair at close range.

And now she remembered where she had heard the voice before. She remembered it from all those telephone interviews and conversations over the years.

"They're the 'D.' twins," she gasped. " 'D.' for David. I've been talking to them on the phone for years. Interviewing them."

"And revealing too much about yourself," Dominic said. "When they found out about that trust fund, they must have lured your mother up here."

"Then she didn't commit suicide. I knew she wouldn't do that."

"They were patient," Dominic said. "They fed your guilt all these years. They waited for your twenty-eighth birthday, and

244

then they used their cosmetology skills and played on your fear and guilt. Just like they did with those other people in New York."

"I feel like a fool," Katherine said. "They had me believing everything."

"You did what anyone would do. People believe what they want to believe. You were vulnerable, that's all."

"But I'm a psychologist."

"That doesn't make you any different."

"I should have known better."

"They fooled everybody. I didn't figure it out either. And they had Henzes fooled too, with all their bits of evidence from the grave."

"But I know about identical twins. I've studied all the works on them. I even lectured on the mental problems common to monozygotic twins. I should have thought of it."

She stopped, remembering the lecture when the figure she had thought was Mother took a seat in the back of the hall. She was lecturing about monozygotic schizophrenic incidence rates. There was hatred in that face, the same hatred she could see now in the twins.

"You treated us as if we're laboratory animals . . ."

". . . but we were the ones studying you," they said.

The first twin remained across the room with the pistol, protecting his brother, who searched among the shattered glass of the sterilizing case. He came up with a scalpel, bringing a smile to both their faces.

"And you were stupid, like your friend here . . ."

". . . supposed to be a policeman, and he never suspected a thing."

He wiped the scalpel and advanced toward Dominic. There was nothing Katherine could do to help.

"You made a mistake with that fire you faked in Katherine's bathroom," Dominic said. "I knew it was a hoax then, but I just couldn't figure it all out."

"You never suspected anything . . ."

". . . you're just trying to keep us talking, to delay your death."

245

Dominic struggled against the wire that held him. It was useless. They had trussed him so all he could move was his shoulders.

"It wasn't a fire," Dominic said. "That's why the arson squad couldn't figure it out. When I looked under the sink, there were cobwebs where the water pipes connected. If it was a real fire, they would have been burned. I figure you used some kind of industrial electric paint stripper, and went over it one section at a time. It must have taken you all day, because the electric bill showed a big surge."

"It took a long time," said the twin with the scalpel. "But it worked. Having two minds instead of one makes it easy to stay ahead of ordinary people."

"People used to make us feel we were strange, because we weren't ordinary, like the rest of you . . ."

". . . that's why we took jobs in different cities, so that we could be accepted."

He lowered the scalpel to Dominic's groin. With one hand, he spread the skin on Dominic's inner thigh.

"You came to Katherine's room through the window. I knew that by the way the window was jammed every morning. And the smell, that was easy to manufacture with some simple chemicals. But how did you kill Eddie? That was the one time I wasn't really certain what was going on. I almost started believing in the supernatural when we found him."

The twin paused with the edge of the scalpel pressed against Dominic's thigh.

"That was something special, wasn't it . . ."

". . . we thought we might as well have some fun."

"That's fun for you guys?" Dominic said. "Killing somebody as helpless as Eddie is fun?"

"He's probably happier now . . ."

". . . because he doesn't have to put up with the insults anymore."

"We know what he was going through . . ."

". . . more than you ever did."

Dominic tried to move his bare leg away from the scalpel. It was impossible. The twin squeezed the flesh and started to cut. Dark red fluid oozed out of the opening in his flesh, coating the blade of the scalpel.

"You're feeling more pain now than he did . . ."

". . . all he felt was a nice warm glow."

They both grinned at the same time, as they recalled the event.

"It was easier than we thought . . ."

". . . we invented our own death ray."

"We took the magnetron tube from a microwave oven . . ."

". . . put a reflector around it . . ."

". . . and put it against his head when he walked into the room."

"You get hard-boiled eyeballs in just twenty seconds . . ."

". . . and brain death in two minutes."

". . . then we put him on the bed and left him there with two other magnetron tubes aimed at him."

The room echoed with strange, high-pitched laughter.

"We microwaved him . . ."

". . . just like you microwave a hot dog."

The twin with the scalpel started cutting at Dominic's thigh again. Dominic's body strained against the pain, his muscles tense, his face contorted. He was making an effort not to scream.

"It won't hurt as much if you relax," said the twin with the scalpel.

"We have to cut through the muscle to reach the femoral artery . . . ," said the one with the gun.

". . . so we can drain you more quickly," explained the other.

Dominic twisted his body, managing to slip out of the twin's grasp for a moment.

"I'm trying to make a nice, neat incision . . ."

". . . we don't like to do sloppy work."

With a deft movement, he plunged the scalpel deep into Dominic's thigh. A scream pierced the room. Dominic arched his back in agony as the blood from his femoral artery spurted out between the surrounding muscle. It came in pulses, timed to the beat of his heart. The flow of blood quickly covered the lower part of the stainless-steel table, flowing into the drainage gutters.

The twin with the scalpel jumped back to avoid being splattered with Dominic's blood.

"Whoooeeee . . ."

". . . it's more fun working on live bodies."

Dominic struggled to try to stop the flow of blood, pressing his legs together, twisting and squirming with the desperate frenzy of a man facing death. The wires holding his arms cut into the skin until he was bleeding there, too. But it was the ponderous flow of blood from the artery in his leg that drew the attention of the twins.

"Three minutes . . ."

". . . and you'll be gone," they said.

"No!" Katherine shouted. "Please. You can't kill him. I gave you the money."

She started for the table.

Two shots rang out, reverberating off the hard surfaces.

Katherine stopped.

The twin was pointing the gun at her face.

He was too far across the room for her to reach. The table was between them. Dominic was already struggling more slowly. His blood was pouring through the drainage slot in the bottom of the table. His life was pouring out of him, and there was nothing she could do. He looked at her, pleading for help.

There was nothing she could do.

Two more minutes and the last of his blood would be drained. One more minute and the damage would probably be irreversible.

"He's finished now . . ."

". . . all we have left is to take care of you."

The twin with the scalpel came across the room. His brother held the gun on Katherine. So far as they were concerned, Dominic was already dead.

They both giggled again in concordant laughter. It was amazing how parallel their emotions and thoughts ran. Monozygotic twins taken to the extreme, Katherine thought. They worked in total harmony, having perfected their duality to abnormal lengths.

"We need a bigger knife . . ."

". . . for you to commit suicide," the said.

Protected by his brother's gun, the twin bent over to find a knife among the shattered glass at Katherine's feet. Katherine stared at the back of his neck, at the hollow where the soft flesh was visible below his blond hair.

It offered her the only chance she would have.

She felt for the long icicle of glass that was still caught in her sleeve.

Suddenly everything was clear.

Stress and fear had overloaded her mind to the point where she was entering hyperkinesia. Her mind was working at a furious pace, synapses shooting off their electrical impulses between dendrites faster and faster, until the information was moving faster than it could be processed by the billions of neurons in her mind.

As a result, all the activity in the room seemed to slip into an illusion of slow motion. Her own senses were heightened to the keen edge of madness. She focused on the twin in front of her. Her hand gripped the glass so tightly, she felt it cut into her skin.

She would have to position the knife edge of the glass perfectly to prevent it from shattering against the occipital lobe of the skull before it could do any damage.

In her hyperkinetic trance, she brought the shiny tip of the glass up underneath the atlas point, into the small opening between the temporal bones and the back plate of the skull.

She felt it penetrate smoothly into the aperture of the spinal cord opening. Even before it reached the cerebellum, the control point for all bodily movement, his head began to fall forward.

She shoved the blade deeper into the vault of the skull, through the cerebellum and into the brain stem itself. Even a bruise to the brain stem could cause an irreversible coma. She shoved the glass into the center of the brain stem, twisting and shredding his life until she knew she had torn through the reticular formation by the vomit that spewed from his lifeless mouth. Thinking of Mother and what they had done to her, Katherine gave the jagged glass another violent shove until she felt it snap against the frontal bone of his cranium.

She looked across the room to see his twin doubled over in concordant agony.

Just as she had hoped, he collapsed on the floor like his brother.

Parallel lives, parallel deaths.

She jumped over the twin and ran to Dominic's side. The blood was still spurting from his leg. She jammed her thumb into the open wound to stop the flow. His eyes fluttered awake at the pain. She pressed her head against his chest to listen for the heartbeat. It was slow and shallow, but it was there.

"Thank God," she moaned, "thank God."

She was kissing his naked chest, tasting the mingled salts of his perspiration and her tears.

Later, when the paramedics had stabilized Dominic with plasma and treated him for shock, she sat stroking his hand.

"I still can't believe it," the chief of police said.

He watched as the coroner examined the second of the twins.

"It's in the literature," Katherine said. "You can look it up. The Louisville Twin Study, the Berlin Twin Study, and the Mormon Death Studies of Twins."

"It couldn't have happened the way you say it did."

"He died of concordant shock. Monozygotic twins have the same heart rate, brain-wave patterns, emotional responses. The literature is filled with identical twins who feel pain when one of them is hurt. The Effenbecks took twin bonding to an extreme. They tried to pretend they were one person with two minds. It didn't surprise me that the shock of seeing his brother die would put him into cardiac arrest. That even happens to normal people at times."

"I'm not talking about these creeps," the chief said. "What I don't understand is how you got out of that grave."

"I told you. Father Ambrose dug me out. It's a good thing for me he was making his cemetery rounds."

The chief frowned and shook his head.

"You two have explanations for everything. Microwaves and arson and phony fires and all this psychological razzle-dazzle about twins and a couple of million dollars. Frankly, I find it hard to believe, but at least it's all backed up by the evidence. We're holding the money at the station. But you don't expect me to believe that story about how you got out of the grave."

"You can ask Father Ambrose yourself," Katherine said.

"I can't," the chief said. "He died in his sleep last night. He was dead twelve hours at the time he was supposed to be digging you out of the grave."

Katherine gasped and looked to Dominic for support. His eyes were skeptical, too. She looked back at the chief.

"But he was there. I swear it. He dug me out of the grave. If you go back there, I'm sure you'll find his fingerprints on the shovel. There's got to be proof. It really happened."

The chief sighed.

"It seems to me we've been through this once before," he said. "You've got a history of seeing ghosts, Professor. Why don't we just forget about it."

He left them and went to confer with the coroner.

Katherine turned back to Dominic.

"He doesn't believe me," she said. "But Father Ambrose was really there. I saw him. He sent me here."

Her voice was getting desperate.

"You believe me, don't you, Dominic?"

Dominic nodded and closed his eyes.

She took his hand and gripped it, knowing in her heart that she would never let him go.

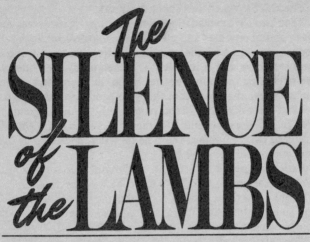

The SILENCE *of the* LAMBS

THE ELECTRIFYING BESTSELLER BY

THOMAS HARRIS

" THRILLERS DON'T COME ANY BETTER THAN THIS."
—*CLIVE BARKER*

**"HARRIS IS QUITE SIMPLY THE BEST SUSPENSE NOVELIST
WORKING TODAY."** — *The Washington Post*